A CIRCLE OF
MURDERS

ISBN: 978-0-9892880-0-2
ISBN-13: 978-0-9892880-0-2

To all the missing children; may they someday find their way home.

ACKNOWLEDGMENT

To my mother, sisters, and friends for all your
encouragement and support.

PROLOGUE

Eleven Years Earlier

He was dead. The son of a bitch was finally dead. How ironic, Sarra Gray thought, that the top of the Christmas tree lay within reach of his one outstretched arm. His hand appeared to be trying to grasp the white tree top angel just inches from his fingers. Maybe he was reaching for salvation, she thought bitterly. But, only the devil would want Homer James.

There had been a knock at the door. Two men had entered the apartment to face Homer. POP had come from the gun in the killer's hand. That was the only sound she'd heard from her hiding place behind the partially closed bedroom door. Through the crack, she had watched as Homer drop to the floor, his knees buckling first, the rest of his body twisting to fall onto the beige carpet. While the killers ransacked the living room, she had rushed silently to hide behind the false wall in the closet where Homer hid his safe. There was nothing she could do but breathe as quietly as possible and pray the men did not find her. If they did, they would kill her too.

Immediately after closing the door to her hiding place, she heard them enter the bedroom. Drawers, jerked from the dresser, hit the floor. The sound of ripping fabric was easily heard behind the thin plaster of the drywall. She held her breath, terrified that if she could hear them, they might hear her as well. Then, they were in the closet. Voices muttered low, indistinguishable words. The noise of hangers raking back and forth along the rod was far too close. Sarra prayed and waited in terror to be discovered.

Suddenly, everything went silent. Not a whisper, not a sound did she hear to indicate the men had left the room. Nor did a door slam to let her know they were gone from the apartment. There was only the absolute quiet. Trembling with fear, she waited for what seemed like two hours before daring to emerge and peek into the other room. They were definitely gone.

Hurriedly, she returned to the closet and grabbed a bag from the floor. Slipping behind the wall, she worked the carefully learned combination. Into the bag, she dumped the numerous bundles of one-hundred dollar bills, a stack of DVDs, several ledger books plus two large brown envelopes, contents unknown. Even though the bag was heavy, she picked it up and returned to the living room.

Outside, the wind howled and whipped sheets of snow into dancing dervishes across the penthouse balcony. Lamps toppled from end tables, cast bright yellow, oblong shapes across the floor. Slashed sofa cushions were tossed in a heap before the balcony doors. Books with ripped pages and bindings were everywhere. Jerked from wall hooks, the back paper covers of the paintings had been slashed open. Sculptures had been broken and tossed in pieces to land on any available surface.

Homer lay just as he had fallen. A dark red stain had spread across the front of his white shirt and oozed in a widening circle beneath his body. The crotch of his gray trousers was stained with urine, and his bare feet looked pale next to the beige carpet.

She wasn't sorry he was dead. She knew all too well how he took people and twisted them into monsters, trapped them and drained them of all hope, then tossed them out like garbage. "That bullet deserved a better target, you bastard," she hissed. "You got an easy death."

She had to get out of the apartment. It was only a matter of time before the killers returned to find what they were looking for. Hurrying across the butchered living room, she stopped a moment to stare down at the body, stunned that she felt so little grief for the man. She expected to feel something other than jubilation at his death. After all, he had saved her from her father. But, she felt nothing. Not even a twinge of regret.

The odor of blood, sharp and coppery, mixed with the smell of evacuated bowels and bladder emanating from the body, made her gag. Nauseated and repulsed, she crouched down and forced herself to search Homer's pockets for the car keys. She hated to touch his body, but she had to have those keys. There would be two sets, one for the Mercedes and one for the old Chevy. Cringing, she reached into Homer's right trouser pocket. Luck was with her. The key ring was in the first pocket she explored. Pulling them out, she flinched as the jingle of the keys sounded abrasively loud in the quiet room. She clasped them tightly, then hastened to the front door and set the tattered blue flight bag on the floor.

Quickly, she jerked a jacket off a hanger from the coat closet. Her hands shook so much she almost dropped the old Navy pea coat, but snatched it in midair and slipped her arms into the sleeves. She pulled a black knit cap down over her ears and made sure every long strand of dark hair was tucked securely beneath it. At this late hour, it would be bitterly cold, and her clothes were not the warmest. What she was wearing would have to do. Time was too short.

A gray angora scarf wrapped around her lower face and neck for added protection, she stuffed the bottom of the gray wool sweater into the top of her jeans and tugged the thick coat closer, buttoning it over the scarf. Lastly, she put on leather gloves, thankful for the cashmere lining. Apprehensive, she cracked the apartment door, glanced up and down the long corridor then sighed with relief. It was empty.

The hall lights seemed dimmer than usual, and at each apartment doorway, the shadows looked darker and more menacing. With a quick gulp of air to quell the fear knotting her stomach, she heaved the heavy blue flight bag over her shoulder and slipped out the door, closing it quietly. She sprinted toward the red neon exit sign at the end of the hall and thanked God for the carpet that muffled the sound of her boots as she shot past paintings, potted palms and shadowed thresholds to the end of the hall. No doors opened. No one peered out to check. The exit door opened silently. With another prayer of thanks, her feet flying, she bounded down twenty-five flights of steps, her hand sliding along the railing to keep from falling. She did not stop until she reached the underground parking garage and only then paused to catch her breath. Her heart pounded in her ears and, inside the leather gloves, her palms felt sweaty.

The garage door was all that now stood between

her and escape. She hesitated for a second, and then cautiously opened the door. Now was not the time for her to meet a neighbor returning home late. Or a noisy security guard checking the garage. Tonight, she was lucky. The vast gloomy parking cavern was filled with cars, which meant that most of the building's occupants were in for the night. Still, she waited a few more minutes to make sure.

Seeing no one, she dashed to the far side where Homer's white Chevy was parked beside his large black Mercedes. Her hands were shaking so much it took three attempts before she succeeded in unlocking the Chevy's door. Tossing her bag into the passenger seat, she climbed in and started the engine. As she backed out of the parking space, she cringed as she swiped the back fender of the Mercedes. It didn't matter. The Mercedes belonged to Homer. He would not be filing a police report.

At the street exit ramp, she was forced to stop for traffic. The flow of cars was not bumper to bumper as usual, but substantial enough to impede her getaway. She froze in terror for a second, her gloved hands clenched on the steering wheel. A dark sedan was parked against the curb across from the exit. Her headlights illuminated the faces of two men in the front seat. It was just a brief glimpse, but enough for her to identify the man behind the wheel like the one who had put the bullet in Homer.

She hunched down at once. Her only chance depended on their not seeing her face behind the wheel or recognizing the vehicle. She merged into the traffic as slowly and casually as she could so as not to attract attention. The two men appeared to be studying the main entrance to the apartment building, and they did not even glance in her direction. Body trembling, she drove away, praying she was leaving all her nightmares behind.

Once she crossed the river into New Jersey, she ditched the car in an alley then took a taxi to the Newark Greyhound Bus station. There, she bought a ticket to California. After the bus had left the depot, she leaned back in the seat and tried to relax.

Her freedom had come at a terrible price. Three people had died so that she could escape. Anyway, only three that she knew about, two women and one gutter rat. All she could do was pray that no one else had been killed. Death was an appropriate punishment for Homer, but her only friend, Rose Ann, had not deserved the death she had received. Ro had been just as innocent a victim as the other woman. Thinking about that made Sarra's heartache.

What punishment would be extracted for her part in all of it? She didn't know what it would be, but she was sure that somehow retribution would find her. Her loss was nothing. The others had lost everything. Still, the giddy awareness of her freedom bubbled up within her and would not be smothered. If that joy would always be mixed with pain and guilt, at least now, she was in charge of her life and future, and no longer being controlled by a madman.

One other thought nagged at her. What if Homer's body was not discovered until someone was attracted by the foul odor of his decaying corpse? Maybe, a small spark of compassion still burned within her. She decided she would telephone the police at the first stop. It was a small act of redemption, but the right thing to do, she thought.

As the bus headed west, she gazed out at the moonlit, snow-covered landscape, passing homes with roofs outlined in colored lights. Wreaths hung on doors, and decorated trees blazed in the windows of houses with ordinary families. She felt a surge of envy for all the warmth those exteriors portrayed. In three days it would be Christmas, and she was alone.

Still, she had reason to be grateful and was thankful to be alive and now have her freedom. She knew, however, that although Homer was dead, the men who had killed him were still out there. Because she now possessed the contents of Homer's safe, she would always need to be on guard, no matter where she managed to hide.

CHAPTER ONE

June 5

The bitch refused to die. Again, she had returned to torment him. Not this time. He was ready for her. Wherever she tried to hide, he always found her. He alone was her judge and jury. And he alone would convict her of the crimes she had committed because no one else had ever bothered. Her sentence? Death, of course. That was a fair punishment. It was up to him to see that the sentence was carried out. Slowly, though.

In a surge of temper, he tightened his grip on the girl's throat and slammed the back of her head against the wall. Her eyes rolled back in her head, and her body went limp. He released her throat and watched her chest rise as she inhaled air. Still alive? Good. He had come too close to ending it. Not yet. Not yet. She had to suffer as he had suffered.

He stripped off the dirty, skimpy white shorts and cut the bikini underwear with the razor sharp blade of his knife. Slowly, using the point, he flicked the buttons, one at a time, from the pink cotton shirt. As the material gaped open, a white bra was revealed. He slipped the blade under the band between her breasts and sliced through the fabric and pushed the garment aside. He finished stripping the girl, posed her body, with her knees bent and her legs spread wide in an invitation, then made each of her hands cup her breasts. He leaned over her still form studying his work. At last, she was laid out and exposed for what she was: a whore, a slut to tempt and torture him as she had been doing his entire life. No more. He couldn't take any more.

Even now, inches from death, she still controlled him. He could feel it. He could feel himself grow hard as he stared at her smooth young form, the flawless olive skin; each perfect breast peaked with a dark aureole around the nipple. No. With one gloved hand, he twisted and tore at them, making her moan. Then he fanned her thick dark hair out on the pillow. He wanted her. He needed her.

All his life, she had tortured him, teasing, hurting and rejecting him until he was forced to act. Forced to show her how he could take her without her touching him at all. It was part of her punishment, that and watching her die for what she had done. And then the pain would go away, and he would have peace. They would be safe.

Naked, he positioned himself between her legs, his erection hard, enormous and aching as he sheathed his penis with a condom. He grabbed and raised her hips as he thrust into her. Her eyes flew open, her legs kicked out. She cried out, a screeching wail, and beat at his arms and chest. He slammed a fist against her mouth. Still, she fought and so he drove even harder into her. He held her down with one hand on her chest, pressing her deeper into the mattress, and used the other to smash her face again, then again, until she went lax. His excitement grew until he was slamming into her without mercy. He cried out a name as he climaxed and his semen filled the condom. His head dropped as the pain faded and breathing hard, he leaned over his prey, his fury and passion spent. He looked down at the face of the human wreck beneath him.

He did not remember moving his hands to her neck, yet it was clear he had because his fingers now were clenched around her throat. Her large brown eyes were wide and vacant, and her ragged, bloody mouth hung open and slack. He let go of her throat and stared down at her for a moment, then calmly rose, going downstairs to the bathroom to shower and scour his body with disinfectant. After dressing in new black slacks and a black shirt, he slipped on his loafers. Donning thick rubber gloves and a rubber apron, he returned upstairs where he opened a small bottle of bleach and poured a generous amount over her belly and thighs, carefully making sure he doused her pubic area. No evidence would be left behind. He was always careful about that. He wrapped her body in a cheap throw rug, not wanting any part of her to touch him. Now that she was gone, it was merely a matter of taking out the garbage.

CHAPTER TWO

June 6

For northern tourists, Half Moon Bay was a haven from winter's snow and ice. Fourteen miles wide, the peninsula was attached to Florida's mainland by a natural land barrier called Raider's Bridge. During September and October, the population doubled from fifty to one hundred thousand or more. Also famous for its white sandy beaches, it offered easy access to all the tourist spots from Orlando to the Florida Keys.

The Bay, as the locals call it, was an easy town to navigate. All the avenues ran east and west and streets north and south. Lined with palm trees, with white wrought iron lamp posts and green benches placed under shady oak trees, Central Avenue cut through the downtown area from the Bay to the Gulf.

Central Avenue also divided the wealthy from the working class. On the north side, the affluent residents lived on exotically named streets such as Le Cafe' Boulevard, the Isle of Shells, Treasure Lane, and Captain's Row. The houses began in price from a paltry nine hundred thousand and went up from there.

Celebrities regularly came to perform at the Arts Center, but if they wanted to party, it was at Crooks Castle. The big pink hotel had the best rooms, dining, dancing and was close to the Performing Arts Center. Legend had it that the original builder was the second son of an English Duke who had turned to piracy to make his fortune, then settled in Florida and built his fortress on the Gulf. The building had been a private home, a hotel, and stood empty for too many years until it became an eyesore for the town. Luckily a wealthy investor purchased the building and all the land including the marina. Currently, it had been successively refurbished and converted back into a pricey hotel, with extensive additions to the north side.

South of Central, where the local working-class lived, the homes were compact masonry ranch style dwellings with two or three bedrooms and were substantially less expensive. The streets were lined with oaks, poor man's orchid, crepe myrtles or other exotic flowering trees.

Some parts of town were not so nice. On Highland Street, in the more impoverished section, there was an abandoned, two-story derelict monster where rotting drapes prevented the sunshine from penetrating the shadows of a muggy interior. The heavy odors of dust and mildew emanated from the building like the smell of rotten food. Outside, the front yard was a jungle of weeds that grew around an old refrigerator that had been dumped next to a rusting Pontiac parked in an unkempt gravel driveway. A dirt path led from the rickety front porch steps, past a rotting clothesline to an equally overgrown rear yard that backed up to a deep drainage ditch.

Dawn was barely breaking across the hot morning sky when Homicide Detective Jarrett Blackwell parked his restored 1976, burgundy El Camino truck behind a new gold Toyota Camry. The Camry belonged to Harvey Coleman, the Medical Examiner. He could see the big man through his front windshield and wondered how Harvey's short three hundred and twenty-five-pound bulk was handling the heat and the humidity. Not too well, from the looks of the underarms of his white, short sleeve shirt, the sweat stains clearly visible. Harvey's tan trousers looked just as rumpled.

The M.E. stood resting his thick forearms on the open car door of the Toyota. As a white and red striped ambulance pulled up and parked behind the El Camino, Harvey closed his car door and turned to wait for Jarrett.

Six blue and white police vehicles were parked at the end of the street behind a red Fire Rescue truck. Yellow crime scene tape had already been put up to mark off the large overgrown triangular lot. Tall cabbage palms lined the street side of the lot, and a large oak tree shaded the front of the house. No breeze at all.

Jarrett saw a familiar black Chevy sedan parked in front of Harvey's car. He glanced around but did not see any sign of his six-foot-four partner. Caruso Jones must be canvassing the neighborhood for other witnesses and information.

"Is Forensics on the way?" Jarrett called as he got out of the vehicle and then retrieved his large yellow flashlight from behind the driver's seat. "Damn it," he muttered. Was there ever going to be a break from the heat, even at this hour of the morning?

The odor of wood smoke permeated the morning air, at times strong enough to burn the insides of his nostrils. He was not sure if the smell was from a local fire or a carryover from other fires that kept erupting up and down the state. The drought was so severe the Governor had banned all sales or individual use of firecrackers for the entire state, other than for specific scheduled Fourth of July events. Florida's west coast had been lucky so far, but Jarrett had plenty of other problems to keep him focused. Young girls were turning up dead, one each month since January. So far, they had few leads, and the bodies kept piling up.

He removed his jacket and tossed the garment on the front seat. After stripping off his tie, he unbuttoned the top two buttons of his white cotton shirt. Sweat had beaded on his back and now was trickling down to soak the waistband of his lightweight tan slacks. Even his deck shoes felt hot on his feet.

"Forensics is here," Harvey said as Jarrett walked up beside him. "They're down in the ditch with the body, and the paramedics just got here. I was waiting for you to show up before I take a closer look. I didn't want to chance falling down that bank." Harvey added with a chuckle, "Don't think you or the boys are in the mood to haul my ass back up!"

"No, I don't need to give myself a hernia, Harvey! Besides, it's too damn hot to be hauling anyone up from some ditch. What have you got so far?" Jarrett asked, slapping at a mosquito buzzing around his face.

"I have the crime scene unit snapping pictures, taking video and checking for evidence. It's a bad one. The girl looks to be between fourteen and sixteen." His tone changed. "Her face looks like ground hamburger, Jarrett."

"How many more young girls have to die before we catch this bastard?" Jarrett muttered.

"So far, the patrolman who was first on the scene has thrown up three times," Harvey said with relish. "I think this is his first body."

Jarrett gave him a dirty look. "What are you doing here, Harvey? You rarely come to a crime scene."

"I just happened to be over at Bay Memorial when the call came over the radio. Thought I'd come to see you guys in action, so to speak." He changed the subject. "Heard you took a trip to Kentucky. Was it related to this case?"

"No, just a personal matter." Jarrett shrugged off the question. "Who's the Reporting Officer?" he asked. He would never discuss anything personal with a gossip like Harvey. Everyone in the department would know his business within hours. Besides, it had been a wasted trip.

"Johnson called it in but didn't touch anything. It was hard to see her at first. So he aimed his flashlight beam over the bank, and then proceeded to throw up." Harvey said, slapping at a mosquito biting his neck. "According to the kid, the old woman who made the call said she was up and heard a car door slam." He pointed in the direction of a one-story masonry house next door that was in desperate need of repair and a paint job. "She said it sounded as if it was in front of her house. At three in the morning that worried her, because she knew this house was vacant, having been foreclosed on. So she left the lights off and peeked out the front windows. That's when she saw a big dark car parked in front of this rat trap.

"No one she knows in this block owns a big shiny

car like that. Then, she sees someone haul this big bundle out of the trunk and carry it around the back of this house. She couldn't see too clearly because it was so dark, and she didn't have her glasses on. Anyway, she thinks it was a man. . . She goes back to bed and gets up two hours later to let her cat out. The big car is gone, but she gets this bad feeling that something bad had happened. So she called the police. Better late than never, I guess. Anyway, her backyard runs parallel to this one," he added.

Jarrett spotted several uniformed officers standing in a group near the front of the house. Across Ninth Street, he could see television trucks parked near the intersection with their antennas stretched high above the street. Like vultures, the reporters had heard the call over the police band and now hovered, eager for a glimpse of a body, or an interview with a cop about the crime, trying to get a jump on the story.

He didn't like reporters, and with good reason. After his mother's murder, they had made him and his father's life miserable with their relentless and invasive pursuit. Knowing it was futile, he hoped they would go away. But, they rarely did.

The fat man started walking behind the paramedics across the damp grass. "Let's go see what we got."

Jarrett followed, pointing the flashlight beam ahead, trying not to destroy evidence they might miss in the near dark. They stopped at a spot near the crest of the trench. From what could be seen in the light's beam, the victim appeared to be a nude young girl. As Harvey had said, she was young and seemed to be a fragile, small, skinny little thing. She had been dumped at the bank's edge and rolled into the ditch. Grass stems bent in one direction showed the path the body had taken down the slope. Her descent had been stopped by a bush ten feet down the steep embankment.

The girl lay on her stomach, her upper back to her waist partially hidden by green branches. Two paramedics carefully made their way down the bank and moved to bend over her checking for vital signs.

Jarrett pointed the light at her head. The left side of her face was visible, and even he had to fight the bile rising in his throat. From what he could see of her profile, her face was badly beaten and resembled ground meat just as Harvey had described. An enormous black bruise surrounded the left eye, and there were wounds densely clotted with blood and dirt high up on the cheek. Her mouth was so swollen it was difficult to tell what was left of her lips.

Rage rushed through him. The kind of animals that killed and robbed young girls of their innocence deserved the same sort of bloody fate, he thought. And, just as infuriating, cops spent countless hours busting their butts to solve such cases, only to see many of the criminals walk away on some minor technicality or through a plea bargain. For those who received a prison sentence, jail time was a comparatively easy trip. He felt that the punishment should fit the crime, especially in cases involving children. However, that was not up to him and never would be. All he could do was track down the monsters who committed these atrocities and leave the punishment to the courts.

Jarrett knew the system was far from perfect. His own father's death had proven that. Anger still raged inside him over the injustice of that whole mess and the waste of his father's life. He kept it tightly locked down where it festered deep inside. But at times like these, it took all his strength to maintain his control.

He had become a cop so that he could do everything in his power to stop such insane brutality. But, far too often, some sadistic bastard shoved it in his face, and then, he was forced to watch the perpetrator walk free. The only way he could help this child now was to find her killer and enough evidence to nail him down. He backed up a few paces and took a deep breath to cap his temper and clear his head.

In front of him, Harvey squatted on the lip of the ditch and tried to make a visual inspection from there. The M.E. was working hard not to lose his balance and disturb the crime scene by falling over the wooden rail and rolling down the bank. Flashes from the photographer's camera blinded him for a second.

"Ah, damn. I can't see a thing," Harvey yelled, blinking as spots danced before his eyes, aware that he would have to wait to fix the exact time of death. Even with the sun coming up, he was having trouble seeing. "Son of a bitch," Harvey exclaimed and huffed, pushed upright and stood rubbing his eyes. He picked his way to where Jarrett waited. "Her face is pretty mangled, which may make identification difficult. I can't say definitely until I get her on the table and, from this distance, I can only guess, but I'll bet she was strangled and raped just like the others. She's young like they were."

Taking his handkerchief from his pocket, Harvey mopped the sweat from his eyes and beefy face and then blew his nose. "It's a piss poor world anymore, Jarrett when children are brutalized and tossed away like so much garbage. It's a damned perverted waste." He eyed Jarrett and shoved the handkerchief into his back pocket. "As soon as I finish the autopsy, I'll get the report to you." Then, "God, I wish we'd get a break from this heat." He patted Jarrett on the shoulder and started to walk toward the road, then stopped. "How many does this one make?"

"She's the seventh, assuming she's connected to the other cases," Jarrett told him harshly, scowling. Even one body was one too many. Seven young girls, between the ages of fourteen and sixteen, had been abducted, molested, beaten and murdered. Each had been someone's daughter and, from what they'd been able to piece together, likely runaways and an easy target for a predator. The girls had believed they were streetwise and safe. Sooner or later, too many such kids frequently turned up as rape, overdose or homicide victims. It pissed him off. He was no closer to finding the killer today, with this girl, than he was with the first one. And they could have been if the woman next door had promptly called the police.

As Harvey continued walking towards his vehicle, Jarrett stayed to watch as the two paramedics continued to work on the body. One of the men straightened removed the stethoscope from the girl's back and looked at his partner with a puzzled expression. "I have a faint heartbeat," he shouted. Then, barely audible, a faint moan came from between her torn and swollen lips. They all stopped, stunned, as a weak breath was gasped from the bloody mouth.

"My God, she's still alive!" One of the technicians called into his radio. "We have a live one here. Get down here with a stretcher, fast!" He yelled. "She's alive, but not for long. There's a pulse, faint, but a pulse. We have to transport now, or we'll lose her."

Jarrett stepped aside as the ambulance driver and police officers raced to the aid of the paramedics with a Stokes basket stretcher and ropes. Once they had the victim safely secured, and up the steep incline, the EMT yelled ahead to the ambulance driver. "Call Bay Memorial and tell them we're on the way." The two men raced with the girl to the waiting ambulance where needed equipment waited.

Jarrett's stomach lurched and knotted strangely as he caught a glimpse of long dark hair. "My God, it can't be!" he whispered. "She'd be older, surely." He shook his head to dispel the surge of dread, the sudden feeling that he was seeing . . . "Harvey!" he shouted and ran to stop the fat man from leaving. "The girl just made a noise. I don't know how, but she's still alive. They're taking her to Bay Memorial. I'll meet you there," he yelled at the lowered window.

Harvey stared at him for a moment. "My God, you're kidding me! I can't believe it! What luck!" He grinned quickly. "Okay, I'll see you there." Starting his engine, Harvey pulled out behind the ambulance as it sped away.

Jarrett hurried to his own vehicle then followed

Harvey to the emergency room entrance. Arriving several minutes after the ambulance, they stepped into a wild scene as nurses and doctors rushed the stretcher into the Trauma Room just inside the automatic doors.

The doctor, a tall man with dark curly hair, dressed in green scrubs, his face obscured from view by a mask was busy working on the patient. One by one, he snapped out orders for IV's, drugs and a portable x-rays. As the medical staff sprang into action, the police officers and detectives were forced out of the room to stand outside the doors and wait. This victim, Jarrett thought, could be their first break in a case that was giving them all ulcers and gray hairs. All these months with relatively little evidence, here was their first real chance to stop the killings, if the girl survived. If she did, could she identify her attacker? All he could do now was wait and hope.

Other ambulances with patients arrived and were assigned to rooms. Jarrett, unable to stand the waiting, stepped outside to catch a breath of fresh air. He watched nurses, clerks and other personnel who were arriving for the morning shift change at seven.

This was the first time he had been to Bay Memorial's Emergency Room since he had stopped dating one of the nurses who worked there. His relationships were short affairs, mainly because he couldn't bring himself to open up the way women seemed to want. They dated him knowing he was, as he described himself, skeptical, reticent, and jaded. Each one thought she could change him. However, it was the woman who usually ended the affair after they reached a point where he could not, or would not become more deeply involved.

Jarrett stared at his surroundings without really seeing them, immersed in his thoughts. He had believed in love once, had chased after it like the naive kid he had been. It had proven to be an illusion that had cost him everything and everyone he cared about. And, ever since then, he had refused to expose himself to that level of pain again. That had not stopped him from dreaming of green eyes and a face that had driven him to what felt like the brink of a mad obsession.

It had happened eleven years ago at his parents' Christmas party. He had been young then and idealistically romantic. He had had a beautiful fiancée and all the advantages of family wealth and close, devoted parents as well. Then, he had watched as, coming up the steps near the front door of his father's mansion on Long Island, New York, a young woman had slipped on the ice. Because he had lunged to help, she had fallen into his arms. The moment he had looked into those green eyes, he was lost.

Even after all these years, he vividly remembered the later image of her coming across the dance floor in a cream-colored, crocheted lace dress that had made his blood burn with desire. From a distance, she had appeared nude beneath the gown. All he had done during that particular party was to make an ass out of himself by following her from room to room. Like a young, immature love-struck schoolboy, he had pulled her aside and professed his love to a girl he did not know. A stunning girl. An illusion. He had not known how evil she could be as he held her for a single dance. That dance was followed by the destruction of all he had ever known. That memory still tied his guts in knots.

Those experiences had not stopped his fantasies, however. Even now, at night, he still had dreams of the exotic, intoxicating fragrance of her, of long dark hair that made him wild with the desire to run his fingers through it. He had visions of kissing her sensuous lips or making love to her and knew how her lips would taste and that her skin would feel like silk.

It was all nothing more than illusions.

He shook his head to dispel the images that fogged his brain and resurrected memories that were best kept buried since he couldn't get rid of them. Besides, Jarrett thought, he did not have time to get tangled up with anyone. It was better to focus on the work at hand. He and his partner had needed a break on this case and had finally gotten one. Maybe the Captain and the Sergeant would get off their backs for a while and give them room to work. The murders were considered a high profile case and had generated a lot of public interest, so Captain Whitmore and Sergeant Angst were always pressing for the latest reports.

There had been little to go on until this morning. The butchered and murdered girls always had long dark hair and pretty faces. They were all teenagers, but their disappearances did not follow a set pattern. Each had been abducted from a different location, at a different time on a different day of the month. But, all had disappeared from Half Moon Bay. Their bodies had been dumped in trash bins from one end of town all the way to the Bay, so far. This girl was different. Jarrett was not sure if this crime was connected to the others since this victim had been found in a ditch, but he would know soon enough. Harvey, he knew, was good at his job. He would take the information from the doctors and make a comparison to the other cases. If there were a connection, the M.E. would find it. Jarrett leaned back against the side of the building and took a deep breath. He was thinking too deeply for this hour of the morning.

The sun was fully up, now. It was not quite seven. The steamy heat he could see rising from the pavement was caused by morning dew. It was going to be another scorcher of a day, he thought. He dreaded it because the heat seemed to bring out the worst in people. He would try to take a week off once this case was solved and the killer was securely behind bars or preferably dead.

He looked toward the Bay and watched the distant flashing of a white sail against the dark blue of the water. Some people had all the luck, he thought, being out for an early morning run across the Bay then south to the Gulf of Mexico. He missed sailing, especially those never forgotten daylong jaunts with his dad.

He shut his eyes, unable to avoid seeing, again, his last view of his father. Matthew W. Blackwell had been draped over the desk in his study with a small black hole in his right temple and a bright red bloody pool around his head. He had died from a self-inflicted gunshot wound, believing he had somehow murdered his wife while in a drunken stupor.

Those old memories dredged up too much pain, and so Jarrett tried to focus on the Bay and the sailboats instead.

When he had first driven into Half Moon Bay nine years ago, after two long prior years spent traveling from town to town, he was still searching At the time Jarrett had not known if he was still looking for the girl involved in his parent's death or merely trying to find his own way. All he had known for sure was that he longed for one day that was filled with peace of mind. He had parked his truck outside the Black Pearl restaurant and had sat for hours at a table on the deck, staring out at the marina.

Even then, the day had been hot and the large umbrella shading the table had been a relief from the sun. Line after line of sailing sloops and several good-sized yachts had been moored in the marina, their tall masts swaying in time with the waves that rocked their hulls. High mountains of white cumulus clouds had floated above the horizon, intensifying the blue of the sky as seabirds rode the air currents over the water.

Behind him, in the tall palms that lined the roadway the screeching of Quaker parrots mixed with the chirping of sparrows could be heard. Later, he would discover the parrots would announce their flight over the city at all times of the day. Some claimed the birds had escaped after Hurricane Andrew tore up the southern tip of Florida and had never returned south. On a dark stormy day, their racket was almost a guarantee that the sun was going to shine again.

As he had sat there, the pain that had ridden him hard for over eleven years had been eased by the smell of the salt air and the sound of the birds. He had munched on a turkey sandwich, watching the gulls and pelicans which had perched on nearby pilings, waiting for a morsel of food to be tossed their way. Signs along the deck rail had forbidden feeding them. He had been tempted to ignore the warning. The longer he had sat there, the more at peace he had felt. That was when he had decided to stay. It was that simple. Within two days, he had found an apartment, notified his attorney to wire him money, and where to send the monthly check from his trust fund.

A whiff of wood smoke brought Jarrett back to the present as the sound of laughter was carried up from the street. He glanced toward the corner of the hospital building in time to see the backs of two women, one with long red hair, and the other with dark mahogany hair cascading below her shoulders. Dressed alike in navy skirts and white blouses, they strolled past and out of view. His heart lurched, and the old ache flared.

"No!" he muttered violently. Up until this string of murders, he had found some sort of peace during his stay in Half Moon Bay. He refused to let his obsessive search start all over again.

"No what?" Harvey asked, coming up beside him.

"Nothing!" Jarrett growled.

Raising his eyebrows, the M.E. retorted, "Sorry I asked!"

Jarrett frowned and inhaled sharply. "I saw a woman that reminded me of someone I met a long time ago, that's all. Not her, obviously. Sorry for taking your head off." He had been thrown off balance by the sight of all that dark hair, first with the victim, now with this other woman. He had deluded himself into believing he had buried those tangled love, hate feelings, and that he did not care anymore. It had all roared back all because of long legs, a shapely, slender backside and precisely remembered long curly dark hair.

Jarrett concentrated on blocking Harvey's curiosity. "What's the word on the girl?" he asked.

"Comatose. Dr. Corbett is admitting her to the Pediatric Intensive Care Unit. He won't know anything definite until tomorrow. If she lives through the night, she may make it. Otherwise, all we can do is sit and wait," Harvey said.

Jarrett nodded. "I'll order a guard on her room around the clock. No one is to know what happened to her. As far as anyone here is concerned, she was mugged and is over twenty-one. Keep all information on your end quiet. I'll control this end," he finished and hurried back inside to speak with the doctor and to squelch any leaks to the press.

He had spotted the TV trucks parked on the street, which meant the reporters were still around and inside. They had to be put off at all costs. Once he established the routine concerning the girl, he leaned against the counter to relax for a moment and wished for a cup of hot black coffee. His shoulders sagging with exhaustion, Jarrett wondered what progress his partner was making at the crime scene. Caruso probably had every person in the neighborhood up and interviewed, and had swept the area with the proverbial vacuum cleaner.

Any possible piece of evidence could point to the

killer, and it all had to be tagged, documented and processed as valid, or eliminated. It took time, valuable time before the next victim turned up. First, they had to identify this girl. Given that the assault had happened last night, maybe Missing Persons had a report that might be just now coming into the office. He had little hopes of identifying the car. The eyewitness had not been sure of the make and had been unable to see the license plate. There were no tire tracks either.

Jarrett rubbed his eyes. He had not slept well before getting the call at four-fifty that morning. Now it was after seven. He needed to go home and sleep for about three hours, but it was impossible. There was too much work to do. He removed the cell phone from his pocket and started to dial his office, but stopped, finger poised above the numbers, staring, as before him, coming through the door from the ER waiting room was, beyond question, the same woman who had destroyed his life, who had ever since haunted and filled his nights with turbulent dreams. His mind reeling, Jarrett whirled and fled out of the glass doors before she could see his face. Once outside, he leaned against the building with his insides knotting up and his heart pounding.

It was her. She was actually here in this town. By sheer, freakish luck, Jarrett's search was now over. All he had to do was walk back through the automatic doors and confront the woman he had been obsessed with for the past eleven years. Which was a bad idea, and he knew it. He could not face her. Not yet. His feelings just had been ripped open by the sight of her. To lose control now might make her run if she saw him. If that happened, he might never get the answers he desperately needed. He was not going to take that chance. Their meeting had to be carefully planned. And they would meet. Keeping that in mind, Jarrett pushed away from the building and headed for his truck. He needed to find Caruso and proceed with this investigation. But now, and amazingly at last, he knew where to find her.

CHAPTER THREE

Sarra was dreaming. In the dream, she was a little girl, and the combination of hot sand and the smell of brine permeated the breeze off the water. Some seagulls winged along the beach, while others appeared motionless, riding the air currents high overhead. She pointed to the waves lapping at the shore where sandpipers scurried along the water's edge before a magnificent stone castle. Oh, how she wanted to play in the water with her bucket and shovel.

Beside her, a beautiful dark-haired woman shook her head, and then she spoke to an older boy who was standing next to them. Kneeling, the woman hugged them, kissed first the boy, then her cheek. Love was a warm, safe cocoon within her arms.

Suddenly the dream changed. All the warmth and sunlight faded as the woman walked away. There was only the boy. Another pair of arms was holding her tight. She struggled, but they were too strong. Then, she wasn't a child any longer. A man with dead shark eyes and an evil leer towered over her, pinning her down on a bed.

Sarra Gray bolted upright, breathless, fists clenched, her skin cold and clammy.

Dream, she thought in a panic, it was a dream. It was the same old nightmare which had been part of her sleep for as long as she could remember. Each time, she reacted as if it was the first, waking violently, then fighting to catch her breath and slow the pounding of her heart.

Since leaving Kentucky, the dream had changed.

Now, she dreamed about the woman first, then that whole sequence slid into and was shattered by the hideous entrapment of her night of terror; the night when she had learned how brutal and vicious a man could be. Whenever she allowed herself to relax a little, to begin to feel safe or secure, the horror she had experienced years ago took over from the first dream to twist and pervert it. It was a warning that her assailant was still free. Once again, that nightmare had interrupted her sleep, and now she sat in bed, tense and uneasy.

Around her, the house was quiet. But her senses still tingled. Across the hall, a nightlight in the bathroom gave off a faint glow. Otherwise, her room was dark. She sat still, listening. She could hear nothing unusual. There was something though. . . She could feel it. The back of her neck felt tight, as though she was being watched.

Quietly, furtively, she got out of bed and padded barefoot through the house ignoring the chill from the air conditioning on her bare arms and legs. She hugged her purple satin nightshirt closer around her. First, she checked the bedroom where her daughter, Amanda, and Sarra's best friend, Pearl Ann Burke, slept in twin beds. The windows were locked, and both of the room's occupants were sound asleep.

She paused to gaze at the sleeping woman and child. They were the most important people in her whole world. Pearl Ann had given her shelter, unconditional love, and support many years ago when she had no place to hide, and no one to help her. Her past life had been built on a web of lies and secrets. Sarra dreaded even the idea of having the woman she called Gran discover the truth about her previous life, let alone what she had been forced to do to survive years ago.

In Madison, Kentucky, she had found anonymity because Pearl Ann had given her a new identity by claiming she was a distant relative from New York. For eleven years Sarra had loved her new life, had enjoyed the small town and its friendly residents. The big old, three-story wood framed house with its wrap-around porch had been a real home. Pearl Ann had made it so, and for Sarra, it was the first real home she had ever known. After Amanda was born, the three of them had become a family, with Pearl Ann sharing the care of her daughter. To Pearl Ann, having lost her husband to cancer and with her daughter long missing as an untraceable runaway, the baby had given new meaning to her life. Over the years, as they had grown closer, they had filled a void in one another.

Sarra knew she had changed dramatically during those years. A mostly illiterate young girl, under Pearl Ann's tutelage, she had gotten her GED, and then attended and graduated from college. She had made something of herself. But it was her growing reputation as a small town portrait artist that had led two killers to their doorstep. As a surprise, her painting, The Fallen Madonna, had been submitted to a portrait artists' contest in New York by Pearl Ann. That simple, thoughtful act had been their downfall. It had forced them to flee for their lives.

After that, Sarra had finally told Pearl Ann that she had been a witness to a murder and that the killers were still after her. When Gran had insisted she go to the police, she had refused, too afraid to tell the complete truth, saying that the police couldn't protect her. So, they had traveled south to escape. Here, Sarra prayed fervently, they had a chance to be safe, for a while anyway.

Her nerves still ragged, Sarra tiptoed out of the bedroom and left the door cracked. Amanda hated a dark room. So did she. She moved on to check all the windows and doors. In the dining room, she stepped to the side door and flipped the light switch in the garage to peer through the diamond-shaped window. It was empty also. She even checked the bathroom, at which point she knew she was silly. No one was hiding in the bathroom. But, she could not relax until every nook and cranny in the house had been checked. All was quiet. Still, which, for some reason, made her tension worse.

The spare bedroom was empty as well, except for her wooden artist's easel, a large box filled with canvases and a small table stacked with tubes of oil paints and jars filled with brushes. Still feeling paranoid, she even opened the door to the large closet and turned on the light. There was no one there either. She rechecked the front and back doors, feeling a fraction safer as she returned to bed.

Tomorrow would be a busy day at the Bay Memorial Emergency Room, where she was employed as a Registration Clerk. Without enough sleep, Sarra knew she would be dragging by noon. The bedside alarm clock read four-thirty, she noted with disgust. Work started at seven. She turned off the light and closed her eyes, but sleep refused to come. From a distance, she heard the faint sound of a siren and wondered if it was an ambulance on the way to the hospital.

Day after day at her job, she witnessed disasters, including the cruelty people inflicted on one another. What affected her most were the abused children, helpless victims brought in who had bruises, burns, fractured bones or internal injuries. The medical staff could tell when the welts, swelling and wounds or abrasions were inflicted by the parents or relatives. In such cases, the police were immediately called in to investigate. Sarra wondered why some women had bothered to have children.

She forced those thoughts from her mind and tried to fall back to sleep. After tossing and turning for the next forty minutes, she gave up, threw the blankets aside and headed for the shower. Afterward, dressed in her uniform of a navy suit and white blouse, she slipped on her matching pumps. After leaving a note for Pearl Ann about dinner, she grabbed her purse and headed for the door, locking it carefully behind her.

In keeping with the current heat wave, the sun was already cooking the morning air and blazing above the horizon as Sarra drove north to work. The tourist traffic was as heavy and fast as always, but as she drove past it, she slowed a little to glance at the early light skipping across Egret Lake. The lake attracted numerous species of Florida's water birds. This morning its surface was like polished glass that reflected the puffy clouds floating in the blue sky. A great blue heron and one graceful white egret stood poised and still at the shore's edge, waiting for breakfast to swim close enough to spear. Two knobby eyes and a long snout floated on the glassy surface a short distance away as an alligator eyed the birds. Life was a cruel cycle, she thought as she drove on toward the hospital.

On reaching the employees' garage, she parked on the fourth floor and then joined Addie Newsome for the block-long walk to the ER. The hospital was a Level II Trauma center. The emergency room's central workstation, surrounded with circular, waist-high, white wooden counters, cabinets, desks and chairs, had the latest computer equipment, and screens for tracking patients. It was always crowded with nurses and doctors writing notes on charts or ordering tests, while others hurried back and forth carrying out orders. The one constant factor was the noise, comprised of the low roar of voices, beeping machines, radio calls, rushing people and the on-and-off sound of approaching sirens.

Sarra was required to know the name and location of every examination room and cubicles in the ER. Her job was to obtain information on each patient. This data had to be taken down fast, and entered in the computer system, with a chart printed and delivered to the secretary as quickly as possible. Some days, it was as if the ambulance drivers were in a race to see who could bring in the most patients. The dregs of humanity, as well as the best, came through the ER doors. She had realized that fact after two days on the job.

Upon arrival in the ER, a quick trip to the lounge for a cup of coffee was essential. As she settled at her desk, Sarra noticed a number of uniformed police officers standing outside Trauma Room A, while another man in a white shirt hurried out the automatic glass doors. The set of the man's shoulders reminded her vaguely of someone, but she had no idea who. He was probably one of the doctors on staff at the hospital, she thought, and then wondered what poor soul was now being worked on in Trauma. From the looks of things, it was already a busy day.

Another three hectic hours passed. The paramedics brought in a young man with a knife wound running from the left corner of his mouth almost to his ear. The bandage pressed to his face was soaked with blood. Sarra filled out the emergency sheet with information obtained from the driver's license and insurance card from his wallet. Turning to go, she almost ran into a doctor in green scrubs.

"Excuse me," she said and hurried back to her cubicle to enter the patient information into the computer. Within minutes, she rushed the printed chart to the Unit Clerk. She returned to her desk, checked the clock, and prepared to go on her coffee break. As she walked past the surgical room where the injured man now lay on a bed, she stopped and stared at the doctor working on the facial wound of the patient. This was the first time she had seen this surgeon in the ER, although all she could see was a partial view of his face and a mass of curly dark hair above broad shoulders. He sat at the bedside, stitching the slash on the man's face.

As if feeling her gaze on him, he looked up and stared at her with widening eyes. Then his skin paled above the surgical mask. Sarra started. The doctor was acting as if he recognized her. That was impossible, she thought. She had never been in Half Moon Bay before and did not know anyone other than Addie and her next-door neighbor Barbara. Maybe she was overreacting, and the surgeon just did not like anyone disturbing him as he worked. Perhaps that was it. She turned and hurried away, anxious to be out of his line of sight. Sarra was well aware that trauma doctors could be temperamental at times.

Fifteen minutes later, she returned from the cafeteria to find the same doctor seated in one of the typing chairs. He stood up when she walked through the door. Oh God, she thought, I'm in trouble.

"I thought I was seeing a ghost," he said stepping toward her, staring. "But you're real. I can't believe this!" He fidgeted, clearly excited. "This can't really be happening, but you're here."

Sarra eyed the man warily, edging around him, trying to decide if he was crazy or just mistaking her for someone else. He was a good-looking man, handsome enough to be a movie star or a model, the sort that would tempt most women to feign an illness just to be seen by him.

"Can I help you in some way?" she asked carefully, frowning.

"Yes, you certainly can! Will you have coffee with me so we can talk?" He gave her a sudden, radiant smile that would have enthralled many a patient.

Sarra did not trust anyone who looked that good in blood-stained scrubs, and she certainly was not about to trust this stranger. "I just came back from break. I can't go again. Thank you just the same," she said briskly. It was a legitimate evasion. But, she had to wonder why he was acting so delighted to see her? She was sure they had never met. She started to sit down, but he grabbed her arm and turned her to face him again, deadly serious now.

"You don't understand. It's important that we talk," the doctor insisted, keeping a firm grip on Sarra's wrist as if afraid she would run away.

Sarra immediately pried his fingers loose and fought to keep both her fear and anger in check. "Doctor, I really have to get back to work," she told him sharply. "If you insist, we can talk while I'm working."

Undeterred, he glanced around the small office, at the watching eyes and pricked ears of co-workers and patients. "No," he said. "We have to talk in private. Look, can you come to my house for dinner tonight?"

Relieved, Sarra gave him an understanding smile. Ever since starting to work at the hospital, she had been hit on by male nurses, paramedics and even some of the police officers, but this was the first doctor. She gave him the same answer she had used on the others. "Well, Doctor, I must admit you have a new approach in asking for a date, but I'm busy tonight." She turned away and called out the name of the next patient. A moment later, a large woman in a flowered print dress sat down in the chair at the counter.

Behind her, the doctor's voice rose in frustration. "Look, I'm not asking for a date, damn it! I'm a married man." He yanked a prescription pad from his shirt pocket and scribbled something, tore off the sheet and handed it to Sarra. "It's imperative. I need to talk to you! Here, I have patients to see, and I don't have time to explain further. That's my home address. Please, I beg you, be at my house at seven. My wife, Helen, will be there in case you're worried. This is vital," he paused to catch his breath. "I'm gambling that you'll show up out of curiosity. Seriously, we have a lot to discuss." He walked out the door, leaving Sarra standing with a piece of paper in her hand and her mouth gaping open.

She almost started after him to tell him she would not be accepting his dinner invitation, but he had already disappeared through the exit doors. Slowly taking her seat, she glanced at the slender redhead who was grinning at her from the next desk. "What are you smiling about, Addie?"

Addie Newsome was the only other woman outside of Pearl Ann that Sarra felt was a friend. While Sarra was reserved even with the patients, Addie was open and friendly with everyone. From the social derelicts dragged in by the police to those dressed in designer clothes, it didn't matter, it was her job to ease their anxiety, and she did so superbly. A tall, slender woman, with big brown eyes, and an easy manner, and a wide grin, Addie was striking, rather than beautiful, and was good at her job. She had put Sarra at ease from the first day they met. Now they worked side by side in the same registration section.

Occasionally, they ventured out together to the Den, a dimly lit piano bar on Beach Drive, to hear Addie's friend Sandy sing and play. Pearl Ann had insisted Sarra needed to "get out, enjoy some music, relax and laugh for a change." It was true, she did enjoy herself. Besides, Addie was fun to be around. At the moment, she was beaming.

"Well?" Sarra demanded.

If it was possible, Addie's grin widened. "I'm just surprised at Straight Laced Corbett, that's all. I've worked here for over nine years, and you're the first woman I've seen him take a tumble over. You have no idea how many women here have the hot's for Doctor Gene Corbett."

"You're wrong Addie," Sarra frowned, recalling his insistent invitation and wondering why she'd never seen him around before. "He said his wife would be at home, so he can't be after me that way." Her mind raced with questions. Why did the good doctor feel a talk was so vital? About what? He was right though, she was curious, she admitted, but she wasn't stupid enough to risk everything by going to some stranger's house.

"Yeah, I heard what he said." Addie gave her a knowing grin before turning her attention to the man who stood with a bloody rag wrapped around his hand in front of her desk.

Sarra stuffed the piece of paper with the doctor's address in her skirt pocket and returned to work. All too soon she was caught up in the fast-paced routine of the emergency room as ambulance after ambulance rolled in with all sorts of trauma cases, broken bones, heart attacks, car accidents, and the odd gunshot wound. At noon, she grabbed a quick lunch, the doctor and his request forgotten. By three-thirty, she was more than ready to scrub the sweat of a hard day from her tired body.

After their shift ended, on the way to the parking garage, Sarra pulled the slip of paper from her pocket and read the address. She handed it to Addie and asked, "Where is this street?"

Addie read the address and let out a soft whistle. "That, girlfriend, is one of the prime sections of Half Moon Bay! That's what they call the "pink streets" north of the Castle just off the Point. It's an older section of town with those big fancy homes on the water. You have to have lots of money to live there."

Sarra arched an eyebrow. "So, Dr. Corbett is wealthy, is he?"

"If it were me, I wouldn't have to even think about it. I'd go and hope the man hated the wife. That man is gorgeous, with those piercing hazel eyes and that thick curly black hair. And that mouth of his! I could kiss that mouth forever! He positively gives me shivers," Addie said, grinning wickedly.

Sarra laughed at her friend and shook her head. "My Gran says beauty is skin deep, but ugly goes all the way to the bone. I'd have to get to know him before I decide if I like him or not. Besides, married is married. I don't want any part of that kind of a mess," she countered and frowned as she thought of how he seemed to have recognized her. How? She would not let curiosity draw her into a dangerous situation, or one she would live to regret. But, she had to wonder, what was so important?

There were times she wished she could be more like Addie, daring, able to live for the moment. But, it was impossible. She had to be wary of everything because the safety of her daughter and Pearl Ann depended upon it. She decided she would discuss the doctor's invitation with Pearl Ann before making a decision.

Addie sensed her hesitation. "Oh, come on, Sarra. You could at least have dinner and find out what he has to say," she persisted. "You could snoop for me and find out if he likes redheads." Patting her dark red hair, Addie's eyes danced with mischief. "Besides, I hear he's unhappily married. His wife likes to throw temper tantrums. She's thrown some good ones in the doctors' lounge."

"All right. I'll think about it. I am curious about what the doctor has to say. But, you're dying to know about his wife and that house, aren't you? You've worked here nine years, and he's been on staff at the hospital all that time?" Sarra asked as they entered the elevator and rode up.

"He's been on staff for eight years, for sure. He's a trauma surgeon. Don't see him around much, though, only when there's a patient with major injuries. He hasn't been in on our shift for quite some time until today. I've been lusting after that gorgeous body of his for each and every one of those years! I know he is a Florida native," she continued as they exited on the fourth floor of the garage. "He was born and raised in Half Moon Bay. So, please, for me, go find out if he's unhappily married or not."

As Sarra unlocked the door to the Camaro, Addie continued on toward her vehicle, then stopped, turned and called out. "Call me later and let me know if you go."

Sarra waved, climbed in and started the car. The Camaro did not have an air conditioner, so by the time she pulled into the driveway, a cooling shower was all she could think about. She did not want to think about the doctor or his invitation.

Five months ago, she and Pearl Ann had rented the house within a week after arriving in Half Moon Bay. It was perfect. Set on a quiet side street off the main artery of Ninth Street, the house was only five miles from the hospital. The branches of four tall oak trees created a canopy of shade over the front yard, offering relief from the blazing sun and tropical heat.

The backyard was fenced with a concrete block wall topped with another three feet of white stockade wood fencing. The gate was fastened with a hooked latch, low and out of reach from outside. All this afforded privacy and a certain amount of security. In the center of the yard, a lattice-covered stone patio was sheltered by a giant maple and two other oak trees. Large pots of geraniums, impatiens and asparagus ferns lined the terrace to add vivid color to the lush green of the lawn. A passion vine with deep blue flowers climbed one corner patio post and spread across part of the lattice roof. On the opposite corner, a black-eyed Susan vine, with its deep gold, black-centered flowers, wound up the post and across to merge with the other plant.

Watching two squirrels chasing each other around the trunk of the maple tree and listening to a mockingbird's song had made them relax. The quiet serenity of the walled garden had offered a momentary peace. Breathing the spicy scent of jasmine in the air, this, they had decided, was the house for them. Sarra had signed the papers for a year, paid for three months' rent in cash, and the realtor had happily turned over the keys that afternoon.

The house had three bedrooms, two baths, a large kitchen and dining room, with an extended living room next to what Floridians called a Florida room. Once, it had been a screened porch that had been converted into an enclosed room with large windows. The house had been cleaned, freshly painted, and was unfurnished. For the first week, they had slept on air mattresses they purchased at Walmart. Garage sales provided an odd collection of furniture, including a used sofa, a recliner and, a small kitchen table with mismatched chairs. They had improved the inexpensive pieces by adding bright gold and orange pillows and then had added faux wood slat blinds and sheer curtains to the windows to shield the interior from the intense sun. Area rugs now hid the terrazzo floor.

Sarra had wanted the place to be as homey as possible. The masonry block building with its vaulted ceilings and simple design could never replace their Kentucky home, but for now, anyway, it was a decent and safe place to live. The only other mandatory purchases had been quality mattresses on twin-size metal frames. Pearl Ann had insisted on sharing the biggest room with Amanda. Sarra took the mid-sized room as her bedroom and turned the smallest room into an art studio. They had left the walls bare except for one painting, The Fallen Madonna, which now hung above the living room sofa.

It was a self-portrait, started when she was pregnant with Amanda and finished after her child's birth. It had been a Christmas present for Pearl Ann. The background was of overlapping diamonds of color from black along the outside edges that morphed into purples, lavenders, and various shades of pink and finally became a soft white that surrounded and backlit the figures of a mother and child dressed in soft rose gowns. Of all the commissioned portraits she had done in Madison, this, she believed, was her finest work.

It was easier to blend in and disappear among the denser, more populous and much larger town of Half Moon Bay, where thousands of people were crowded onto the peninsula than it had been in Madison. They were just three more snowbirds who had moved south to get away from the frigid northern winters. Since their main income consisted of Pearl Ann's Social Security check, the last of their savings had been growing short. It had become necessary for Sarra to find a job.

Other than her daughter and Pearl Ann, painting was Sarra's passion. She didn't want a career, just a job she could leave quickly, if and when necessary. With her limited office skills, Sarra had been lucky to land a job at Bay Memorial Hospital. The pay was standard for the area, low, but between her salary and Pearl Ann's check, they would not starve. If their situation were to become desperate, there were other assets she had tucked away in that old flight bag for an emergency.

Sarra knew that in this town, she could not use her art to supplement their income. Even though her portfolio was extensive, she could not risk it. Her artistic ability was what had sent them on the run. She had not touched a brush to canvas since they had arrived and hated not being able to paint. That had to change. She could do the paintings she longed to do, and do them for herself. It was her stress outlet. Even if she never exhibited her work, she needed to paint. There were portraits of Amanda and Pearl Ann she wanted to paint. One painting, in particular, she badly wanted to try.

Tucked away, her sketchbooks were filled with drawings of Kentucky landscapes and familiar faces. There was one face that she had sketched over and over until she knew every plane and angle and nuance. His image haunted her dreams. Too often she had wondered about the young man she had met all those years ago, on her night of terror. He was probably married with children, happy and content with his life. Sometimes she had even allowed herself to fantasize about him, imagining that she was his wife and Amanda was his child. But, fairy tales did not have a place in her life. Wondering what might have been would not change the facts. Thoughts like those only left her feeling desolate inside.

Their lives had touched so briefly and then had gone in different directions, lost moments that could not be recaptured. "Put the past behind you," Pearl Ann was fond of saying. It was good advice, and Sarra tried to follow it. But, she also knew from bitter experience that sometimes the past refused to stay buried.

As the days passed, they had developed a routine. Knowing it was a strange town and that children left alone were vulnerable, Sarra kept Amanda close to home.

She would watch television or play with the little girl next door. As for herself, Sarra knew a few coworkers. Except for Addie, she did not make any effort to extend her circle of acquaintances. She minded her own business and kept that business to herself. That was the general idea, anyway. Now some doctor she didn't know wanted her to come to his house for some sort of important discussion. It frightened her.

The house seemed too quiet when she entered. There was a message taped to the refrigerator from Pearl Ann saying she was taking Amanda to buy new shoes. Sarra smiled. She loved being a mother and having Pearl Ann with her, but there was never a moment for herself. She didn't want a lot of time, just an occasion such as this one when she had the house all to herself so she could enjoy some peace and quiet. Pearl Ann must have sensed that need today and decided to give her a break.

After locking the door, she stripped off her clothes and dropped them across a wicker chair on her way to the bathroom. She showered and washed her hair, thankful for her natural curl. The Florida humidity, however, made it curl more than usual. Quickly drying her hair with the blow dryer, she donned her pink terrycloth robe as protection against the blast of frigid air blowing down the hallway from the vent in the ceiling. She had time for a short nap, she decided and yawned. Stretching out on the bed, she wrapped the spread around her and closed her eyes.

CHAPTER FOUR

Two hours later, Sarra awoke refreshed just as an excited Amanda charged into the bedroom clutching a shoe box.

"Mom, you have to see the new Reeboks Gran bought me!"

The child landed on the queen-size bed with a bounce, flipped the lid off the box and shoved the shoes toward her mother. In a face that strongly resembled Sarra's, large dark eyes watched for the appropriate reaction. The child's dark curly hair was pulled up in a ponytail, and her red and white striped shirt and tan shorts showed mustard stains. Hot dogs.

"Those look really comfortable. Are the shoes a good fit?" Sarra kissed the top of her daughter's head and glanced at Pearl Ann standing in the open doorway.

"Perfect!" Amanda exclaimed, and then added, "What's for dinner? I'm starved!"

Sarra rose from the bed handing the shoe box back to Amanda. "You're always starved. From the looks of you, I'd say you've already had an early dinner." Her tone became serious, "I may have to go out for a while to see a doctor about something."

"Are you sick?" A worried frown creased the child's forehead. She snuggled closer to her mother and wrapped her slender arms around Sarra's waist.

Her daughter had become a worrier since they had left Kentucky. My God, Sarra thought, having to flee for their lives, especially without understanding why, would put a mark on any child, certainly one as young as ten. They had lost the only home they had ever known, and their beloved dog, Skipper.

As soon as Pearl Ann had shown her the magazine article about her painting, Sarra had known they had to leave as quickly as possible. But, Pearl Ann had refused to budge until she knew why they were being forced to run. The older woman already knew that Sarra had been raped and that Amanda was the product of that rape. But Sarra had never divulged the circumstances associated with the vicious assault on her person.

That day, she had been forced to explain more but had managed to reveal only the bare minimum of information. She had almost convinced Pearl Ann it was necessary to leave Kentucky to save their lives. Then, the men sent to kill them had shown up and nearly succeeded.

Amanda still had nightmares from the horror of that experience. More than anything, Sarra wanted to see a smile return to her child's face. Somehow, she had to make that happen. She hugged Amanda.

"No, I am not sick," Sarra said and quickly added. "You worry too much, Pumpkin. This nice doctor has invited me to his house for dinner. Maybe he's going to offer me a better job. What do you think of that?"

"Fine, I guess." Amanda's worried expression faded. She slipped off the bed and then ran past Pearl Ann through the door and down the hall to her bedroom.

"I think we may have a problem," Sarra said softly moments later as she and Pearl Ann headed for the kitchen. She quietly explained what had transpired at the hospital. "I can't imagine what is so important." She continued, "What scares me is that he seemed to recognize me. If I don't go, he may come looking for me again at work. We don't want that."

Pearl Ann frowned. "You've never seen him before at the hospital?"

Sarra shook her head. "No, never, not even in the hallways. Today was the first time."

"Well, I doubt a reputable physician means you any harm, and you said his wife was going to be there," Pearl Ann said cautiously.

"Addie says he was born and grew up here in Half Moon Bay. She's known him for almost eight years." Sarra hesitated. "That's the only reason I'm even considering this. Do you think I should go? I'm curious as to what he has to say."

Pearl Ann studied her for a few moments. "Sarra," she said, "not every man is dangerous. We need to have a real life, you know." She pushed a strand of short curly gray hair behind one ear. "We can't hide forever," she added with a stubborn set to her jaw.

Instantly on the defensive, Sarra countered with, "Just because I believe in being careful, is not exactly the same as hiding. Look what happened in Kentucky."

Pearl Ann did not respond at once. She knew Sarra was right. They wouldn't even be in Half Moon Bay if she hadn't submitted that painting to the contest without her knowledge. What had been intended as a wonderful surprise had gone dreadfully wrong. If it hadn't been made public, the man who had raped her would never have come looking for her. They would still be safe instead of on guard all the time. It was her fault, Pearl Ann thought, and she had paid dearly for her mistake. "We have to stop running at some point, Sarra," she said firmly.

"I hear what you're saying, and you're right." Sarra agreed reluctantly. "But, don't you think it's strange for a married doctor to invite a complete stranger to his home? A person he's never met before?" She fretted, preparing the coffee to brew.

"Obviously. But, there's probably a simple explanation. Perhaps the doctor thinks you're a long lost cousin or something." Pearl Ann said.

Sarra scowled, "Believe me, Pearl Ann, there is no way that Dr. Gene Corbett could possibly be related to my father, Harry Gray." Harry had lived with the most unspeakable filth from New York's sewers. If he were related to anyone, they wouldn't want to claim him. Then why did she? Sarra wondered. Because he was the only family she had ever known.

"Maybe he isn't related, but I admit I'm curious as well," Pearl Ann said. "And you're obviously anxious about this. Besides, you never completely relax. Amanda senses this you know. Today she even asked me if those bad men were coming back to hurt us."

Rendered more distraught by what she was hearing, her nerves already raw, Sarra blinked back tears. "My God! It's so stupid! Amanda shouldn't have to suffer because of my mistakes."

"Well, she does! This has all got to end, Sarra," Pearl Ann stated sharply as Sarra turned away to fiddle with the coffeemaker and hide her face. "I always said the police would likely catch that man who attacked you.

That still applies, even now." She had brought up the police years ago when she had first learned about the rape, but Sarra had flatly refused to consider it.

"I won't chance it, Pearl Ann, you know that, so stop pushing me!" Sarra bit out. She knew far too well that when threatened with death, a person will do anything to stay alive, especially if she is only sixteen years old. That didn't mean her nights had been peaceful since. Anything but! She was still plagued with horrible dreams of being beaten and raped.

Pearl Ann's face tightened with exasperation. She was scared. The girl had to be persuaded to get the police involved. If she didn't, and those men found them, Pearl Ann was afraid she might lose her, and she couldn't bear to lose Sarra. She had lost her own daughter Rose Ann. One day she had been home, the next, gone, vanished into the oblivion of a man's false promises of stardom. They had searched for her but without any luck. They never heard one word or uncovered a single trace. Her husband, John, had died never knowing if his daughter was alive or dead. Then, two weeks before Sarra had appeared on her doorstep, Pearl Ann had been notified that Rose had been murdered in New York City and dumped, like a piece of garbage, in one of the rivers.

"All right," Pearl Ann said, "but keep in mind what all this running and hiding is doing to your daughter. To all of us for that matter."

"I am thinking of Amanda. And you," she added. "I want to keep you both safe."

"Hiding is not being safe! We can be careful and still enjoy what this town has to offer." There was so much to do, the theater, the beach, the Pier. . . "We can have fun," Pearl Ann countered in frustration. "It isn't normal to stay housebound all the time, and it certainly isn't good for Amanda. She's a child, Sarra, young, healthy, and shouldn't be fearful and anxious, the way she is. Go to this doctor's house, find out what he wants. Maybe it is about a job." Pearl Ann added, relaxing a little. "Besides, you might have a better dinner than us. It's going to be a soup and sandwich night here. So go. Take the chance, enjoy the meal."

"Maybe, but . . . . " Sarra left the sentence hanging as she leaned back against the counter.

"No buts! We have to live, and I for one will not go on living like a caged animal!" Pearl Ann snapped back, trying to control her temper as she watched fear run through the younger woman's eyes. She softened her tone. "If your rapist does find us, well, it will be time to stop running and take a stand. You have to realize that, or we'll all be raving maniacs soon."

Sarra ignored the last. "Yes, fun, but cautious fun. We have to be on guard for Amanda's sake."

Pearl Ann fought to keep her patience. "Yes, I know, but I repeat, you have to face it all at some point." She inhaled and then added. "I still believe going to the police is our only chance."

"My God, Gran, you know I can't! I absolutely can't," Sarra was vehement. There was too much she had never told Pearl Ann. Secrets were like an infection in the soul, a boil that festered and spread until the core had to be lanced before all the pus could ooze out. Keeping secrets from Pearl Ann was just like that and as painful, but absolutely necessary.

Pearl Ann held up her hands and gave up. "Forget I mentioned it." She reached for her cup, took a sip of coffee then carried it to the sink.

Sarra watched her. "Well, put that thought out of your head. I will not have my daughter exposed to my past and possibly taken away from me. I won't risk it."

"All right, Sarra!" Pearl Ann set her cup down with a clatter. "But, remember one thing, you're going to have to stop running sometime. The police can help." From the look on the girl's face, she knew it was useless to press the issue further. Things were going on in Sarra's head that she didn't understand and she was not about to disclose. "Never mind! Go get dressed, or you'll be late. I'll take care of Amanda. But think over what I've said."

"I'll think about it," Sarra agreed over her shoulder as she hurried to her bedroom.

Pearl Ann watched as Sarra disappeared into the back bedroom. She was a far cry from the tough sixteen-year-old who had rung her Kentucky doorbell long ago and had inquired about renting one of the upstairs apartments. That child had not trusted anyone and had been scared to leave her rooms until hunger had literally forced her out.

She had finally asked for directions to town and a grocery store. That had been her first act in soliciting, then accepting help. Then, the early morning sounds of Sarra vomiting in the upstairs bathroom had carried down through the old radiator vents. Pearl Ann had guessed immediately the young girl was pregnant. It had taken nearly a month to get her to admit to her condition and to come to dinner. She had accepted the invitation only after Pearl Ann had climbed the stairs and insisted. That had been the beginning of what had developed into their close friendship.

Beyond reluctantly admitting that she had been beaten and raped by a man in New York, Sarra had confided little of her past. It was only after the art exhibit fiasco that she had confessed she also had been a witness to a murder. Pearl Ann had been left to wonder what other things were tormenting the girl, and hope that someday Sarra would trust her enough to tell her everything. But the girl never had. Only time would force her to face her past. She could wait. Pearl Ann shrugged and began preparing soup and sandwiches for herself and Amanda.

Unfamiliar with the streets on the Point, Sarra was aware she needed to leave the house no later than six-thirty. With a practiced hand, she applied her makeup, but choosing a dress took more time. Amanda and Pearl Ann helped her, finally settling on a soft pink cotton dress with a scooped neck and capped sleeves. It had been a birthday gift. She pulled her black hair off her neck and secured it with combs, slipped on her pumps and grabbed her purse. It was past time for her to leave as she kissed Amanda, hugged Pearl Ann and closed the door behind her.

With luck, she would find the doctor's house without too much trouble. At Fourteenth Street north, she turned right and drove up Third until she crossed First Avenue South. From Addie's directions, the doctor's home was on exclusive Le Cafe' Bayou, a brick street on the far north side of the Bay where million dollar homes graced the waterfront.

She found the street well north of the Castle and was surprised to see the road surface was actually paved with dark pink bricks. Side streets branched off toward the east and west. Directly before her, Half Moon Bay spread out, shimmering with reds, oranges and variegated shades of purples, in the late evening sun. All the houses were large two, or three-story dwellings with well-manicured lawns and lots of foliage. Some were Spanish in style; some were modern, while others were Colonial with tall white columns and circular driveways. They all exuded wealth. She found the correct street and parked in front of the house with the number the doctor had written on the slip of paper. Doctor Corbett, in tan Dockers, a white shirt, and loafers, came out of the front door and rushed down the steps. Apparently, he had been watching for her.

"Thank God you came!" He greeted her as he opened the car door. "I realized after I left the emergency room, I didn't know your name or where you lived." He took a deep breath and continued more slowly, "I was afraid that if you didn't accept my invitation tonight, you might disappear on me." He gave her a quick smile, "Good grief, I'm rambling. I'm sorry." He took her arm gently. "Come inside, and I'll introduce you to my wife."

"She's here?"

"Certainly, I wouldn't invite you to my home without my wife being present." He smiled again at the look of relief on her face.

Sarra flushed with embarrassment. "I apologize.

You know how talk is around the hospital."

He chuckled and ushered her into the foyer. "Yes, I do. My wife is upstairs on the deck. She thought you might like to eat outside overlooking the Bay," he said and led the way up a flight of stairs.

It was an imposing three-story house of Spanish stucco. Sarra followed the doctor into a large living room and stared at her surroundings. At least thirty- five feet in length, the walls were painted a pale pumpkin with accents of deep teal. An off-white cotton-covered sofa, flecked with the pumpkin and teal colors, sat in front of a white brick fireplace. The same colors were repeated in the upholstered side chairs facing the sofa. White, wrought iron coffee and end tables and a curved bar with a polished marble top, completed the room. The rich oak floor served as a backdrop for the bright colors throughout the room. At the opposite end of the room, broad, sliding glass doors opened onto a screened deck overlooking the Bay.

A tall, attractive woman with red hair stood leaning against the railing, her emerald green dress elegant and classically simple, complimenting her looks. At their approach, she turned and greeted Sarra with a smile and a handshake. "I'm Helen Corbett. Welcome to our home," she said graciously, and then added, "Gene tells me he thinks you're his long lost sister."

"What?" Sarra froze for a moment and then whirled to face the doctor.

"Damn it, Helen!" Gene Corbett barked. "She knows nothing about this."

"I'm so sorry," Helen said, "I thought Gene had already told you." She gestured toward the table. "Please, ignore what I said. Won't you sit down and Gene will explain everything."

Sarra cut in. "What is she talking about? I'm no one's sister." She looked at Helen. "In fact," she said, a feeling of dread trying to grab hold as she turned back to face Gene, "let's forget this entire dinner idea. I'd rather go home."

"NO!" Gene yelled, grabbing her arm as Sarra started for the door.

Sarra stopped in her tracks and glared at him.

He hurriedly shifted his grip and, indicated the deck with his other hand. "Please come and sit down. Let me explain." Then, more gently, "I want my nightmares to end."

Nightmares. . . . The word struck a chord. After hesitating, Sarra allowed him to lead her to a large, white glass-topped patio table and chairs.

Gene let go of her arm and turned to his wife. "Helen, I know you didn't mean to blurt it out, but, I remind you that this young woman knows nothing. I haven't told her anything. I wanted to do it here, privately." He indicated, "My wife, Helen."

"Well, as I told you, I'm so sorry I said anything," Helen said, her beautiful face remorseful, but her gaze intensely studying Sarra. "My God, if it turns out you are his sister; it will be a blessing for poor Gene. It will help erase the guilt he's carried for so many years." She shifted and returned to again lean against the deck railing, her eyes never leaving Sarra.

The doctor ignored the last and turned to address

Sarra. "Please sit down and have a drink while I try to think of the best way to begin this. What will you have?"

Sister? Sarra eyed him suspiciously, ready to bolt. His wife's concern was apparent by the way she continued to study her. And the good doctor? Where in the world would he get the crazy idea she was his sister? Curiosity won out, and she sank carefully onto one of the cushioned chairs around the table. "Scotch and water, please. If you have it."

"I do." He smiled and reentered the house. He returned a moment later followed by an elderly oriental man in a white jacket carrying three drinks on a silver tray. Gene took one glass and held it out, and, when Sarra accepted it, seated himself. The servant silently set down the other two drinks and disappeared into the house. Sarra watched Helen Corbett scoop up one of the glasses and seat herself at the table as well with a smile direct at Sarra.

"I don't even know what to call you." Gene said then, leaning toward her, "I want to call you Micki, but I suspect, that wouldn't mean anything to you."

"That isn't my name," Sarra told him, feeling her heart pound as she tried to remain calm. There was something about him. . . "You can call me Sarra. My full name is Sarra Gray. I know you're Dr. Gene Corbett and your wife is named Helen. Now that we have the introductions out of the way, what is this nonsense about me being your sister?" She was beginning to get a dull headache from lack of food. She hadn't eaten since eleven, now it was almost seven-thirty.

As if reading her mind, the oriental man appeared and set plates of salad down before each of them. Across the table, Helen ignored Sarra and began to pick at the greens on her plate.

Gene shot an annoyed look at his wife. "I have every reason to believe that you are my sister, as my wife has stated. But we won't discuss that right now. I want you to hear me out before you come to any conclusions." He settled back in his chair and held up a hand as Sarra stiffened further, then took a sip of his drink. "Hear me out, please," he repeated. "It's a tragic story. . . .Sarra. An old one." He inhaled as though bracing himself. "The events of that day are etched in my brain. . .

"In the late eighties and early nineties, my father was one of the last physicians to treat patients out of a small Veterans Administration Outpatient Clinic north of Crook's Castle. When Dad worked at the clinic, Mother would take us to meet him for a picnic lunch on the small beach near the marina, which was nearly every day." His voice softened with recollection as he sipped his drink. "My little sister, Monique, in particular, loved those picnics. Crook's Castle was her fairy castle, and she was its princess. So, every other day, she would cry to go to the beach at the Castle.

"Dad got his discharge from the Army and opened his own practice in town. He did very well. We had a home over in Driftwood. It's another residential area on the north side that, at that time, was considered to be one of the nicer places to live. It's still a nice area."

Gene handed his glass to the servant for a refill while he studied Sarra's face. "The resemblance is truly amazing," he said staring at her until she felt heat creep up her face. He shifted in his seat and glanced at his wife whose eyes still continued to watch them both. Ignoring her, he turned back to Sarra. "You've seen the Castle, haven't you?"

"Yes," she said, "I've been there." The big pink building meant nothing to her. Yet, what Gene had told her so far was making her stomach churn. She was having trouble focusing on his words and caught herself clenching her hands under the table until her fingernails bit sharply into her palms. She forced them open and placed one on top of the other in her lap, fighting to relax.

"Well, in 1989 it looked a lot different," Gene was saying. "The basic building was the same, but it wasn't as grand as it is now, and not the same color. The salmon pink was quite faded back then and altogether missing in places on the walls. The area was not as densely populated either, and Crook's was in bad shape. There was even talk of it being demolished at the time. A lot of the windows were boarded up, but it was still a fairy tale castle to my sister." He paused and inhaled as if collecting himself.

"That particular day in August was beautiful. It was hotter than blazes, but there was a cooling breeze off the water. Mom took us for our usual picnic lunch on the beach. Dad was supposed to meet us there. Anyway, we lived in an old, two-story Spanish style house with this tricky driveway. The only way out was to back out." Gene shook his head and smiled as he remembered. "Mom hated that driveway. You had to ease out carefully, and sometimes that was risky. You couldn't see anything coming from either direction. Anyway, that day Mom was in a hurry. She backed out too fast and plowed into our neighbor's new car. God, she was upset.

"Our neighbor, Mr. Craswell, was very generous about it and took the blame. He said he was in a hurry to get some relatives to the airport. I remember seeing a woman holding a little girl on her lap in the passenger seat. Another man was in the back seat as well. Mr. Craswell assured Mom he would take care of the damages. Then he drove away.

"We had a big hamper full of food and soft drinks, so we went on to the beach. We spread out a red blanket on the sand near the Castle. Dad never showed up. I think Mom was worried he was going to be mad at her for damaging the car. We were in our swimsuits, and Mom wore a long flowing beach skirt." He paused again and looked down at his hands. "It was way past time for lunch. Monique was getting fussy and wanted to eat. I was old enough to look after her for a few minutes while my mother went to call Dad." He swallowed his voice roughening. "My God, I was twelve years old and big for my age. There was no reason I couldn't take care of her."

Sarra saw Gene's tension, how he fidgeted, opening and closing his hands restlessly. A knot had formed in the pit of her stomach, and there was a new throbbing behind her eyes. She was terribly afraid of what she was hearing but more afraid not to listen to the rest.

"Monique didn't want to stay with me," Gene continued unevenly. "She wanted to go with Mom. Mom had told her couldn't and that she would only be gone a few minutes to make a phone call and was coming right back. She hugged and kissed us both on the cheek then walked away. Monique wouldn't stop crying. So I walked her up to the street so she could see where Mom went. We watched her walk down the road. Then she turned and waved to us and entered the restaurant near the Castle.

"I was holding Monique's hand when she jerked away from me and ran after our mother. She ran straight into the road." He paused for a second and then continued. "A car was coming, and I was terrified she was going to be hit. I ran after her screaming. God, she was fast for three and a half. . . The car slowed to a stop. A man leaned out and grabbed my sister around the waist. I tried to stop him, but he knocked me down, and I hit my head." He paused and looked up again. "I woke up in the emergency room with a doctor stitching up a cut on my cheek. The police were there. My mother was in hysterics, and my father was in a state of shock."

Her heart beating wildly, Sarra was afraid to breathe.

Gene stared steadily at her watching the reaction on her face. "My sister was never seen again nor was her body ever found," he said. "There was no ransom request. Nothing! The police never found her or her abductor. She vanished completely." He hesitated, "Until now. There is no doubt in my mind that you are my sister, Monique."

CHAPTER FIVE

Sarra tried to remain calm, but her heart was beating too fast. Her head began to spin and nausea churned in her stomach. Everything in the room started to blur and fade. Then the strong odor of ammonia burned her nostrils, causing her to jerk her head back. Throwing up one hand to ward off the acrid fumes, she looked up into Gene's worried eyes.

"What happened?" she asked. "Why did you stick that smelly thing under my nose?"

"Smelling salts. Old fashioned, but effective. You were passing out. You turned white." Gene returned to his chair. "Better now?"

"I think so." Sarra shivered and rubbed her arms, her mind racing. "I'm fine, just shocked by what you've told me," she said cautiously. She shook her head, frowned, and then looked straight at him. "If your story is true, it would explain the nightmares I've had most of my life. They sort of match, but that's probably just a coincidence. I couldn't be your sister."

Gene leaned forward, "Why not?"

"Don't misunderstand," Sarra said slowly, carefully. "It would be great to discover I have a brother. I'm sure you would be a wonderful brother to have, but. . ."

"Wouldn't it be wonderful if you are his sister? And just think, finding a wealthy brother at that," Helen interrupted softly, and then gave Sarra a warm smile, but the warmth never managed to reached her eyes before she glanced away.

Sarra stared at her but did not respond. Helen

Corbett was a little suspicious, as she would be in her place. And the woman had a right to be.

"Helen!" Gene gave a disapproving. Helen shot him an innocent expression and raised her hands as if in wonderment. "I'm telling you again," Gene repeated, "Sarra knew nothing about all this. I'm the one who invited her here, and I'm the one who's certain that she's my sister." He shifted to give Sarra an apologetic smile. "Where were we?"

Sarra stiffened further. "Well, I'm sure your wife might be concerned that you are mistaken. Frankly, so am I." Sarra leaned toward him. "Do you have any proof, Dr. Corbett?"

"I have something in the upstairs office I think will convince you." He stood up, glanced at his wife, who suddenly looked startled, and offered his hand to Sarra. "Come with me, I'll show you something that should take care of any doubts you or anyone else might have." He looked at Helen again. "Not even you, Helen, can wonder at this proof, so you come as well."

Helen rose to her feet and followed Gene.

Sarra followed them up the stairs to the third floor and down the hall to a large room filled with shelves crammed full of books. A massive, scarred old desk sat facing the large window overlooking the Bay. It was definitely a man's room, cluttered and comfortable with the smell of leather and polished wood. Two worn leather chairs sat by the fireplace, and a well-stocked portable bar stood against one wall. It looked like a haven away from the pressures of his profession, as well as being a place to work in peace and quiet.

The two women waited just inside the door while Gene crossed the room to unlock and enter a large walk-in closet. After rummaging in it for a minute or two, he reappeared with a large rectangular object wrapped in white cloth and tied with string.

"You would be around twenty-seven this year, am I right?" he asked Sarra. He appeared more relaxed as he came toward her.

"Yes," she said, wondering how he was so sure of her age.

"Well," he said, as he untied the string and removed the cloth from the object. "This should remove all doubts from your mind." He turned it around so they both could see. It was a painting.

It was a portrait of Sarra.

The same mass of long, curly, dark hair surrounded familiar delicate features. The large, expressive eyes were the same shade of green. The shape of the nose and the full lips were the same as well, and the image exuded such a gentle warmth. Sarra gasped with shock. The look in the eyes. This was the woman from her dreams, a duplicate of herself, dressed in a white satin dress. Yet, somehow, yes there was a subtle difference. One she couldn't quite catch.

"Who is it?" she whispered, suddenly hoarse and feeling peculiar.

"Where did that come from, Gene? I've never seen it before," Helen asked.

She sounded far away, Sarra thought. Gene gave Helen a brief glance.

"It's a portrait of our mother." He looked at Sarra

again. "I've always kept it put away, until now." He inhaled raggedly. "Now do you believe me, Moni," he corrected, "Sarra?" He leaned the portrait against the desk.

Still staring at the painting, Sarra nodded, unable to speak.

Gene took a step toward her. "Would you mind if I hugged you?" he asked, a little hesitantly.

Sarra stood with her hands clenched tightly together, unaware she had been doing so since entering the room. She rubbed the muscles of one palm with the other as Gene moved closer. He was so eager. "I suppose not," she got out, then, "I guess it's possible I might be your sister." She felt awkward and stiff as this man who claimed to be her brother put his arms around her then held her tight. She could feel his emotional intensity, but it wasn't until she felt his damp cheek on her forehead that she realized he was crying. She relaxed and rested her head on his shoulder as he trembled briefly. A few moments later, taking a deep, ragged breath, he gave her another firm squeeze and released her.

Sarra looked up at him. "I don't know what to say," she said slowly. "I know I should be asking a thousand questions, but I can't think straight. I need to go home until I can clear my head."

"You are home," Gene beamed at her. "This is your home now. I want you to move in here with us."

"I can't do that! I have obligations." Sarra shook her head. She didn't want to mention Amanda or Pearl

Ann. "I need to go to my house. Besides, your wife doesn't want a stranger underfoot." She stepped back, putting distance between them. "I really need to think. This is all too much too fast. Things like this don't happen. . ."

Was it really possible that everything she had ever believed was a lie? That the man she had known as her father, Harry Gray, wasn't? Who was he, if not her father? There were too many questions. Her head whirled with confusion.

Helen interjected crisply. "Gene, let the girl go home until she can digest this startling bit of revelation you've dumped on her," she added more slowly and looked at the picture again only to frown. "I had forgotten how beautiful your mother was, Gene." She looked at Sarra. "You certainly have the same look. It's too sad you'll never get to meet her."

"What does she mean? Where is your mother?" Sarra asked, still wrestling with a world that had flipped on its axis.

"Damn it, Helen!" He rounded on his wife.

"Oh God, I've done it again," Helen said, frowning in astonishment. "Again, I'm so sorry."

Gene reached to take Sarra's hand and gripped it tightly. "I'm sorry, Sarra. This is not how I wanted to break the news, but, yes, both of our parents are dead. I'll tell you all about it later. Let's go back downstairs," and led her from the room.

"I'm sorry, Gene. I know you must miss them." Sarra offered politely, too numb to feel any sense of connection.

He stopped suddenly and looked at her.

"Strange," he said. "I was expecting to have to comfort you."

"I'm sorry." She said again, feeling thoroughly awkward. "I would have liked to have met them, but they would have been strangers to me. Can you understand? I don't mean to sound uncaring or cruel." Still floundering, she added, "I'm sorry. I'm making it worse. I'm not thinking straight. I really have to go." She started toward the door.

"Only if you come back tomorrow. We have a lot to go over," Gene insisted, moving with her. More than you can possibly imagine, he thought as he studied her.

"Like what?" Sarra asked. The possibility of her being his sister didn't change the fact she had a job.

He smiled warmly at her. "Well, for one thing, you are a wealthy young woman. Dad started a trust fund for you right after you were kidnapped. He never gave up believing you would eventually be found. It was added to by our grandparents, and with good investments over the years, it comes to a lot of money. I've managed it for you, always hoping this day would come." Still talking in a continuous rush, he led the way back downstairs.

As she followed, Sarra glanced up to see Helen watching, her face unreadable in the shadows at the top of the stairs.

"You'll never have to worry about your future or a job again," Gene rambled on. "That's why you have to come back tomorrow. We have a lot to talk about and catch up on, not to mention all the papers we have to go over." Gene paused. He was talking fast to keep her from having a chance to say no. "Good grief! I invite you to dinner and then don't feed you. In the excitement, I forgot about dinner. You have to stay and eat."

Sarra pulled away and grabbed her purse. "No, really, I can't eat anything now. Thanks anyway." She wanted desperately to escape and get home. She needed Pearl Ann to help her sort this out. "I have a horrible headache, and I really need to lie down." Even her eyeballs hurt. It could not be true. Life was not a Cinderella story. "Um, I'll come back tomorrow. We'll talk then."

He didn't want her to go, but he knew it was too much for anyone to absorb in one evening. He sighed and surrendered. "Okay. But I expect to see you tomorrow. I won't lose you again." When she nodded, he said, "I'd like to call you Micki or Monique, but that would sound strange to you. So I'll just call you Sarra for now?"

"Fine," Sarra responded numbly and headed for the door with Gene in close pursuit. She had to get out of this house now. Her life as she had always known it, from what Gene claimed, should never have happened. It was too much to comprehend that, without that one act so clearly linked to a far too familiar and reoccurring dream, all of the pain and horror in her past might never have existed.

"Are you okay to drive?" Gene touched her cheek lightly with two fingers. "Give me your phone number and address. As I said, I don't want to lose you again."

Sarra ducked out of reach. "I'll be fine. I live off

Ninth Street; it's not too far from here. I'll take something when I get home." She shook her head, seeing his anxiety. "It's all too much for me right now. I promise to see you tomorrow." She hesitated, then dug in her purse and tore a blank deposit slip from her checkbook. "You can reach me at this address and phone number." She handed him the slip of paper, then turned and hurried out to her car.

Gene watched until she was safely in the car, waited as she drove away then closed the door and marched straight back to the deck where Helen now sat eating her dinner. For once, he didn't care if the neighbors could hear this night's row.

He started it. "What in the hell did you think you were doing? Do you really think I didn't notice how you deliberately let things slip?"

Helen didn't even look up at him.

Planting himself in the chair across from her, he took a fortifying drink of the scotch he had left at the table. "Answer me, damn you! What was all that subtle hostility about? You know nothing about that girl." Then, because Helen wasn't reacting, "Hell, I don't know what's wrong with you anymore."

Helen sat her fork down and eyed him coldly. "There's nothing wrong with me," she said frigidly. "You're the one who had all that psychoanalysis, not me. You're the one who's gone off half-cocked, believing that this person, this stranger you met for the first time today, is your sister. You're not realistic, Gene." She paused for a moment. "Don't you think it's a bit peculiar that a woman the image of your mother suddenly shows up? As for her looks," Helen snorted contemptuously. "You know very well what a good plastic surgeon can do! And, not only does she appear in the same town you live in, but she works at the same hospital? And, even more conveniently, not only the same hospital but in the emergency room where you see ninety percent of your cases? What are the chances of these four facts happening at the same time?" Gene opened his mouth, but she continued before he could speak. "I cannot believe this is all coincidence. Then, like a complete idiot, you tell her about the trust fund." Her disgust was audible. "There's a lot of money in that account."

Gene stared at her, his eyes narrowing. "Money! Is that what all this is about? That damn trust fund?" Staring at her, he leaned back in his chair and took a large swallow from his glass, his eyes riveted on Helen's face.

Helen softened her tone and sighed. "Gene, darling, I don't mean to sound hateful, but you must understand. You left yourself wide open. You mustn't believe everything that girl tells you. In six months on your sister's birthday, and if she has not been found, the trust fund reverts to you. This woman says she knows nothing about your sister's kidnapping, but I have my doubts about her. It's all too convenient, don't you think?

"That money belongs to you," she continued insistently. "That girl has no right to any of it. You've worked hard for what you have. You can't just give away over five million dollars. That would be stupid. You need it to further your practice." She reached across the table, took his hand and caressed his fingers, earnestly. "I won't sit around and see you lose what is rightfully yours." Releasing his hand, she rose from her chair. "All this has destroyed my appetite. I'm tired, and I'm going to bed." Giving him a quick, seductive smile, she added, "Don't stay up too long. You know I hate to fall asleep by myself."

Gene remained seated, staring futilely at the drink in his hand, the fight gone out of him. She always did that to him, too, reduced his anger to rubble. Trouble was, he could never quite figure out how. Helen was right about one thing, he thought. He had spent years in psychoanalysis before coming to terms with his guilt over Monique's sister's abduction. It had taken him a long time to admit there was nothing he could have done to prevent what had happened. That it was okay to be angry over losing the sister he had adored.

He now understood how he had punished himself after the kidnapping. He had over-compensated, trying to be the perfect son, the good neighbor, and the best surgeon. Failure had not been an option. It had taken a long time for him to forgive himself for those inevitable, even minuscule subsequent failures that had occurred. But, he had set a standard for himself while he was growing up and, to a large extent, still tried to fit the mold of expectations for the person he had created. His thoughts turned to Helen.

Since when had his wife become so concerned with his welfare, he wondered suspiciously, sipping his drink and ignoring the meal he had yet to taste. She enjoyed his status as one of the leading trauma specialists in Half Moon Bay and the kudos associated with the conferences he was compelled to attend. With Helen's position as President of the Auxiliary for doctor's wives, they always had to participate in this or that black tie affair for some charity fundraiser. He realized she craved recognition from her peers and liked to socialize with the famous locals but, damn it, she refused to accept that their budget might have a limit.

As a trauma doctor, the hours could be rotten at times, but he made a good living. Even though he had agreed to it, Helen had almost exhausted a good portion of his own inheritance with the purchase of this house and, not to mention, furnishing it. The two new cars in the garage had compounded matters. Talking hadn't done any good. He had been forced to take control of their joint checking account after she had suddenly and without telling him, hired Lee Chung as a live-in houseman. There had been quite a fight over that one, which, somehow he had lost. They had never needed a full-time servant before. They didn't now, Gene thought. They had a cleaning service that came every week. For parties, caterers took care of everything. And they were not cheap. But that was not enough for Helen.

One night at dinner, Lee had mysteriously appeared and served the meal. At first, he thought the man was from one of the homeless organizations Helen was associated with. That was until Gene saw the check stub for the man's wages. That had been six months ago before he had taken over the checkbook and the bills.

He remembered how he had fallen in love with the beautiful, sassy redhead the first time he met her at his attorney's office. Fun, sexy as all get out, and witty, she had never hidden the fact she wanted a better life for herself. But after three years of marriage, he was now facing the fact that Helen did not love him and probably never had. He kept telling himself he was in love with her. She was his wife. Wasn't his marriage supposed to be like his parents? He was no longer sure if that was true. Their relationship had not been working for some time he now admitted.

In one of the many efforts to save his marriage, he had allowed the servant to stay. He had kept, and was still paying for, the new cars, and he continued to pay her charge cards at expensive dress shops. They even stayed in this damned house which, he was convinced, was not worth what it had cost. Now, Helen had begun to mutter about moving to a mansion out on Treasure Lane. Even with his income, he could not afford a three million dollar monstrosity. Well, he thought grimly, Helen would just have to settle for this house. Treasure Lane was out of the question. Besides, they already had more than they needed.

Drink in hand, he got to his feet, ignoring the meal that no one had eaten, left the deck and wearily climbed the stairs. Instead of going to the bedroom, he went upstairs into his office and closed the door. He picked up the portrait to reposition it against the fireplace and sat down on the sofa to stare at the painting. He raised his glass and said softly, "Monique found me, Mom. I didn't find her, as I promised. But we're going to be together from now on. I'm going to make sure of that. That's all that matters, isn't it, family and being together? Anyway, that's what you taught us." He sighed heavily,

"I don't know about Helen, Mom. I just don't know what I'm going to do about her."

He suddenly knew what he wanted to do. The trouble was that divorcing Helen would very likely ruin him financially. Setting his glass on an end table, he picked up the portable phone from his desk and made a quick call to his attorney, Arthur Craswell. After finishing the call, he settled back again on the sofa, stretched out his long legs and closed his eyes. Exhausted, he was sound asleep within seconds, oblivious to the storm that was brewing in his bedroom down the hall.

CHAPTER SIX

Home again, and emotionally exhausted, Sarra was relieved to discover that Pearl Ann and Amanda had gone to bed early and were already asleep. She did not feel equipped to call Addie and talk about the unbelievable revelations that had taken place. After taking a couple of aspirin for her headache, Sarra went to bed and tossed and turned for an hour before her eyelids grew heavy. Finally, she slept, but the nightmares came again, once more filled with harsh voices and pain from the past.

It was a winter nightmare this time. Relentless icy cold gripped New York City. In the hotel room she shared with her Daddy Harry, the wind whipped at the flimsy curtains, and the radiator gave little if any heat. Cockroaches fought for their share of the left-over pizza on the dresser, and the scratching in the walls indicated the presence of rats. A bare, forty-watt bulb hung on an electrical cord from the ceiling, provided the only light. Neither sky nor trees could be seen from the room's single window, only a brick wall. The outside world was just as gray, cold and brutal as Harry.

Even though it was the middle of the day, she was curled up under the dirty linens and smelly blankets she shared with her daddy. At least she could get warm for a while. She cried out when Harry suddenly jerked her up from the bed and stood her on her feet. Shivering with fear, she faced him and saw that there was another man in the room. He was tall, clean, dressed in nice clothes and smelled spicy. Harry's dirty garments always stank of sweat and booze. Harry himself had a rank, sour odor. She was forced to turn around slowly while the stranger watched her, the look in his eyes scary, nasty. Then, with one quick jerk, Harry stripped the thin dress off her body, leaving her exposed and naked.

Sarra awoke to her own muted, pleading cries. She sat up, inhaled sharply as tears flowed down her face, to feel a sickened, aching knot in her chest and a raw, strangling sense of loss. The tears did not stop. Her breathing became a ragged gulp as she swallowed against the pain that kept welling up.

She cried for the face in the portrait that Gene had shown her and grieved for herself and the woman who might have been her mother. Their mother. If Gene really was the boy from her dreams, she realized as she wept, she had blamed him for being snatched away from their family. Instead, he had tried to save her and suffered from the attempt. Crying slowly dissolved the resentment Sarra had held towards that innocent boy through the years.

Unable to sleep, Sarra spent the remainder of the night fighting the demons of her past. By dawn, feeling worse than when she went to bed, she wearily rubbed gritty eyes. She got up, stumbled to the bathroom and let the warm water of the shower beat her into something more akin to wakefulness.

Makeup applied and hair brushed, she started to dress in her uniform, then changed her mind. Instead, she phoned the hospital and told her supervisor she would not be into work, claiming a migraine to make use of a sick day. It was not really a lie. Her head was pounding.

Slipping on a cotton blouse and matching green slacks, she had a sudden surge of longing for the cool peaceful mornings in Madison, sitting on the porch with Pearl Ann, quietly sipping coffee. She wanted their lives back to what had been for her, normal.

But when had her life ever been normal? Before meeting Pearl Ann, her life had been colored by different levels of fear. All she had known with her father, Harry Gray, was being perpetually cold, always hungry, and the unpredictable bruises, welts, and pain from the back of his hand or his belt when she didn't do as told. With Harry, squalor and terror were so ordinary, they were a norm she had not questioned.

It was only after fleeing New York, arriving in Kentucky and finding Pearl Ann, that she learned what it felt like to live a truly normal life. A life like people on TV had. The big old two-story, Kentucky home had been filled with talk and laughter, love, and most of all, happiness. But, that house was gone, blown to smithereens, and now she was here in Florida. Living in the past never helped anyone, she told herself. Besides, it hurt too much. Hers was not a past she felt Gene would choose for his sister.

Barefoot, Sarra headed for the kitchen to make coffee. Later, while waiting for the others to wake up, she sat sipping her third cup and tried to decide what to do next. Her world was changing too fast. It terrified her. There were too many secrets and too many people involved. And she was the axis around which it all spun. Opening her purse, she finally pulled out the paper with

Gene's address and phone number on it. She rose and reached for the wall phone and dialed, hoping Gene had not left to go to the hospital.

Helen answered on the third ring.

"Helen, this is Sarra," she said leaning back against the counter. "Is Gene there?"

"Yes, just a moment, I'll get him." Sarra was surprised he was still at home. She heard Gene's name being called. Moments later, he picked up the phone.

"Good morning." He sounded fresh, cheerful and eager; the complete opposite of how Sarra was feeling. "Did you get rid of that headache?"

"Somewhat." Sarra paused to collect her wits. "About us meeting today, why don't we just forget about it? I..." She jerked the phone away from her ear as he loudly interrupted.

"NO!" Gene protested. "Look, I won't lose you. I can't let you disappear again."

Sarra interrupted him. "Listen to me! Assuming I am your sister, you know nothing about me. You have no idea where I've been or what I've done in the last twenty some years. You don't know me." If she cut it off now, he would not find out about her past.

"Sarra, I don't care! All that matters is that, by some miracle, we've found each other. Do you know how lucky we are? This almost never happens with families that have children kidnapped. Most of the time, those children are found dead or are never seen again. We're getting a second chance. Please," he insisted, "I beg you, don't throw it away. If not for yourself, then for me. Give me back my sister." She heard his voice crack, then there was a pause before he continued. "Let me make up for all the years you've missed. Please."

Sarra didn't respond at once. Listening to him, how could she tell him no? She desperately wanted it all to be true. She wanted the relationship of having a real brother, a real family member, a relative to whom she belonged. Her resolve wavered. "All right," she said reluctantly. "But, remember, I tried to warn you." She would have to tell him everything, she thought. Pearl Ann was right, time was running out. Secrets and lies never stay hidden. She sighed deeply, giving in. "I know I promised last night to come back to your house today, but could we meet somewhere else?"

"Certainly. How about meeting me at my lawyer's office. That way Arthur can start the paperwork on proving that you are my sister." He gave her the name and address. "I'll see you there at ten. Okay?" She could tell he was anxious, wanting to be sure she would show up.

"Fine. See you there at ten," Sarra said, and hung up the phone, then glanced up at the wall clock. It was eight-thirty.

Pearl Ann's chipper "Good morning" from the doorway startled her. She had been so tangled up inside she hadn't heard her come down the hall. Sarra hurried to pour coffee into another cup, stirred in milk, carried it to the table, and set it down on the placemat, bracing herself as she did so. "The coffee's fresh and hot. You'd better sit down." She glanced toward the hallway. "Is Amanda still asleep?"

"Yes," Pearl Ann said.

"Good. You aren't going to believe what happened last night."

"Why? Did that doctor make a pass at you?" Pearl Ann asked as she took her seat. "I thought you were sick when I saw you were still at home."

"No, I'm fine. I called in, though. And no, Gene didn't try anything. He was a perfect gentleman." Sarra paused to regroup. "Remember once back in Madison, you told me I needed to find my history? Well, I may have found a big chunk of it last night. Dr. Gene Corbett believes I'm his long lost sister." She waited for the shock of her statement to sink in.

Pearl Ann stared. "What?"

Sarra rephrased. "Pearl Ann, he believes I'm his sister who was kidnapped as a child back in 1989. He has a portrait of his mother, and it's the same woman from my dreams. She looks almost exactly like me. I believe it's possible she was my mother. I mean, the resemblance is freaky. If it's true, she didn't abandon me. Apparently," Sarra went on to relate all that happened. She also explained about the trust fund, and that she had arranged to meet Gene shortly at his attorney's office.

"I have to leave now," she concluded. "It's after nine, and I don't know where Mr. Craswell's office is. It's not about the money, Pearl Ann. I don't care about that." She didn't. It didn't seem real in any case. Besides, Sarra was always aware of the fortune she had taken from Homer's safe and had kept carefully hidden all these years. Close to a million dollars, or thereabouts. Payment for services rendered.

"I know that Sarra," Pearl Ann said.

"Anyway, I don't want Amanda to know anything

about this until everything is settled. Okay?" Sarra insisted.

Looking solemn, Pearl Ann nodded. "I think that's best," she agreed. "I'll take her to the library, or maybe the mall. She still needs a few things for school this fall. It isn't that far off, anyway." She paused, hoping it was all true that Sarra had found her real family after all these years. "It sounds wonderful, but be careful," she added, aware of her own particular loss.

"It does, but is it?" Sarra hedged. "I would like for it to be true, but it could be bad for us too. It might mean we'll have to move again."

"No," Pearl Ann said at once, and very firmly. "I'm not leaving here. I like this town, and I will not go running away."

"It might be dangerous to stay," Sarra protested.

This time, Pearl Ann glared. "I don't care! I've had enough! There are police to protect us. And I, for one, am more than willing to go to them!"

Sarra caught the warning and frowned, "We'll talk about it later, okay? I just want to find out if what Dr. Corbett says is true. If it is, then we'll make whatever decision we need to." She and Pearl Ann rarely argued and usually only when the older woman floored the brakes and refused to budge. This was going to be one of those times. Sarra wasn't sure what she'd do. She loved and depended on Pearl Ann too much to leave her behind. And there was Amanda to think about, also. Maybe she was right, Sarra thought, uncertainty scrambling everything, perhaps now was the time to stop running.

"I'll let you know what happens," she temporized. "Danger is lurking out there for us, Pearl Ann. Never forget that fact," Sarra said, leaving the other woman still sitting at the kitchen table with a stubborn expression on her face.

Arthur Craswell's office was on the second floor of one of the older buildings in Half Moon Bay. The downtown area, which, during the seventies and eighties had stretched from the Bay to Thirty-Fourth Street along Central Avenue, and had been famous for its shops, now barely covered a four-block square.

There were shops along Beach Drive to accommodate tourists. At the end of Second Avenue, a long bridge extended out over the Bay and led to the rustic wooden Pavilion Pier. It reminded Sarra of an old northern fishing village with its quaint shops and stalls that sold everything a tourist could want.

Promptly at ten o'clock, she walked through a door marked L. Arthur Craswell, PA. She had expected the dark wood, and heavy, antique furnishings considered usual décor for an attorney's office. Instead, Gene was pacing a floor covered with a pale blue carpet. The receptionist sat behind a classic, French provincial desk in front of cream-colored walls and raised a fancy white French phone when Sarra entered.

Gene rushed forward to greet her. "I was worried you wouldn't show," he said and moved as though to hug her, thought better of it and gave her a boyish grin. "I seem to worry a lot where you're concerned. Arthur's waiting for us." He went to the inner door and led the way into the inner office.

Arthur Craswell's office was as opulent and bright as the reception area. Bleached wood bookshelves covered one wall, filled from ceiling to floor with leather-bound volumes with titles printed in gold. Two elegant, cream-colored, wing-backed leather chairs sat before an antique, ornate Louis XVI desk. Even the carpet was a soft shade of off-white.

Against one wall, on a table, a vase filled with a mixture of bright red silk flowers provided the only color contrast in the room. Sarra felt a stab of apprehension as the room summoned up memories of another time, another place. It was in New York City, high above Central Park, a memory she had fought to bury, of a wide slash of red on white. Gene's sudden firm grip on her hand kept her from bolting out the door.

Arthur Craswell was a direct reflection of the wealth of the room. Dressed in a dark blue Armani suit with a crisp white shirt and red tie, he was a tall man with thinning gray hair and dark brown, opaque eyes which narrowed when he saw Sarra, his lips almost curling in a sneer. He rose to greet them, his eyes expressionless.

Puzzled, Sarra studied his face. She had never met him before, yet she had the eerie feeling she should know him, and that he didn't like her at all.

"My word, Gene, you weren't kidding." He said coming around the desk to shake Gene's hand. "She looks just like your mother, but then," he left the statement hanging and motioned to the chairs facing his desk. "Sit down, sit down. I have all the papers right here. After you called me last night, I dug them out of the files and had my secretary type them up first thing this morning. So, we're all ready." He smiled then added, "All I have to do is compare handprints and take a DNA sample to be tested, and that will settle the matter."

"What do you mean, compare handprints?" Sarra asked warily.

Craswell looked at her. "Gene's mother had hand and footprints made when you both were born," he avoided calling her Sarra's mother, but then explained, his voice detached. "Initially, they were reproduced as a heading for her notepaper, which was a popular thing to do then, with your names listed under each set of prints. When Gene's sister disappeared, and after his mother was murdered, his father found a packet of the notepaper with the original print card on her desk."

"Murdered?" Sarra gasped and stared at Gene. This shocking information overshadowed the fact that Arthur Craswell had not once referred to her as Gene's sister.

Gene flinched. "Christ, Arthur, Sarra knows nothing about that. I haven't had a chance to tell her everything. Thanks to Helen, she knows that our parents are deceased, but none of the particulars. It was enough of a shock for her to find out that she is my sister." He reached for Sarra's hand again and squeezed it, then spoke gently. "I'm sorry you found out this way, Sarra. Our mother was murdered many years ago, three days after you were kidnapped, in fact. Her killer was never found. I'll go over all the details later. But right now, we need to get this paperwork out of the way, all right?

"All right," Sarra conceded warily and pulled her hand free. "But I do want to know everything." She turned to look at Arthur Craswell. "What do you need from me?"

He returned to his chair behind the desk and sat down. "As I said, I have the handprints made when Gene's sister was born," he said. "When Doctor Corbett Senior found the notepaper, he gave a sheet to the police in hopes of tracing the little girl by her fingerprints. He also had a set of prints enlarged in the event she was ever found." The attorney gave her a cool, practiced smile. "And lucky for you, young lady, it would seem you have been."

"Now," he continued, "all I need is a set of your fingerprints to compare with the originals. If they match, you'll receive your inheritance. If they do not match, then Monique Corbett's share of the inheritance reverts to her brother, Gene, here in about six months." He leaned back in his chair, and continued, "You understand, there is a sizable fortune involved here. I have to be absolutely certain that I release it to the proper person, Miss Gray?"

"Of course, Mr. Craswell, I understand you perfectly." Sarra fought to conceal a surge of fear. "So the police have a set of my fingerprints?" she asked before she could prevent herself. And then, before Craswell could respond, "And this will prove positively that I'm Gene's sister?"

He inclined his head. "That and, as I mentioned, a DNA test. But the fingerprints will be sufficient for the moment. Fingerprints by themselves are proof enough. I want the DNA for backup. A couple of strands of hair would do for that." He took a large black stamp pad from his center desk drawer along with two large white cards.

"Then do it." Sarra agreed, reminding herself that New York City was a long way from Half Moon Bay. Besides, a lot of years had passed. Now, perhaps people had forgotten. Maybe Pearl Ann was right, and they were safe here.

The attorney transferred her fingerprints to the cards and identified each hand and finger. When it was finished, he showed her to the bathroom and gave her alcohol to remove all traces of the ink staining her fingertips.

"With today's computer technology," Craswell said, when she returned, accepting the few strands of hair she held out, slipping the cards into a folder and the hair in an empty envelope, "I should have the results in a day or so. Until then, if I need anything else, I'll give Gene a call, and he can notify you."

"But, Arthur," Gene protested, "can't she sign the papers now? If the prints don't match, you can tear them up. I don't want her to have to wait or come back. We have a lot to catch up on, and I would like to get started."

Craswell shook his head. "No, Gene. To turn over that much money is not something to be done casually. I have to be certain Ms. Gray is who you believe her to be. I won't take any chances with your sister's money. Don't be so eager that you forget I have a responsibility to you and to your late mother and father."

"All right." Gene conceded reluctantly. He turned to Sarra. "I have to be at the hospital for a while. Do you want to meet me later for coffee?"

"I'm still trying to digest all that has happened, and I need time to do so. Can we make it tomorrow?"

Sarra said at once.

"Sure," Gene reluctantly agreed.

Sarra stepped forward to shake the attorney's hand. His gaze was cold, she thought, and far too penetrating. She countered with a polite smile and quickly allowed Gene to escort her out of the building into the warm sunshine, then watched as he got in his car and pulled away from the curb. She stood staring after the black Infiniti until it disappeared.

Murder? She was still shocked by that. His, their, mother was murdered? And, he had said, within days after his sister's, her, abduction? And, it was still unsolved. . . There was an eerily sinister resonance which compounded the overwhelming impact of the portrait Gene had shown her. She had felt as if she was staring at a ghost. Granted, it had happened long ago, and that for himself, Gene had primarily come to grips with it, but, Sarra knew suddenly that she needed to know everything about the woman who was supposed to be her own mother.

She realized then that neither Helen, Gene, nor the attorney, had mentioned the given name of either of the deceased Corbett members. It was important somehow. Quickly she reentered the building and found Arthur Craswell just walking out of his private office, a folder, and papers in his hands.

"Mr. Craswell," she called. He turned toward her. "Would you tell me the first names of Gene's parents?"

He hesitated for a moment, accessing her coolly, and then shrugged. "His mother was French. Her name was Angelique Rondeau Corbett. She was one of the dearest women I have ever known. Gene's father was Howard Turner Corbett, one of the most successful surgeons in Half Moon Bay."

"When did they die?" Sarra pursued even as it occurred to her that she could visit the newspaper to research Angelique's death. Gene had said his mother had been murdered three days after his sister's abduction, which gave her the approximate date, August 1989.

Craswell stiffened. "Dr. Corbett stated quite clearly he wanted to discuss that with you, himself. It would be inappropriate for me to disclose any further information. I suggest you talk to him." He turned away to his secretary clearly dismissing her.

Sarra stared at his profile for a moment. She didn't like Arthur Craswell, mainly because he gave her the feeling he had disliked her on sight and certainly did not trust her. Without a word, she left the office and found her car then drove home. No one was there when she arrived, and the house felt unexpectedly lonely. Changing into a tee-shirt, white cotton slacks and sandals, she curled up on the sofa and picked up the phone to call Addie at work, as she had promised.

CHAPTER SEVEN

June 7

"Girlfriend!" Addie hissed into the phone the moment she recognized Sarra's voice. "What in the world is going on? There are newspaper and TV people all over this hospital trying to get information about you." Then. "Sarra, are you in trouble? Can I help?"

"What are you talking about? What television people!" Sarra demanded, jerking to her feet to pace as panic streaked through her. The thought of her face splashed across the national news meant that this tenuous new safety had evaporated. Gone. They'd have to run. And Gene? It slammed home that he'd be in danger too. My God, she thought, she'd have to warn him.

"It started early this morning," Addie was whispering. "I had just gone on break and was having my first cup of coffee when Jerry, the paramedic who moonlights here in the ER, you know, the one that's been trying to get me to go out with him?"

"I know who you mean," Sarra cut in.

"Well, he says the TV people are asking for you and want to interview you. Mostly, they've been chasing after Dr. Corbett all morning. One of them even asked me if I knew you. I managed to get away. You know it is hospital policy that employees are not allowed to talk to the news media. Anyway, what did you do at his house last night anyway?"

Sarra could hear voices in the background. She

hesitated, swallowed hard, then plunged in. "Addie, Dr. Corbett thinks I'm his sister who was abducted years ago."

"What! So that's what this is all about! I thought maybe you, and he had killed his wife or something!"

"God, Addie."

But Addie continued, "If you're at home, quick, turn on your television. Your face is plastered all over the noon news."

As Sarra leaned to switch on the television, she heard Addie's rushed whisper. "Gotta go. Call me at home later. The big shots and Dr. Corbett just came into the ER with the television people." The line went dead.

Sarra hung up the phone and sat down to stare in horror at the news. It was a recap of what Gene had told her about the abduction. But the reporter also gave brief details of Angelique Corbett's death, embellishing it with film footage of the crime scene and a full-color photograph of the victim. The resemblance still amazed Sarra as she heard him say. "Three days following her daughter's kidnapping, Angelique Corbett's body was discovered by the next door neighbor, floating in the Bay behind the Corbett home."

The reporter went on to describe how a fatal car crash had taken the life of Howard T. Corbett only nine months ago. Sarra was shocked to realize that she had missed meeting the man\ who was possibly her father by such a short time. The details of the accident were not as striking as those of the murder. Failed brakes at an intersection. . .

Unable to cope with more, Sarra switched off the television then tried to call Gene at the hospital. He couldn't be reached. And so she left her phone number and a message for him to call her at home as soon as possible.

After fixing a peanut butter and orange marmalade sandwich and a cup of hot tea, she sat at the kitchen table, staring at the food and thinking. How had the news media picked up on the story so quickly? The only people who knew were herself, Gene, his wife Helen and the lawyer. Not the lawyer, she thought. Either Gene or Helen had to have given the story to the press. Why? Gene was so determined that she was his sister, but Helen had taken an instant dislike to her.

Having a facsimile of her face spread across the local and, probably, national news was a disaster. And if the wrong person saw it? She let that thought drift, not wanting to consider it even briefly.

Sarra started violently as the phone rang. It was Addie again. "Dr. Corbett asked me to call you and tell you to meet him at his home. He said the only way to get rid of the news people is to have a press conference, or they'll never leave you two alone."

"You tell Gene for me he can forget that," Sarra said heatedly. "I will not talk to reporters. You can also tell him that if it was his wife who opened her mouth, I will strangle her!"

"Look Sarra. He's right," Addie insisted. "If you don't talk to these reporters, they'll be calling you day and night. I know what it's like. I went through it when my brother killed himself a couple of years ago. You wouldn't believe the questions they asked."

Suicide? Addie had never mentioned that before, Sarra realized, thinking fast. "You may be right, Addie," she countered, all nerves. "But I can't talk to them. There's a reason I moved here, an ex-boyfriend. I had to get away."

Addie was silent for a moment, accepting the implication. "Well, what do you want me to tell him? Doctor Corbett is your brother, isn't he? That's what he's telling everyone."

Sarra relaxed a little. "I didn't know anything about his missing sister until I went to his house last night. And, for all I know, Doctor Corbett has made a big mistake. My resemblance to his mother might just be a fluke. You probably know more than I do. You've lived in this area longer than I have." She paused. "Thank you for being my friend, Addie. Now, please tell Gene no press conference. I will not talk to any news media. And, no pictures," she added. "Thanks for your help. I'll keep in touch with you." Sarra hung up the phone, ate her sandwich without tasting it, and carried her cup and plate to the sink. She leaned back against the counter, thinking hard. Helen. It had to be Helen. But what purpose could she have in calling the news media? The phone rang again. Fed up, Sarra picked it up.

"Sarra, I'm so sorry. The press is having a field day with the story." It was Gene. "I don't know how they found out. But maybe it'll give hope to other families."

Sarra frowned. "Gene, you don't know for certain I'm your sister," she said sharply. "Until that is a proven fact, I won't talk to anyone about anything." She took a deep breath and tried to explain. "Please understand. I'm a very private person. I live a quiet life. I do my paintings, I work at my job. I don't like or want a lot of excitement in my life." She had visions of her face broadcast on the news and in the papers of New York City. It wouldn't be long before someone would come looking for her. Worse. How long before the police showed up to start asking questions about New York? They had to run. But, to where?

"Sarra, you don't have to. I'll handle everything. Don't worry," Gene cut through her thoughts. "Unfortunately, all anyone has to do is look at one of the many photographs taken years ago of our mother to have a picture of you. Her face was in the papers constantly after her death. There's no way you'll be able to hide from this, I'm sorry to say."

His breathing sounded loud in the receiver as he waited for her response. He was right, of course. The photograph on the noon news had already been shown. The newspapers would rehash and milk the story embellishing it with other file photos. There was no way she could escape that now. It seemed she was being forced to stop running.

Sarra thought a second, and then asked, "Gene, have you given any thought as to how the information about me was discovered by the news media? The only other person who knew was Helen. I'm quite sure your wife leaked it."

He was silent for a moment. "Helen? I don't understand why she would do that," he said slowly. "All I can do is apologize for it happening. I'm sad to say, the story would have come out sooner or later. But we'll face everything together." He was silent for a few seconds. "Look, I'm being paged. I'll talk to you later," he added.

Sarra hung up the receiver and went to curl up on the sofa. Turning it on, the television was now playing a daily soap opera, and she stared at the screen without really seeing it. Instead, her thoughts drifted back to her years in New York City. If she really was Gene's sister, then who was Harry Gray? Was he the man who snatched her from the beach? She couldn't imagine Harry being that daring, at least he wasn't when she had known him. She had called him Daddy for as long as she could remember, believing him to be just that. Now, she ransacked her earliest memories for any detail or scrap of information about the nasty man that could enlighten her further.

There had been a woman with him for a time, she recalled, when she was little, a woman who had smelled of booze as much as he had. Sarra couldn't remember her name. She did remember that the woman had been kind to her, but then the woman had died. How Sarra had no idea, and everything with Harry had become worse. He drank more and was always hitting her. Or, he would yell at her about how her mother had left because she, Sarra, was terrible. He had never shown the kind of fatherly warmth she had seen some men in the park show their children. Harry had been just mean and cruel.

She had no memories of him working. Nor had they stayed in one place for long, always moving from one seedy hotel to another. Sometimes, one of Harry's assorted girlfriends would watch her for a few hours while he went out. They were kind to her. One or two even gave her clothes; she recalled a brightly colored blue dress. When he returned, he always had money, and then the drinking would begin again. She had been hungry most of the time, Sarra remembered. Harry hadn't given her regular meals. Mostly, she had scrounged scraps, leftover pizza, half a sandwich, and fries, cold and soggy. Sarra pushed those memories away, unable to deal with them at the moment.

Where was Harry now? Sarra wondered, recalling something else. The night he had hauled her out of bed and sold her to Homer was almost the last time she had seen him. The very last time had been later when he had come to Homer's apartment. She still did not know what had been going on between Homer James and Harry Gray. Nor had she ever wondered about it before, until now. Maybe the answer was hidden in the back of her bedroom closet.

In all the years since Homer's murder in New York, she had rarely opened the flight bag she had taken from the apartment, only when she needed a little money. Nor had she opened any of the envelopes she had removed from Homer's safe. Everything remained exactly as it had been, at the bottom of the bag under the money. She was tempted to get the bag and look at the contents now, yet something stopped her. For some undefined reason, she was afraid of what was on those computer discs and in the envelopes.

Sarra nervously twisted a strand of hair. All this sudden publicity was terrifying. George would use anyone to get at her. He would even use Pearl Ann and especially her daughter. Her rapist was not the type to give a damn about a child. He certainly would not hesitate to harm Gene Corbett.

Sarra knew she had to talk to Gene about all this. But how? She was surprised to realize how much she liked Gene Corbett. She really wanted him to be her brother, to be part of the family, like Pearl Ann and Amanda. He was honest, open-hearted, and generous to a fault, and vulnerable, for that reason. She did not want to be responsible for anything happening to him. Uneasy as she had been at the time, the way he had hugged her last night had been palpably warm and caring. As for the trust fund, it was hardly something to dismiss. Sarra didn't feel it was right for her to even think about it.

She grabbed the portable phone and dialed Addie at work. The phone rang four times before Addie picked up.

"ER Registration," Addie answered.

"It's me." Sarra caught herself trying to whisper. "Don't say anything. I need to get a message to Gene, er, Doctor Corbett. Tell him to meet me at the Pirate's Den on Beach Drive this evening at eight o'clock. Do me a favor, and call and reserve a booth at the back under your name. Tell him it's vital I talk to him." Not for a moment did she doubt he would be there.

"Listen, girlfriend," Addie whispered, "the reporters are gone, but you would be wise to stay away from this hospital. Everyone and their cousin are watching your brother. Do you want me to pick him up and bring him to the restaurant?"

"Good idea. That way he may be able to avoid

the reporters. Just make sure you're not followed. Have Gene drive to your apartment and leave from there." Sarra hated getting Addie involved, but she was the only person in this town, other than Gene and Pearl Ann, whom she could trust.

"God, Sarra. From what I hear on the news, you're going to inherit a lot of money. What have you got to hide from?" Addie listened to the silence. Sarra had never talked about her private life. Other things though had led Addie to count Sarra as a good friend. "Okay, you tell me later what you want me to know. I won't question you further. And I'll get Doctor Corbett to The Den without anyone seeing us."

Sarra exhaled with audible relief, "Thanks, Addie. I'll explain everything I promise." She replaced the receiver and checked her watch. It was after twelve.

The sudden shrill ringing of the phone jarred Sarra. She wasn't expecting another call. This time, it was Pearl Ann. "I didn't want you to worry. I thought you could use a day to yourself. I'm going to take Amanda to a movie and grab a bite to eat. We'll be home around five or six. Fix yourself some dinner," she said.

Sarra braced herself. "Come home early, if you can. We really need to talk. I'm meeting Doctor Corbett and Addie for dinner at eight."

Amanda called to her over the phone. "I love you, Mommy."

"Give her a kiss for me, Gran. Just get home as soon as you can. I have a lot to explain and not a lot of time to do it."

"What's going on, Sarra?" Pearl Ann's tone changed, filled with concern.

Sarra hesitated, and then asked, "Have you seen any news?"

"No," Pearl Ann said, "I've been too busy with Amanda. Why?"

"Remember how you told me I had to stop running," Sarra said. "Well, my past is about to catch up with me. I have kept secrets from you, and I pray you won't hate me for what I must tell you."

"Hate you?" Pearl Ann exclaimed. "I know you. How could I hate you?" then gruffly, "You have been more of a daughter to me than my own."

Sarra remembered what little she had been told about the daughter that Pearl Ann had not heard from, or seen in fifteen years. Rose had run away when she was fourteen and never returned or contacted her mother. That was another thing she kept from Pearl Ann. "You say that now," Sarra responded, "but wait until you've heard my full story."

Pearl Ann didn't say anything for a moment. "We'll be home in twenty minutes." She ended the call. Twenty minutes later, almost to the second, they walked through the front door.

Sarra had made coffee and sat at the kitchen table, waiting. An excited Amanda wanted to show off the new clothes Gran had bought her, but Sarra cut her off. "Sweetie, Gran and I need to talk. It's important. I want you to go to your bedroom and play on your computer until we're done. Okay?"

All the sparkle left the child's eyes and, without a word, she hurried down the hall with her packages to shut herself in her bedroom.

"I hated to do that," Sarra said and looked at Pearl Ann. "She looked so happy, and now that anxious expression is back on her face."

"Does she have a reason to be worried?" Pearl Ann asked, and then before Sarra could answer, she added grimly, "I have a feeling we both do."

"Get a cup of coffee and have a seat." Sarra indicated the kitchen table. "This is going to take some time."

Pearl Ann filled a cup, added cream and carried it back to the table. Taking a seat, she said, "Okay. I'm listening."

Sarra sat down across from her, swiped both hands across her face and looked up. "I told you long ago I was raped by a man named George. I also told you I witnessed a murder and had to run from New York. That is how I ended up in Kentucky."

"Yes, I know all that."

"God! Where do I begin?" Sarra said, steeling herself. She paused before continuing. "I guess I should start with the man I thought was my father. His name was Harry Gray. I don't have any consistent memories of any other person except Harry."

"What about those dreams of your mother?" Pearl Ann asked, aware of Sarra's dreams of a woman and a young boy, which she had always believed to be Sarra's mother.

Sarra shifted, uncomfortable. "I thought it was just that, a dream. Harry had always told me that I was bad and that's why my mother left."

"The man should have been shot." Pearl Ann fumed. "You never tell a child such a thing!"

"I don't know what happened to Harry," Sarra said, feeling no remorse. "He may very well have been shot. He beat me every time he was drunk, which was almost daily. Actually, I hope he's dead." She went on to awkwardly describe all of it, the squalor, the stink, the hunger, Harry, all of it.

"You never told me that." Pearl Ann whispered, appalled when Sarra finally stopped.

"It gets worse. I never knew my exact age or date of birth. But I believe I was around seven or eight when Harry sold me for five hundred dollars to a man named Homer James." Sarra shuddered but described how she had stood naked before Homer and had been made to turn slowly so he could appraise the goods. How he had poked. How atrocious she had felt, how dirty, while the two men bartered for her as though she was no more than an old car. How they had argued because Harry had wanted a thousand dollars and all Homer would give him was the five hundred.

This time, even the silence felt contaminated. Pearl Ann broke it. "This Harry actually sold you?" she stared in disbelief. It physically hurt, she thought, hearing this. In her world, people valued and cared for their children. But, sometimes, as she knew all too well, love was not enough. It hadn't been enough to save her own daughter.

Sarra continued then to explain how she had felt upon being rescued from Harry. It hadn't mattered that Homer had paid cash money for her. All that had was that Harry was no longer part of her life. "What you don't understand," Sarra said, "is that with Homer, I had plenty of food, clean, pretty clothes and a warm, nice place to live. He even had me schooled, reading and writing. Because of that, I thought Homer loved me. Well, I vowed to be so good, Homer would love me forever. It wasn't until I was thirteen that he made me share his bed. . ."

"He, um?" Pearl Ann whispered.

Sarra shook her head. "No, I was willing enough. That was my way of showing him how grateful I was. I felt special and loved. Homer had a lot of other girls who came and went from the apartment. I thought because of that, he loved me best. All I had ever known before was being beaten by Harry, as I told you. Homer didn't treat me like that at all."

She was so impersonal about all this, Pearl Ann thought. "What happened to change your mind about Homer?" she asked, sickened.

Sarra swallowed, "I think he had my best friend, her name was Ro, killed. He sent her out on a date, and she never came back. Two days later, her body was found in the river."

"Homer was a pimp, then?"

"Not just any pimp." Sarra grimaced. "He made sure his girls were taught proper table manners, correct posture, how to walk and talk, how to dress appropriately and how to handle money. What we lacked in formal education, he made up for by teaching us every possible way there was to please a man. Men who wanted a woman for a night, a weekend, or a special party, called Homer. He supplied the classiest escorts to some of the most influential and wealthy men in New York City and Long Island. Other girls, not me. I was special, you see."

"So, what did he do to you?" Pearl Ann frowned, not sure she wanted to know, but felt compelled to ask.

Sarra studied her hands on the table in front of her. "When I was sixteen, Homer received a call for an escort to some big Christmas event on Long Island." She paused, and then continued deliberately, "I tried to talk him out of sending me. The ultimatum was a shock. I had to go to the party and do as I was told, or I would be sent out on the streets. That's what he did with the girls who were, well, disobedient. That, or they vanished.

"Anyway, a limousine arrived to pick me up that evening. My escort turned out to be a man named George. My job was to seduce the host of the party. I was to arrange to get the man in a compromising sexual position, and George would be waiting with a photographer.

"After I arrived, at the entrance, I slipped on some ice and fell into the arms of a man. A young man. . . He saved me from more than a fall." Sarra swallowed. "He changed my life that night. He wouldn't leave me and followed me from room to room." Her tone softened as she thought of the single dance they had shared. "He was," she inhaled deeply but didn't finish. "We danced and then for some crazy reason, he told me he had fallen in love with me, and then asked me to marry him. He meant it." Sarra shook her head. "I couldn't believe it. At that moment, I felt so beautiful, so special, and clean.

But it changed to shame. I was dirty because I knew then what I was, and what I'd been sent to do. I ran away from him."

Sarra rose awkwardly and began to pace the kitchen floor. Pearl Ann followed her every movement. "George found me," she continued with difficulty. "Refusing to do the job was a big mistake. I tried to. He hauled me upstairs to the master bedroom, beat me until I couldn't move. Then he raped me. I don't know how, but George got the man, a Mr. Blackwell, upstairs. He seemed drunk, or drugged," Sarra shrugged, "I don't know which, maybe both. The poor man was out of it, anyway, and couldn't have known what he was doing. He kept calling me Vicki while he, err. Anyway, they got their pictures. I was ordered to get dressed and go wait in the car. How I got downstairs, I don't know.

"I remember running past all those people, holding my dress together, and then climbing into that limo where the photographer was waiting. George joined us shortly after. I called him a bastard. He slapped me across the face, stuck his cigarette to my breast and told me to forget everything I had seen or heard. The limo driver dropped me off at Homer's apartment, and they drove away."

Pearl Ann rose and went to embrace Sarra. But the girl backed away, hands up. "Don't! I can't handle it right now. I have more to tell." She looked away, her face pale. "The next morning, in the newspapers, I read that Mr. Blackwell's wife, Victoria, had been murdered and her husband was the prime suspect. Homer was terrified. I tried to talk to him, show him I had bruises and a cigarette burn. And when I told him about the rape," Sarra's voice got hoarse, "he slapped me and told me I was nothing but a whore! That's what he'd bought and trained me for. What did I expect, to be treated like a lady?

"I was stunned, Pearl Ann. I believed that he loved me. That I was his special girl, you see. He'd told me that often enough. It was all a lie. I was nothing more than a piece of property. A dirty piece of property now. I vowed then that I would escape from him. I didn't know he would be murdered three days later on orders from George." Sarra shifted to stare at Pearl Ann with pain-filled eyes. "Ro and I had plotted to run away. She must have let something slip. I believe that was why she was killed."

Pearl Ann did not move or speak for a time after Sarra fell silent. She could see from the braced, wary expression on Sarra's face that she expected revulsion, rejection, not understanding. "Sarra," she said carefully, "I'm glad you've told me all this. You only did what you had to do to survive. Anyone would. What any normal person would do." She inhaled slowly and then said. "Are you going to tell this Doctor Corbett everything? If he is your brother, he has a right to know."

Sarra didn't answer at once, then nodded. "I'll give him the highlights. He doesn't need to know all the sordid details. But, you're right, he should be told. I plan to tell him tonight. You realize he may very well change his mind about wanting me as his sister."

"In that case, he wouldn't be much of a brother," Pearl Ann pointed out. "But I doubt that's the case."

It didn't matter, Sarra thought, that she had never had a choice about whom she had been forced to have sex with, or that there had only been three men, Homer, George, and her first and only trick, the unfortunate Mr. Blackwell. Given the circles Gene moved in, the only thing his level of society would see was her as a prostitute, not the person she had become. Gene Corbett did not deserve to be ostracized because of her. Nor was she confident he would realize that.

Pearl Ann waited a few seconds to see if Sarra had anything more to tell, then asked, "Is that it?"

"Yes, essentially." Sarra had no intention of mentioning the flight bag hidden in her closet.

"Well!" Pearl Ann said slowly. "If that's it, you don't have anything to worry about. You were kidnapped and forced into a life over which you had no control or choice. What matters is not what you did before I met you, but the kind of life you have made for yourself and your daughter from that day forward."

"But I lied to you," Sarra protested.

Pearl Ann sighed heavily. "No, you omitted facts," she said. "You told me about the rape and the murder a long time ago when it was necessary. That's what's important." Her tone changed, becoming harsher. "I love you like a daughter, Sarra. That will never change. I know you, as well, but I expect you to be completely honest with me from now on so we can face" she hesitated, "things together. I mean it," she added.

Sarra nodded and sagged with relief. "I will, Gran. I promise." Then, "Do you have an old hat or scarf I can borrow? I have to hide my hair, so no one will recognize me. It is usually pretty dark in the restaurant. Maybe I can slip in unnoticed."

"I may have just the thing in my closet," Pearl Ann said and led the way down the hall to her bedroom.

CHAPTER EIGHT

The combined heat and humidity sent rivulets of sweat down Jarrett's back until he entered the police department. The lobby provided blessed relief with its frigid air. The desk sergeant buzzed him through the door, and he made his way to the Homicide Division on the fifth floor. He strolled through the large room, past desks grouped together by Squads, Burglary, Personal Violence, Robbery, or Auto Theft. Then, ambling down the long hallway, he entered the room occupied by the Homicide Squad and plopped down in the chair at his desk.

The progress report on the investigation of the attempted murder and rape of the young girl had to be finished. Opening the file, he still felt sick as he looked again at the pictures of the victim, her small body brutalized, torn where it shouldn't be, her face showing swollen, blackened eyes, mangled jaw, and a bruised throat. It had been a vicious rape. The child was still unconscious and in intensive care.

As in the other cases, they had little to go on at this time. No hairs, no fibers, no semen, no idea where the rape actually took place, just the brutal destruction of an innocent young girl. First thing this morning, he had checked for a missing person's report and come up with nothing. This latest victim was still unidentified. At least they had managed to get the newspapers and television reporters to run the story as a robbery/assault with no associative reference to the other killings. It was a minuscule streak of luck that she was alive, unconscious, but still alive.

As he looked at the pictures, he felt a boiling rage coursing through his veins. Jarrett fought it but could feel the fury that, if it were allowed to break free, would propel him into the same kind of violence. Then, he thought, what would set him apart from the monsters and scum he worked to put behind bars? Nothing. That kept his anger in check. The unbridled atrocities committed by people against each another did not surprise him anymore. Lately, it seemed that people would kill over nothing more than a can of beer.

Although adults were accountable for their behavior, far too many placed themselves in the path of destruction. Each one chose his or her way of life with that first step into the criminal underworld to make unwitting victims of those around them. Jarrett had seen the results with the crack addicts and the prostitutes and those others who ended up on a cold steel table being cut open by Harvey. It was all so wrong. That was what infuriated him. But the senseless violence against these young girls, these children, he could not forgive at all. They haunted him as if they were actually calling out to him to find their killer.

Two others haunted him daily, still waiting for long overdue justice. Jarrett felt as though his parents would not find peace until he had set to right the wrongs that had so thoroughly destroyed them. That was the root and core of the anger that simmered and drove him, that festered because it was an unanswered cry of outrage.

His protest to the world was that such atrocities should never be allowed to occur at all. And, because they did, his frustration was palpable because he was well aware he could not stop it all by himself and because there were times when he no longer felt sure of anything.

Not so long ago, Harvey had told him, as Jarrett had stood white-faced, watching the other man coolly dissect one of the other butchered rape victims, that he took it all too personally, and that he'd either burn out or drive himself nuts. No, he wouldn't, Jarrett thought. That deeply held outrage was nurtured because if he ever lost it, he would go numb inside. He would become anesthetized against the very purpose that shaped his own life.

At the hospital yesterday morning, he had believed he had seen the key to his own personal resolution. Evidently, he had been wrong. The woman he'd had scoured every town up and down the east coast hunting for eleven years couldn't just walk right in through the door one day? She had been on his mind, and his imagination had run away with him when he saw this other woman.

There was a sudden loud thump. Jarrett's thoughts were frozen by a photograph clipped to the top of the case file suddenly slapped down on the desk in front of him. He jumped in surprise.

His partner, Caruso, a newspaper folded to the cryptogram and tucked under one arm, chuckled, "Finally scared you, did I? Old 'steel gut' caught unawares. I'd say, Laddie, ye might be slippin' a bit in your old age!"

Caruso Jones was an odd mixture of Hungarian and Irish, whose parents had come straight from the old country. His father, a strict Irish Orangeman, had bestowed upon him a silver tongue and an angelic voice with his love for opera and the ability to weaken women's knees with his singing. It hadn't been a surprise to learn he had two ex-wives. Caruso loved women and remained on good terms with both of his ex's. With men, on the other hand, he was rough, distrustful, and boisterous, the only exception being his partner.

Jarrett glared up at Caruso. At the moment, he wasn't feeling much affection for anyone. "Where did this come from?" he demanded, staring at the photograph. It was the same ghost he thought he had seen at the Emergency Room.

"That's an unsolved murder case which has just been reactivated." Caruso eased into the chair beside the desk, laid his newspaper down and leaned back, clasped his hands behind his head, and stretched his legs out to accentuate his full height of six-foot-five inches. "It's all over the news, how this missing sister of a local doctor has suddenly shown up out of the blue. And, of course, the press dug up some dirt on the murder of the mother twenty-three years ago, hence the reactivation. We've been assigned to talk to the daughter of Angelique Corbett."

"You're not talking about this woman?" Jarrett frowned as he continued to stare at the photograph. "I've been looking for her for the past eleven years. She's not dead. In fact, I thought I saw her this morning at Bay Memorial."

Caruso gave him a strange look. "Well, Laddie," he said slowly, "it can't be the same person unless you've been seeing ghosts and beasties and things that go bump in the night! Mrs. Corbett was murdered shortly after her young daughter went missing." He snatched the folder and flipped it open, then shoved it back across the desk to his partner. "Read, Lad, and see for your own self."

Jarrett scanned the pages then skipped to the autopsy report. "She died from strangulation." He looked up, pushing at the wisps of dark sandy hair that had fallen down over his forehead.

They were an interesting contrast in color and size. Jarrett knew he looked short next to Caruso, even though he topped six feet. Where his partner was a big man with black hair and hazel eyes, Jarrett's muscular but slimmer build, sandy blonde hair and deep blue eyes had garnered him more than one noted resemblance to Brad Pitt.

At the moment, Caruso continued to study him. "Hey, Jarrett, man I'm sorry. I wasn't aware that you knew the victim."

Aware of Caruso's continued and interested scrutiny, Jarrett shook his head. "I don't," he said slowly. "The resemblance shook me up, that's all. Obviously, it's not the same person, but the girl I've been looking for is a younger version of this woman." He closed the folder, rubbed his tired eyes, and changed the subject back to their current case. "CJ, did you have any luck with the other neighbors at the crime scene?"

"Unfortunately, no one else heard or saw anything."

"Damn it!" Jarrett picked up the folder again, unable to detach himself from the photograph, and then said, "Did I ever tell you how my parents died?"

"No."

"My mother was murdered," he said quietly, looking up at Caruso, "and my father was charged with killing her. Because he couldn't remember what happened and because he believed he was guilty, he killed himself. They were devoted, my parents. He was found in a drunken stupor holding her dead body." He touched the photograph briefly.

Jarrett watched Caruso's face. This was the first time he had told anyone about that dreadful holiday season that had left him orphaned and forced to face a brutal reality that he had been ill-equipped to cope with. He had left New York to get away from all of it. Now, looking at the photograph, nightmare images flashed across his mind.

"My mother was strangled, just like this woman," Jarrett continued, shifting his gaze down at his hands. "My father built yachts. He was very good at it. Very successful. My mother was beautiful and socially well connected. We were the American dream family." His tone soured. "You know the type. My father was the kid from a poor background who married a wealthy socialite and was accepted into," he gave a bitter laugh, "New York society. That was us.

"It was Christmas, and I was home from college." He paused, his features softening as he remembered aloud. "My mother loved the holidays. She decorated every room in the house. We had this giant tree in the foyer. It had to be thirteen feet high. That thing had so many lights on it my father kept expecting it to burst into flames.

"It was our usual Christmas bash. Anyway, I was standing outside the front door greeting guests when this limo pulls up." He looked up at Caruso. "I fell in love that night CJ. I mean, really in love. You know the kind that slaps you in the face and almost stops your heart. It's a once in a lifetime feeling when you look at someone and really know that she's the one you want to spend your life with. That's what happened to me.

"There I was," Jarrett continued, "engaged to the daughter of one of the wealthiest families in Boston, and I completely flipped over someone I didn't even know. She slipped on the ice on the front steps and fell right into my arms. I looked into those large green eyes, and I was lost. Then she pulled away, entered the house, and vanished. I looked for her in the ballroom, the library, all over the place and kept missing her. I finally found her in the main living room admiring one of our Christmas trees."

"You had more than one Christmas tree?" Caruso interrupted.

Jarrett shrugged off the question. "Anyway, we waltzed. Right then, I proposed to her. But, not surprisingly, she turned me down, then left me standing there feeling like two kinds of a fool. I couldn't look for her because my fiancée found me and then stayed glued to me for the rest of the evening. Later I caught a glimpse of her running out the front door. I took off after her, but she jumped into this limo with some other man and was gone. That's the last I ever saw of her." He paused as Caruso stared at him fascinated.

"So you've been lusting after this mystery woman for all these years?" Caruso asked slowly. "Christ, Jarrett, the way women fall all over you, I would have thought you would have found someone else by now!" CJ straightened in his chair and, reached for the photograph, studied it closely. "If one of my wives had looked like this, I might have stayed married!"

Jarrett scowled. "I haven't been lusting after her!" he snapped, then looked away. "The police claimed my father strangled my mother after they argued. I know my father. He didn't kill my mother. But, he couldn't prove it. Needless to say, all of this put an end to my engagement. Her society conscious parents could not associate with a suspected murderer or his son."

Jarrett didn't relate how his father also had been accused of rape. The general consensus had been that he killed his wife in a rage after being caught with that same girl. Nor did he mention how the girl's dress had been torn half off when she had run from the house. He couldn't tell Caruso his father had admitted to having sex with the girl.

Caruso leaned forward to place a hand on Jarrett's arm. "Christ, Lad, it's plain to see you've had a tough go of it," he said gently, as he picked up the photograph and looked at the murder victim with a new interest. "You suppose there's a connection between the death of this lady and your parents?"

Jarrett leaned back in his chair. "I don't know," he said honestly. "If the girl at the Christmas party is the daughter of Mrs. Corbett, she must know something. I don't know how involved she is, but I'm damn well going to find out!" He frowned a little. "Would you do me a favor? Request the files on my parents from New York PD. You shouldn't have any problems getting them. They were closed when my father died. If I do it, someone might recognize my name, and I don't want that. Then we can compare the information in those records with this one. Maybe we'll find something."

"I can do that." Caruso agreed, then picked up the phone and placed the call to the records department. After speaking to someone on the other end, he hung up and grinned. "Andy will contact the New York police and have the file pulled," he said, "and copies faxed or FedEx'd overnight. It may take a couple of days."

Jarrett fidgeted restlessly, and Caruso could tell by the look on his friend's face that it was not fast enough. Patience was not one of Jarrett's best qualities. He was inclined to be reckless at times. Caruso was aware that he was a more cautious man. Big men made easier targets. There had been more than one occasion when Jarrett's recklessness had saved his life. His own, more careful approach had also saved Jarrett's. Their respective attributes made them a well-matched, productive team.

"Why did you become a cop?" Caruso asked after a moment, suddenly curious, aware that Jarrett had never talked about his past before. "Didn't you inherit a lot of money?" he added.

Jarrett shrugged, "Attorney fees took most of it. I have a trust fund, but I have to be careful with it." He averted his eyes. "I did appeal to my maternal grandmother for financial help to pay the expenses of my father's defense. Grand Dame Thornton," he added bitterly. "She would be in her eighties by now. She was then, and probably still is, filthy rich. She lives in a mansion in Portland, Maine. I found out later that she owned our house on Long Island." He gave a harsh laugh. "You'll never guess what she told me."

Jarrett continued in a rougher tone. "My grandmother, Ada, put it to me bluntly. She told me that every time she looked at me, she saw my father. The sight of me hurt her too much. I was just like him. And she wouldn't give a penny to help save my father because she knew he was guilty. I left the house she owned, and I haven't seen or contacted her since. I don't hate her," Jarrett shrugged again. "I can't forgive her either, you see." He shifted uncomfortably. "To be fair, I suppose she's had more than her share of tragedy. She lost her husband, then her daughter, her son, and granddaughter."

Caruso winced, but Jarrett ignored it. "Several years ago, her son, my Uncle Albert, was killed in a skiing accident in Colorado. Then, about four years ago, Albert's daughter, the only other grandchild, died. You probably remember the incident. She was lost off a yacht during a storm in the Gulf, Sharon Thornton Adams."

Caruso combined staring with a frown, and then said, "Yeah, I remember that." He nodded and ran the fingers of one hand through his hair. "Jesus, Lad, talk about still waters!" He shifted in his chair, his frown becoming more pronounced. "Wasn't Gabe Parker tangled up in that one? He quit the force shortly after."

"Yes," Jarrett nodded. "I don't remember much about it, but, I do seem to recall that he knew my cousin Sharon. I had virtually nothing to do with that side of the

family. We Blackwell's were the lepers, so to speak."
Jarrett stopped abruptly as another detective walked up.

"You two are wanted in the Captain's office," he
said, spun on a heel and left. With that, the two men
exchanged looks, got to their feet and strode toward the
office at the end of the hall.

Captain Barry John Whitmore was big, black and
ugly. His face was crisscrossed with thin pencil line
scars on both cheeks. His nose was skewed and lumpy,
having been broken more than once; he was as proud of
his battle scars as a veteran displaying a Purple Heart. He
had received the facial slashes while defending a white
woman from her crazed, razor-wielding husband. The
woman had lived, but the husband had died from a blow
to the head inflicted by 'Big John's' fist. That had
occurred in his long-gone days as a street cop. He had
worked his way up to his present position with the
combination of formidable intelligence, sheer effort, and
relentless persistence. Born and raised in Norcross,
Georgia, he had little tolerance for bigots. He refused to
consider himself black, or African American. As far as
Big John, as his men had nicknamed him, was concerned,
he was an American and color blind. He did not discuss
religion, politics or the color of a person's skin, and
expected those who worked for him to show the same
restraint. His standards were not always viewed as
realistic.

He viewed Jones and Blackwell as two of his best.
Put together, they reminded him of himself when he was
a detective. He knew that when he gave them an order to

find a killer, they delivered only their best efforts.

Big John had an unsolved case that had troubled him for a long time. It had been his first case. Now suddenly, the murder of Angelique Corbett was to be resurrected. He very much wanted to see it solved before his retirement. Maybe, after all these years, and with the daughter's reappearance, it was actually possible.

He motioned for Caruso and Jarrett to be seated, and coming quickly to the point, laid the case before them. "I retire in three weeks. That is not much time, but it gives me one last stab at closing this file. I want you to do everything in your power to solve this murder by then. You have the records. Read them over carefully. Use whatever resources you need, but solve it. Our break seems to be that the missing daughter has been found. She's the sister of one of the city's leading physicians, Dr. Gene Corbett, the murdered woman's son. You'll have to tread lightly there. But if you run into a problem, let me know. I'll handle it. And," he added, "you both report directly to me. I'll inform your sergeant."

The two men looked at each other.

"Are they sure it's the same girl?" Jarrett asked.

"Dr. Corbett believes so. He was interviewed this morning." He picked up the folder and handed it to Jarrett. "This is his statement. Jankowicz was originally assigned to this cold case, and he did the interview of the doctor this morning. Since then, he's been reassigned to another case. So, I want you two to handle this one,"

"What about the case we've been working on?"

"Keep at it also. We need that one solved yesterday. However, Angelique Corbett's case has gone unsolved since 1989. Do the best you can. I hope a fresh approach will catch something that was missed back then." He paused and stared at the pair intently. "Are there any other questions?"

The two detectives shook their heads.

"That's all, then. Just keep me informed." The Captain returned his attention to the papers in front of him, oblivious to their departure.

Back at their desks, Jarrett and Caruso faced each other. "Nothing like overload," Jarrett muttered.

"What information do we have on Mrs. Corbett's murder?" Caruso asked.

Jarrett pulled the file from the desk drawer and opened it, to rifle through the contents. "We have the husband's statement taken by the Responding Officer, one Harold Johnson." He continued to read. "According to this, Dr. Corbett returned home from the hospital around ten in the evening. He found his young son, Eugene, asleep on the sofa in the TV room and alone in the house. He was concerned because his wife never left the boy by himself for any length of time. Eugene was not sure where his mother was. The boy thought she might have gone next door." He slowly read on. "The doctor called his neighbor, Arthur Craswell, who was also his attorney. Craswell stated Mrs. Corbett had stopped by for about five minutes around eight and then left. The attorney was present during the interview, as well as his brother, Thomas, and a woman named Thelma Joan Poole."

Jarrett, his interest now piqued, could sympathize. He read on. "The attorney stated that Mrs. Corbett had visited him to offer to pay for the repairs to his car. That was the last time she was seen by anyone. After searching the grounds, the doctor called the police, reported that his wife and boat were both missing. Another neighbor reported hearing a speedboat behind the house. Mrs. Corbett's body was found the next morning in the bay near the family dock. The boat was later found adrift at the mouth of the bay."

"Here's something!" Caruso had been studying the autopsy report. "The lady had bruises on her neck."

Jarrett looked up. "Was she raped?" he asked softly.

Caruso met his gaze. 'No. Apparently, she was hit on the back of the head," he said and looked down at the document again. "She had an abrasion on the back of her scalp. There was not much else in the way of evidence, a few stray hairs, not hers, from a wig, according to the ME, who did the autopsy." Caruso kept reading, abridging the report out loud. "No traces of alcohol or drugs in her system. Trauma to the neck was the cause of death, manual strangulation. Nothing under her fingernails to indicate resistance. Conclusion, she was struck from behind first, and then strangled. The time of death was estimated to be between eight and nine p.m."

Jarrett nodded and went back to reading the interview. "The neighborhood was canvassed, but except for the sound of a boat, no one heard or saw anything. Since Dr. Corbett was well known in the community, a squad car was dispatched, and the area was searched again. Big John was the lead detective then. He was in charge of this case, as well as the abduction of the little girl. The FBI had been called in on the child's kidnapping and had been at the house earlier in the day. No ransom was ever requested. The child just vanished." He frowned and looked up. "What I find strange is that the kid is snatched, and then the mother is murdered a week later. Why? Did anyone check out the husband?" Jarrett began perusing the other reports. Dug out one and scan it. "Here it is. He was cleared. His alibi was solid. The good doctor was performing a complicated operation on a patient at Bay Memorial at the time of his wife's death."

"Did anyone check out the attorney?" Caruso asked. After two divorces, he disliked attorneys intensely.

"Craswell had an alibi as well. His brother was in town and corroborated the statement that Mrs. Corbett never came into the house. The woman, Thelma Joan Poole, was there on business for the attorney," Jarrett, said shaking his head.

"What kind of business?" Caruso muttered. "Everyone seems to have had a solid alibi. Someone had to have seen or heard something besides that motorboat. Is it possible someone was waiting for her when she started the walk home?"

"Did they locate the actual murder scene?" Jarrett asked. "You'd think she'd had to have been murdered close by to be dumped in the Bay behind her home. Besides, she had just gone next door. Not that far."

"Apparently not." Caruso sat back and tapped a finger on the file. "No clues anywhere to speak of.

Between the little girl's disappearance and the mother's murder, the department had their hands full. Not exactly easy cases," he said. "They're not going to be any easier now, either."

"Who was the attorney's brother?" Jarrett pursued.

Caruso shifted and flipped back to that report. "One Thomas Craswell, from Maine."

"Is there a Maine address for him?"

"Yeah. Here. But the man could have moved by now," Caruso said. "Tomorrow, I'll call Maine MVD and check for a driver's license."

"What did you say the woman's name was?" Jarrett asked.

"Thelma Joan Poole."

"Did the Captain make a notation by her name?" Jarrett leaned back in his chair and waited for Caruso to locate any pertinent notes.

"This is interesting," Caruso said. "Big John indicated that she was a local. He put several question marks next to her name. We'll have to ask him about that."

"Is he still in his office?" If Big John were still at work, now would be a good time to see what he remembered.

Caruso swiveled around to look. "No, he went home."

"I guess we'll have to start from scratch. We'll have to interview all the people listed again and see what they remember. If we can find them."

Caruso looked again at the list of names and frowned at the notations beside one, all in Captain

Whitmore's handwriting. "Well, that may be difficult. It looks like Big John kept track of these people. The husband is dead, as well as the witness who heard the boat. There's nothing beside Thomas Craswell's name, except a question mark. We'll have to ask him about that too."

"Maybe we'll have better luck retesting all the evidence," Jarrett said and glanced at his watch. It was nearing six o'clock.

"It's time to pack up and head home," Caruso said. "There isn't anything more we can do on either case tonight. Besides, I promised the Sandman I'd come by The Den and sing a couple of songs. Want to join me there around nine o'clock?"

Jarrett shot him a grateful look. "That sounds good. I'm not in the mood to sit at home tonight anyway. See you there." He closed the folder and placed it in the file drawer. Slinging his jacket over his shoulder, he followed Caruso out of the building and headed to the parking lot.

CHAPTER NINE

In New York City spring had come and gone. The summer heat and smog had settled in between the buildings and the night air was stifling. New Yorkers were familiar with the sweltering air trapped between the skyscrapers. With the heat radiating off so much concrete and glass, not even a breeze off the East River could cool the nights.

In Central Park, the trees were ready for the season's weather and long days. Their small buds had burst open, transforming the branches from bare brown into a rich assortment of forest greens. Flowers scented the air with their blossoms. And, on the weekends, Central Park was filled with large numbers of the city's populace. The breeze smelled faintly of the earth's rebirth, while the bright sun thawed the inhabitants' bodies chilled by the long cold winter.

In his apartment, high above the Park, George Lowell sprawled on his black leather sofa relaxing with a short glass of Scotch. It had been another long day at the Gallery. He was pleased by the day's receipts, but also tired. He had finished the last of the accounts for the commission sales and artist payments from the May and June exhibits. He hated doing book work and was annoyed with his ex-manager for leaving him in the middle of a busy season.

Tonight, after a hard day at the office, all he planned on doing was watching the news before changing to go out for dinner. He stretched out his long legs, pointed the television remote and clicked it on. The evening news anchorman appeared on the oversized screen. As George pushed the volume button on the remote, the man's face was replaced with a picture of a familiar and beautiful woman with long dark hair, large expressive green eyes, and a pretty, sensual mouth.

Shocked, he sat up too quickly and sloshed the remaining liquid in his glass onto his pants. "Damn it!" he swore, jumping to his feet. He brushed at his wet trousers, all the while transfixed by the breaking story of the woman being reunited with her lost brother.

As soon as the newsman switched to another story, he turned off the television and grabbed the phone. After two rings, the other end was picked up.

"Lewis!" George almost shouted, "She's there! The little bitch is in your town. She must have been there since she left Kentucky. I'll catch a flight out tomorrow." He listened and then broke in. "No, I'll rent a car. It'll be safer that way. We'll get her this time!"

Strong protests were uttered on the other end.

"What the hell do you mean, leave it alone?" George shouted. "No, Lewis. Think! We have to get rid of her. Especially now she's resurfaced again, and with all this publicity. She's a slick little bitch, remember."

George had returned to the apartment the night his men put an end to Homer's extortion. Homer's body laid as he had fallen in the living room, the bright red spread out from under his white shirt had already turned dark. The room stunk. George had covered his nose with a handkerchief and made his way through the wrecked chaos of the living room to the bedroom doorway. The two fools who worked for him had left a mess, having dumped the contents of the bureau and dresser on the floor and bed. Angry, he'd been surprised no one had come to investigate the noise they must have made. His men were lucky they hadn't been discovered.

The clincher to the evening had come when he had noticed the light coming through a narrow gap at the back of the walk-in closet. There appeared to be an extra door, something he hadn't seen on his previous visit. Furious, he had found the hidden safe and understood the full significance of its open door and shelves empty.

He also remembered staring out the window watching how the cars below formed moving ribbons of light in the darkness. Homer's little pet whore had raided the safe and was on the run. He had sworn then that she wouldn't escape him forever; that he would find her someday and get back what belonged to him. She had taken Homer's books and tapes as well as his money. His only consolation had been the satisfaction of knowing that one part of his revenge against the Thornton family had succeeded. The whore had been a critical component to his plan.

He had not expected the girl to be successful in hiding from him for eleven years, but he had always known she would surface someday. He had very nearly had her recently too, but she had disappeared again. Now she had resurfaced in a way that made her much more accessible. What a stroke of luck to find she was even closer than he had thought.

George broke in on Lewis' tirade on the other end of the phone. "She has Homer James' files, Lewis." There came another verbal explosion on the other end. He stopped to listen to the outburst. He interrupted it. "I didn't tell you before, because I intended to find and get rid of her. Kentucky turned into a fuck up, I know that. You don't have to remind me. Look, we'll go over everything when I see you tomorrow."

He frowned at the silence on the other end of the line. "Lewis, are you there?" An unintelligible grunt was the only answer he received. "Lewis, remember we only have each other. Think about it." He hung up the phone, a look of delight slid across his face. Then, he called the airlines to book a seat for the next available morning flight south before going to his bedroom to pack.

CHAPTER TEN

Jarrett still drove his father's old Chevy truck. Over the last eleven years, he had replaced parts, repaired and repainted the vehicle too many times to count. In fact, it could be argued that little of the original vehicle still existed. Each time he considered scrapping the old heap, he had been unable to part with this last connection to his father.

After leaving Long Island, nothing had mattered to him. The loss of his parents and home had sent him into months of severe depression. The nasty end of his engagement had only compounded the tragedy in his life as close friends backed away, never to be seen again. He had worked at various manual labor jobs up and down the eastern coast, killing his days with hard physical exertion to avoid thinking, unable to cope with much of anything.

And then there were the nightmares, tangled mirages of a particularly beautiful face and the sweet feel of a soft body that disintegrated into the terrible last images of his dead parents. His father's ghoulish corpse saying over and over, "I don't know, I loved her," all morphed into a chaotic mess that became relentless and exacerbated by people snatching at him, nagging him with questions, chasing him down corridors, through rooms where his mother lay bruised and twisted like a broken doll. And the girl, his girl, running, torn, writhing through it all like some inexplicable catalyst.

In each town where he stayed, his first act had been to visit the police station and make inquiries about the girl. He always claimed he was searching for a lost cousin. He had never found any arrests for prostitution on the girl, or any unknown Jane Does who matched that girl's description.

Eventually, he found himself in Half Moon Bay. It was after his lunch at the Black Pearl that he made his usual trip to the police station. The sun was bright and the pavements hot, and the cold air of the building's interior was always refreshing. He had stopped to make his routine inquiry at the front desk, and before he could say a word, the officer behind the wire cage informed him that testing for the police academy was being held elsewhere, then handed him a flyer. That had stopped him in his tracks as he had realized that by joining the police force, he would have access to all kinds of records across the country. Locating the girl would be much easier.

Jarrett had phoned his attorney in New York and had arranged for an additional five thousand dollars from his trust fund. He rented a small apartment, bought a few pieces of furniture and waited. When the next testing cycle came around, he took the exams and had been a little surprised when the notification came he'd been accepted to the police academy.

Determined to learn as much about police procedures as possible, he had studied hard. Then had served his two years on the streets and taken the tests required for advancement. Finally, achieved his goal of becoming a homicide detective. With an increase in salary, he purchased a small, dilapidated house where he had lived modestly ever since. The building was a far cry from the spacious, mansion on Long Island, but it suited his needs, and it pleased him because he had earned it.

The kitchen had been a disaster. When he had moved in, he had gutted the room and installed new fixtures, white cabinets, and stainless steel appliances. The large window over the sink looked out into the backyard. Each year a grapefruit and two orange trees filled the springtime air with their sweet odor and, in the winter, offered fresh fruit. Out of control, a tangerine tree grew next to the wooden fence. He had thought of installing a pool but rejected the idea in favor of a wooden deck covering most of the small rear lawn.

He converted one bedroom into an office containing his computer and files. The other was occupied by a queen size bed, a nightstand with a tall bedside table lamp and a dresser. The walls were devoid of any family pictures. He furnished the living room for comfort, building solid oak bookshelves, adding a brown, leather easy chair and a recliner that faced the TV, with a couple of end tables, and two tall wooden lamps. The old tan love seat was used mainly by Chance, a mongrel dog he had found one night and adopted.

Hit by a car and left on the side of the road to die, the injured animal had somehow managed, even with a broken hip and leg, to crawl up his driveway, almost to the front door. Hearing the dog's cries, Jarrett had rushed out to a pitiful sight. The animal's hindquarters looked mangled, all torn flesh and protruding bone. He had taken the animal to an emergency veterinary clinic that night and later brought him home after his hip had been repaired and the broken leg pinned.

Chance had taken a long time to recover, and the vet bill had cost as much as a human's visit to a hospital emergency room. In the long run, Jarrett decided it was worth the price. The dog was devoted to him and was good company on lonely evenings. With the house and dog, Jarrett had found some measure of peace in having a place devoid of ghosts that he could call home.

Slowly, he had found some sort of normalcy, even half seriously dating two different nurses he had met at the hospital emergency room. His attempts at developing a relationship with both women had been abysmal failures. He discovered that he had become detached, unable to share his feelings or his past life, and always haunted by the dark-haired beauty he had fallen so hard for. Each woman he dated soon felt his disconnection. Disgusted, they soon ended the affair. Through it all, Jarrett had come to believe that he and the vanished young woman would meet again. Now, it seemed, his tenacity had paid off. Eleven years later, the answers to his nightmares were within reach. Except that it appeared from her mother's case file, that Dr. Corbett's sister might have a few bad dreams of her own.

As he pulled into his driveway, Jarrett tried to push thoughts of the girl from his mind. She had been a ghost for so long, it was hard to realize that he would actually be face to face with the real person within a matter of hours. If he had his druthers, he would be on his way to talk to her now. Which, he had to admit was a bad idea. His thinking was off, he knew, and his emotions were in a shambles. The strange, obsessive love/hate attachment for her which he had half buried had broken through the surface of his hard-won stability.

Now he couldn't get her out of his mind.

He pulled into the driveway, turned off the engine, and got out. He had spent far too long brooding over the puzzle the girl had become. She had been so young, so? Jarrett stopped suddenly. Terrified? Yes, that was it. She had been terrified that night. He had thought she was fearful of him because of his obvious passion and instant proposal. But it hadn't been that at all. The girl had been frightened of something else.

Eyes wide with realization, he fished his house keys out of his pocket and shook his head. This new understanding didn't really help. If anything, it opened up more questions. His parents were still dead and the girl, woman now, was still connected to that.

He opened the front door. Chance jumped and barked as he stepped inside. Patting the dog, Jarrett went straight to the dining room and opened the back door to let the dog out into the fenced yard. Then, he checked his messages on the answering machine. There was a call from his attorney, Lawrence Greenwalt, with a message to call him back. No hurry on that. It was probably about his trust. Another call was from a salesman with important information about his heating and air conditioning unit, and lastly, a reminder from Caruso to be sure to meet him at the Den by nine.

He fixed himself a sandwich and coffee, then let Chance back inside. After a quick shower, he dressed in jeans and a white, short-sleeved, cotton pullover shirt. The dog curled up on his rug beside the bed, gave him a sorrowful look as he dropped his head on his paws, let out a deep sigh, and closed his eyes. Patting the animal on the head, Jarrett left the house and locked the door behind him, then climbed into the El Camino.

It was almost nine when he walked down the steps and entered the restaurant. The Den was not only known throughout the area for the quality of its cuisine but also renowned for its piano bar. It featured notable vocalists and musicians from the local area. Since its opening, the establishment had become a hot spot for the local talent. It had been closed, reopened, closed again, only to open once more under new ownership. The crowds had gladly returned to fill each booth and table, and seat themselves around the piano bar.

A dark, wood-paneled room, approximately twenty-five feet wide and forty- five feet long, the restaurant offered an aged ambiance. A brass divider separated the bar at the entrance from the eatery at the back. Small, tall, round tables and padded high stools surrounded the piano for those wishing only to drink and listen. Six booths and seven tables were set aside for dining.

For the past several years, a colorful, well-known local musician had provided most of the entertainment. An accomplished artist, The Sandman regaled the patrons with his renditions of a considerable repertoire of songs. Laminated copies listing the most popular pieces were placed on top of the piano to enable the clientele to choose a preferred number.

The Sandman was a striking figure. A handsome man with a close-cropped beard and large, friendly brown eyes, he was popular with the female patrons. With his black hat, long ponytail and husky voice, the Sandman presented a romantic and desirable image of a modern-day desperado. He ignored the disappointment his unavailability status caused and smiled politely at the comments made by the numerous women who frequented the piano bar.

"I don't want to keep him. I just want to borrow him for one night. Then, I'll give him back to his girlfriend, that is, if he still wants her" was one of the remarks Caruso had heard. He remembered, in vivid detail, the tall, slender woman with red hair, who had said it and wondered if Sandy had noticed her. She had been striking enough to be hard to miss in any room. Interested, he had intended to question the piano man her identity but had not seen the woman again.

Positioned on a stool near the instrument, with his back against the wall, Caruso saw Jarrett enter the darkened bar and eye the room in search of him. He raised a hand in the air, signaling to him.

After working his way through the crowd, Jarrett stood next to Caruso and ordered a scotch and water from the waitress who appeared at his side.

Sandy took his place behind the piano and smiled at them. "How's it going?" he asked trying to be heard above the general din.

"Great!" Caruso beamed. He had already downed two drinks. Food would be needed shortly.

Jarrett gave a brief "Okay," and took a sip of his drink.

Ignoring the lukewarm response, the piano player looked at Caruso and asked, "Anything special you want to hear tonight?" He adjusted the microphone and immediately broke "Harlem Nocturne" as the opening number.

Caruso grinned. "Sing Buffet's "A Pirate Looks at Forty" for me."

Sandy nodded and, after his first musical piece, continued on to play the introduction to the Jimmy Buffet song. Satisfied, Caruso grinned again, leaned back against the wall and nursed the last of his second drink, glad to relax and let the stress of the day fade under the sound of a favorite song.

As the musician's smooth, powerful voice filled the room, Jarrett began his old habit of looking around and checking for familiar faces. Carefully, he studied each man and woman seated at the bar. The regulars he recognized were out in force tonight. Two men, their voices slurred and rising above the music, obviously had started drinking early. The other tables and stools were rapidly being taken, and a line of drinkers had formed along the brass and wood divider. The dining area was packed with people for the dinner hour.

As the song ended, Caruso tapped Jarrett on the shoulder to get his attention. "What time do you want to call Dr. Corbett about his long lost sister?"

"How about eight a.m. I want to get it over with. I'm not sure I'm looking forward to this meeting." Jarrett pushed his hair back off his forehead. The thought of coming face to face with this particular woman made him decidedly uneasy.

"I thought you wanted to find this girl?" Caruso insisted.

Jarrett frowned. "I do," he admitted, "but, I'm not

sure whether to be relieved that it's finally happening or dread the answers I might get. She's the key to so many things, and I don't want to screw up the investigation." Jarrett looked at the glass in his hand. "Hell. I'm not making any sense. I feel like some kid waiting for his first date!" Disgusted with himself, he inhaled and turned back to continue surveying the room.

Next to him and unnoticed, Caruso picked up one of the laminated lists and pointed to an old 1940's tune, "I'll Be Seeing You." With a quick conspiratorial grin, the piano man nodded and began singing the melody of the love song.

Recognizing it, Jarrett glared at CJ, then turned back to stare into his glass again. The words of the song struck home to him. Yes, he desperately wanted to see the girl again. That was the trouble. He had never stopped wanting to see her. He needed to fill that damned, haunted void inside. Lost in his own thoughts, Jarrett completely missed his partner's suddenly amazed expression.

Caruso leaned back against the wall and, turning to his left, stared in growing disbelief down the long room to the back booth on the far side. Seated by a dark-haired man was the redhead who had once made the remark about the Sandman. He saw her flash a big smile at the man and then turn to speak to another woman who sat across from her. He couldn't see the other woman's face, only a mass of long, curly dark hair.

While Caruso tried to maneuver to get a better view of the back booth, Jarrett slipped from his stool. "Be back in a minute. Order me another drink, if you would." He looked at the musician. "He asked you to sing that song didn't he?" The Sandman merely grinned before breaking into another melody. Jarrett shot another quick glare at his colleague and left.

Pleased with himself, Caruso smiled and watched as Jarrett threaded his way toward the back of the restaurant, headed for the restroom. Then, as Jarrett neared the back booth, he suddenly went tense and stopped in midstride.

Caruso stood up, watching as Jarrett veered sharply and went back to the booth.

Jarrett stared down at the dark haired woman. Struggling for control, he blinked. "You!" He said and leaned forward, placing both hands on the table, his face inches from hers.

White-faced with shock, Sarra shifted closer to Addie and away from Jarrett.

At the same time, recognition hit Caruso as he realized this was the missing daughter of the woman in the file. He quickly walked up behind Jarrett. The resemblance was unbelievable. The two women were like twins. "Miss," he said hurriedly. "I apologize for my friend's behavior. I think seeing you may have startled him."

"Startled!" Gene exploded. "He's scaring my sister. You had better get your friend out of here before I call the police."

Jarrett came to life and growled hoarsely. "We are the police! You!" He continued staring at Sarra, as he stood up, his voice going stark and ragged. "You don't even know me, do you?"

Sarra had known who he was the moment he stopped and looked at her. "No," she whispered the lie, "I don't know you." It was all falling apart too fast. She clutched at her throat where a knot of fear was about to choke her and turned to Corbett. "Gene, I have to get out of here. I have to leave now." While Gene and Addie scrambled out of their seats, she rose from the booth; her purse already snatched up and held tight against her chest, she pushed past Caruso.

His expression taut, Jarrett reached out to stop her.

She jerked away. "Don't touch me!"

He flinched a little, and she pushed past him and hurried away.

Jarrett swiveled to follow, but Gene hurried to block him. "You heard her. Leave my sister alone."

Acid welling up inside, Jarrett took a step toward the other man, then turned to run after her, but was whipped around by a vice-like grip on his shoulder.

"Get hold of yourself, Jarrett," CJ hissed and shoved him forcibly down into the booth. Glancing at Addie's stricken face, he said, "Your friend is upset. Go after her. We do have to talk to her, but not tonight." Keeping a firm grip on Jarrett, he added, "Can you give me her address?"

Hesitantly, Addie asked. "Are you really a cop?" The big man dug into his back pocket and flipped out identification and his badge, which she examined with care. "Sorry, I don't know her address."

"What business do you have with my sister?" Gene demanded, uncertain now, but still angry.

"You are Dr. Corbett, aren't you?" At the other

man's nod, Jarrett pried Caruso's hand from his shoulder. "Let go of me, CJ. I'm all right." Taking him at his word, Caruso released his iron grip. "Jarrett Blackwell. Caruso Jones," he introduced as he stood up, embarrassment crossing his features and reddening his ears. "I apologize for scaring your sister." Jarrett looked at the red-haired woman standing beside Gene. "Miss?"

"Addie Newsome," she answered.

Caruso tucked that bit of information away.

Jarrett nodded and turned to Caruso, "Thanks for stopping me. I have no idea what I was thinking of," he said and took off, heading for the club door.

Hurrying to follow, pursued by Gene Corbett, with Addie in the rear, Caruso caught up, snatched at Jarrett's shoulder again and demanded, "Where do you think you're going?"

Jarrett pulled free then pushed through the door before his friend could stop him. "I'm going to talk to her tonight before she leaves town."

Caruso caught up with him again. "Do I have to knock you out to get you to back off?"

Jarrett stopped abruptly a few feet outside the entrance and turned to face him. "Look," he said, "I owe her an apology. I overreacted, and I know I scared the hell out of her, but I have to see her tonight. She's been running from something besides me for years. If you want, you can come with me. I won't be stopped, CJ. Not this time. I intend to follow her home."

"Hold it," Gene bit out, stepping up beside Caruso. "You can't let him follow my sister like this."

He glared furiously at Jarrett, aware that both men were cops. He couldn't help Sarra if he got himself jailed. "I won't have her hurt any more than she has been already. And, if you're so set on questioning her tonight, I intend to be there." He spun around to take Addie's arm as she hovered, wide-eyed behind the three of them. "You can follow me to her house, I know where she lives. I'll give my attorney a call." He turned back to Caruso. "And you'd better keep this nut under control, or I'll sue his ass off!" With that Gene strode past them, Addie in tow, and crossed the street to his car.

CHAPTER ELEVEN

It was a short drive from the Den to the little house on Fifty-fifth Avenue South. Sarra pulled into the driveway just a few moments before Jarrett parked his El Camino at the curb. She didn't pay any attention to the other two cars as they parked behind him, but hurried to the door, intent on locking herself in the house. Just as she started to insert her key in the lock, the door flew open.

"Mommy, you're home early," Amanda cried, grabbing her mother around the waist. She stiffened as she heard the slamming of a car door. "Who are those men?" Amanda pointed toward the driveway.

The garage lights spread eerie shadows under the trees and Sarra could feel her child's fear.

"Are they bad men, Mom?" Amanda asked as she pressed closer.

Sarra swiveled around to face the men, blocking the doorway and pushing Amanda back behind her.

Pearl Ann appeared next to the child. "Sarra, what's going on? Is everything all right?"

In the street, Jarrett stopped short at the edge of the sidewalk to stare in astonishment at the little girl peering around her mother. Then he saw the older woman behind them. A multitude of questions rushed through his mind. He had never thought about a child or considered the involvement of another person. The girl, woman, who had haunted him for so long had always been isolated in his mind. Whose child was she, he wondered as he came up the driveway? He slowed, and then stopped to look down at Amanda and then at his ghost's ashen face staring back at him.

"Pearl Ann, I have to talk to these men." The ghost said briskly. "Please, take Amanda and put her to bed." Mentally filing the older woman's name, Jarrett watched her hug her daughter and give her a kiss. "There's nothing wrong. I'll only be a second."

At that moment Gene, Addie, and Caruso walked up to stand beside Jarrett. Gene stepped up to Sarra, smiling at the little girl and Pearl Ann, and cheerfully introduced himself. "Hi, I'm Sarra's brother!"

Pearl Ann looked from Gene back to Sarra but said nothing.

"Gene, please!" Sarra snapped and then turned to Pearl Ann. "Please put Amanda to bed." Then, when no one moved, she waved her arms at them. "Oh, for Pete's sake, all of you come inside before the neighbors start to complain!" Taking Amanda's hand, she turned her back on the lot of them and hurried into the house, followed by the three men, Addie, and Pearl Ann. She led Amanda to her bedroom and waited while she changed into her pajamas. As Amanda stared at her anxiously, said gently, "It's okay Amanda. We're safe. No questions please. I'll tell you about it in the morning."

After tucking her daughter into bed and giving her orders to stay put, she closed the bedroom door and joined everyone in the living room.

Pearl Ann was busy in the kitchen making coffee, placing cups on a large tray and cookies on a plate. The two policemen sat together on the sofa, while Addie occupied one of the blue velvet chairs placed on each side of the large bay window. Gene hovered protectively near the hall and moved when Sarra crossed the room to sit down in Pearl Ann's recliner.

She clasped her hands in front of her and looked at her brother. "Gene, please stay out of this for now." Looking straight at Jarrett, she asked. "Who are you? And who is the gentleman next to you?"

Jarrett sat forward, still transfixed. "This is my partner, Caruso Jones. We're Homicide Detectives here in Half Moon Bay. We are working on a case which has been reopened, the murder of Angelique Corbett."

"What?" Gene said in surprise.

Jarrett ignored him and frowned a little as he continued to stare at Sarra. "You do remember me?" he asked, in a calm, gentle voice.

Sarra wanted to deny it. "Yes," she said reluctantly. "I do. We met a long time ago in New York."

Jarrett continued to study her. "I never introduced myself that night. My name is Jarrett Blackwell. I am the son of the man who gave the party."

Sarra froze. "My God!" she whispered, going white. "You can't be!" She looked up at Pearl Ann. The older woman had appeared and now perched on the chair arm beside Sarra.

Thoroughly confused, Gene crossed the room to position himself close by on Sarra's right. "Sarra, you don't have to say anything without my attorney present." He told her and glared at Jarrett. "What do you want?" He roared, ready to do battle. "It's obvious you're scaring the hell out of her."

Jarrett met Gene's gaze briefly and then went back to looking at Sarra. "I just want some answers," he said bitterly. "My whole life was destroyed eleven years ago. I lost my parents, my home. Everything! I need to know why." Scowling, he took a ragged breath as he addressed Sarra. "Did you know my father was accused of raping you?"

Sarra met his eyes and flinched. "I remember I was examined by some doctor, a friend of Homer's. He was my pimp," she added in a whisper, then stiffened. "I don't know how your father could have been charged. I never gave a statement to the police. I never even saw the police. And, I swear, I didn't know until the next day that your mother had been murdered." Her eyes widened suddenly. "It was the pictures they wanted! They took photos when. . ." She didn't finish. She didn't have to.

Still focused on her, Jarrett clearly understood her meaning.

Gene moved away to collapse into an empty chair. Addie sat in stunned silence. Round-eyed, Caruso looked back and forth from Jarrett to Sarra.

Jarrett, still frowning, leaned forward. "You were introduced to my father as Candace James." He glanced at Gene. "Dr. Corbett insists you're his sister. For the record, what is your real name?" he asked, his voice reacquiring some of its professional smoothness.

Sarra glanced at Pearl Ann next to her, then met Jarrett's gaze steadily. "Candace James was a name Homer used for that evening. My real name and the only name I have known is Sarra Gray."

"Did you know that my father committed suicide

within ten days after my mother's death?" Jarrett pursued.

Sarra shook her head. "No. I never knew what happened to Mr. Blackwell." She was fighting to remain calm, but it was all coming too fast. She looked down at her white-knuckled, clenched hands. She unclasped them and set them flat on her thighs, trying to relax. "So much went wrong after that party."

"Did my father rape you?" Jarrett asked hoarsely even as it occurred to him that the little girl down the hall just might be his half-sister. She looked about the right age.

Sarra stared back and then shook her head. "No. No," she whispered. "Please keep your voice down. My daughter. I don't want her to hear this." Her hands clenched again into fists. "No. The man who brought me to the party did" she hesitated, "that. Before Mr. Blackwell. His name was George. I don't even know if it was his real name. That's all I know. I'd never seen him before, either."

Jarrett exhaled slowly, feeling a sense of relief in a way. But there remained the fact that she had had sex with his father. And the child, whose was she?

"Who in the Hell is George?" Gene demanded, his shock and confusion clear.

Caruso leaned forward, glancing from one to the other, interested and attentive to each detail. Addie remained silent, gaping at the group as if she was watching a film or television show.

Pearl Ann calmly rose from her perch, went to the

kitchen and returned with a tray weighed down by a pot of coffee, cups, sugar bowl and cream pitcher. Setting it on the coffee table, she went back to the kitchen and returned with a plate of cookies. "I think," she said pointedly, setting that down as well, "we need a break from all this. Help yourself to coffee and cookies. I want this cut short. I won't have my granddaughter upset, and Sarra is already in a bad way. Do the rest of you understand me?"

Jarrett looked up at the older woman. "We are the police, in point of fact," he told her in gently, "and we do have questions in regards to the case we're working on."

"Which case are you referring to, the murder of your mother in New York, Sarra's kidnapping as a small child, or her mother's murder?" Pearl Ann asked sweetly, as she returned Jarrett's steady gaze.

He looked at her in surprise.

"Exactly," she said. "Sarra has told me a lot about the real hell she has experienced in her young life. I won't allow you to torment her further. Ask your questions and stop beating around the bush."

Jarrett nodded and glanced down at his own clenched hands. "I only want to know if there is anything she can tell me about my mother's death."

Pearl Ann saw that he was fighting his own demons, and relented with a nod of her own. She walked over to Sarra who was huddled in the large easy chair. "Do you want to continue?"

Sarra muttered a quiet, "No," shivered and gave Pearl Ann a pleading look.

Seeing his sister's overwrought condition, Gene stood up. "That does it for the evening," he said sharply.

"I suggest we all leave. It's obvious that my sister has had more than enough. If you two have a problem with that, I'll have my attorney here within minutes. I've already notified him of what is going on. Otherwise, if Sarra is agreeable, we'll come by your office tomorrow to discuss everything and answer all your questions." He looked from one policeman to the other.

Caruso rose. "Fine, tomorrow will be fine."

Jarrett stood more slowly and took a step toward Sarra as Pearl Ann indicated the front door. "If it's any consolation to you," he said, "at the restaurant, I was so shocked at seeing you again. A lot of feelings, you know, I didn't mean. I owe you a big apology for this evening's disaster." He reached out with one hand to touch her shoulder with his fingertips, then, as she flinched away, let his hand drop to his side.

All his old feelings for this woman were roiling around inside. He needed to make this real, to see her outside of his job and office. Jarrett had to sort out how he really felt, to understand fully what had happened. "I owe you a dinner for the one you missed if you will allow it?" he said gently. "We'll straighten everything out when you and your brother come to the station."

Sarra gazed up into his deep blue eyes then looked away. Almost afraid to breathe, she said, "Thank you, but that isn't necessary. Like Gene said, I need a chance for the shock to wear off then I'll be ready to talk to you."

Jarrett smiled a little and stepped back. "That will be fine." He turned and followed his partner out the door.

Once the door was closed and locked, Pearl Ann pulled the drapes closed and began turning off the lights. "So much for coffee!" she said. "We need to go to bed and get some sleep. No more talking. No more thinking about anything tonight. Tomorrow is a different day. We'll face what comes together, Sarra. Remember, you're not alone."

Sarra rose from the chair and slipped into the arms of the only mother she had ever known. Pearl Ann held her tight. "Thank you, Gran. . . I know. It's time to put all this behind us. I'm not running anymore. You've been right all along. I'll go see Jarrett Blackwell and tell him all I know. Maybe it will help solve what happened." She kissed the older woman's cheek, squeezed her again then walked down the hall to her bedroom.

Pearl Ann collected the tray and the plate of cookies. After putting everything away, she turned out all the lights except the one over the kitchen sink. Silently, she prayed that all their troubles were coming to an end.

Still feeling bemused, Gene dropped Addie off at the Den to pick up her car, and then slowly drove home. Between all the phone calls from reporters, arguing with Helen over Sarra and the trust fund, he had slept little the night before. And now, this? He hadn't realized how exhausted he was until he pulled into the driveway.

He stopped the car and sat behind the wheel with the engine running and looked up at the darkened upstairs bedroom window. Was Helen waiting up for him?

He turned off the engine, threw his jacket over his arm, but made no move to get out of the car. He didn't want to go inside. All he could think of was how tired he felt, and how fed up he was of the fights with Helen over money. She knew how much the loss of his sister had haunted him. It didn't seem to matter. All she was concerned about was that damned trust fund. This morning, she had screamed at him, "That bitch is not your sister! All she's after is money that rightfully belongs to you, and you are just too happy to give her every cent! It's disgusting, and I, for one, don't intend to sit around and put up with it."

Even after this evening's confusing fiasco, he would be glad when the DNA test came back and proved Sarra was his sister. That would shut Helen up. He hoped so anyway. After that outburst, she had stormed from the breakfast table, leaving her food untouched. Shortly afterward, their bedroom door had slammed shut. That had been the summit of a mountain of fights.

He understood to some extent, Helen's hunger for a different life, especially after meeting her mother. He had believed there was gentleness, compassion, and kindness in her manifested through the charities with whom she had become involved. Lately, he had seriously begun to wonder. Little things had jarred that belief. It felt like catching someone in a lie. Her lack of sincerity was there all along, swaddled in platitudes, that was offered just enough to evoke unease. Rather like lying back after sex, utterly drained and depleted to realize your partner had not quite scaled the heights with you.

Although, at the time, the cries and clenching had seemed to indicate so, and, despite that, you were too satisfied to pursue the matter.

Helen was good at sex, and thoroughly beautiful. The two had become some sort of total equation in his mind shortly after they met. But, performance was not the same as sincerity. He realized now that for some time he had been feeling alone when he was with her. It dawned on Gene suddenly that it had been several weeks since they had had sex. He was equally startled to note that he hadn't missed it, and realized as well, that he felt no desire for her now.

He was just now recognizing that Helen's physical beauty did not connect to deeper qualities. Gene felt as though he was seeing Helen in a true light for the first time. Her sexuality was a performance, not real. Intimacy and her appetite for sex were not founded on feelings for him, but only in self-interest.

Thinking further, he couldn't remember the last time she had expressed real concern for another person. Things, yes, people, no. Instead, everything she related about one person or another of their acquaintance, however positively couched, had a gossipy, vicarious taint that swiveled away from any genuinely human interest. Was that why he so frequently felt pressured when he listened to her chatter on? As though he was being nudged, or pushed?

His wife, Gene decided, was the most self-centered person he had ever met. Dislike was an actual flavor in his mouth. Fool no longer, he thought. Helen had overplayed her hand with her interest in Monique's trust.

Monique, no, Sarra, Gene thought. Sarra. He was still trying to absorb the shocking bits and scraps that revealed the grim, sordid life that she had led since she was snatched away as a small child. Yet, tonight, at Sarra's house, he had seen the warmth and love between her, the older woman and the child, it was an almost tangible thing. That was what a home was supposed to be, he thought, a sanctuary filled with love and family. All he had was an empty house and bills. No children would ever grace this marriage. Helen would see to that. She had already, he was sure.

He glanced up at the window again before getting out of the car. It was still dark. Helen usually went to bed early and read until she fell asleep with the light on, or until he came home. As he started up the walk, he could see that the rest of the house was darker than usual. He unlocked the front door and let himself in, climbed the stairs to the living room. Only a faint glow of light from the kitchen came into the darkened room. Throwing the wall switch, he half expected to find Helen asleep on the sofa. But she wasn't. He checked the kitchen and even the deck. The downstairs was empty as well.

Back in the living room, he glanced at his watch; it was late. He knew Helen didn't like to stay up past ten. Maybe she was still angry and had gone to bed? Tossing his jacket over his shoulder, he hurried upstairs to the master bedroom.

"Helen?" he yelled, not caring if he woke her. Their bedroom door yawned before him like a black void. Stepping inside, he flipped the light switch. Nothing was disturbed. The king-sized, Ethan Allen bed was undisturbed, the satin bedspread and matching pillows were immaculate and precisely placed, just as Helen liked.

Gene checked the large walk-in closet. Hanging his coat on a hanger, he surveyed his wife's many dresses and suits, the plethora of shoes and accessories to match. Everything was there. As far as he could tell, nothing was missing except Helen.

Puzzled, and a bit deflated because he had been braced for a confrontation, he quickly walked downstairs to the living room, then down the hall to the quarters assigned to Lee Chung. He gave the door three sharp raps.

Too slow to suit Gene, it seemed as if it took forever for Lee to open the door. He rubbed his eyes and gave a half smile. "Yes sir, you need something?"

"Lee, my wife, did you see her this evening?"

"She make phone call, then go out about hour ago. No see since. Anything else, Dr. Corbett?"

"No, go back to bed. I'm sorry I disturbed you." Gene hovered as Lee closed the door then wearily returned to the bedroom. Sitting down on the bed, he picked up the phone and dialed Arthur's number. The answering machine responded after three rings. "Arthur, this is Gene. Please call me as soon as possible. I need you to go with Sarra and me to the Police Department tomorrow or the next day. Also, I seemed to have misplaced my wife and wondered if you've heard from her. Call me tonight if you can. I'll be awake."

Leaning back against the pillows, he continued to cradle the phone against his chest. Weariness slid throughout every fiber of his body. Slowly, he stretched full length on the bed. God, he was exhausted. He'd just rest for a minute and then go downstairs and wait for Helen.

Even as the words ran through his mind, sleep claimed him. He fought briefly to keep his eyes from closing. He never heard Helen's quiet footsteps later when she came to stand in the doorway and stare at him with a satisfied smile. Nor was he aware when she walked away to enter the guest room, closing the door behind her.

CHAPTER TWELVE

June 8

Blissfully, Gene slumbered straight through to morning. It was the wafting scent of brewing coffee that roused him, making him long for a cup. Still half asleep, he rolled off the bed, stripped off his wrinkled clothes and headed for the shower. A towel wrapped around his waist, he emerged a short while later feeling refreshed and fully awake and, curiously clear-headed. He was aware, before entering the bathroom that Helen's side of the bed had not been slept in.

After dressing in gray slacks, matching socks, he slipped his feet into black loafers and donned a clean white shirt, then selected a bright tropical print tie to go with his navy sports jacket. Something cheerful. He was positive when Helen did come home, there would be one hell of a row. He was actually looking forward to it.

On his way downstairs, he encountered Lee on his way up with a breakfast tray.

"I'll eat downstairs, Lee. Thanks for the thought."

"This is for Missus. She come in late. Woke me up to tell me bring breakfast to guest room. I go now, or she be mad." He tried to get by, but Gene stopped him and took the tray out of his hands.

"I'll take Missus her breakfast," Gene told him. "Please pour me a cup of black coffee. I'll be down shortly."

Dismissed, the oriental man shrugged and hurried back downstairs to do as instructed. Holding the tray and in a temper, Gene returned upstairs and marched down the hall to the spare room. At his sharp kick, the door sprang open. Helen was sitting up in bed, waiting, and started as he stormed through the door.

"You wanted breakfast in bed. Here," Gene said, dumping the loaded tray on top of Helen's covered lap. "Enjoy!" China and cutlery clattered. Eggs slid. Coffee and juice sloshed.

"Damn you!" she screeched, scrambling to contain the mess.

"Helen, I was damned the day I married you!" Gene snarled. "Go see Arthur. Tell him you want a divorce. If you don't, I will." He started to leave, then turned back to face her. "Oh, and don't get greedy! I know you've been squirreling money away, and I know where."

She sat yelling profanities at him even as he strode out of the room and slammed the door behind him.

An instant later she flew through the door and followed him to the head of the stairs. "You fucking son of a bitch! You'll never get me to sign any divorce papers! I'll drag this out in the courts until you're broke!" she screamed.

"Do it, and you won't get a penny," Gene called over his shoulder. "Come to think of it, if I stay married to you, I'll be broke anyway, so what the hell!" He headed downstairs pursued by her expletives. He grinned. For the first time in months, he felt a profound sense of relief and actually was looking forward to the day. Liberated. Yes, that was what he felt.

Once in the kitchen, he used the portable phone to

call Sarra and postpone their joint trip to the police
station until the next day. He didn't bother to explain
why. He thought she probably could hear Helen still
yelling at him, even over the phone. Hanging up, Gene
left the house whistling happily.

From their bedroom window, Helen watched
Gene back out of the driveway and drive away. Boiling
inside with anger, she paced the room. Divorce? She
hadn't expected that. He wasn't going to leave her high
and dry! She'd worked too hard for what she had to give
it up now.

She had stayed out until after Gene got home to
teach him a lesson and make him jealous. Jealousy was
useful. Apparently, it had backfired. He wasn't jealous
at all, which was disturbing. She remembered a time
when he'd give her anything she asked for, or do anything
she wanted.

All she had to do was keep him charged, satiated
and glazed. He had changed suddenly it seemed, and it
had begun after they had purchased the house. It wasn't
as if he couldn't afford it, but he'd gotten progressively
fussier about the bills. Cajoling had slid into arguments
which she had been able to manage. Then, when she had
brought up the much nicer house she wanted, they had
had a full-scale row. He had become as stubborn as an
ox. Now he wanted a divorce? No way.

It had to be that damned sister business. Since
finding this Monique, or Sarra, or whoever she was,
nothing had been right, especially his willingness to
literally throw away five million. Helen was confident
the woman was a scam artist. The whole thing was a
well-planned setup. Once she had the trust money, she'd

vanish again. "Well, this Sarra Gray doesn't fool me. She'll never see a penny of that money," she vowed to herself. "I'll make sure of that."

Helen went to her dressing table and sat down. She was in the habit of paying meticulous attention to her appearance, and now she did so again, studying herself carefully in the mirror. A couple of extra pounds had settled around her hips. New crows' feet were forming at the corners of her eyes. Age had not been kind to her mother, and it obviously wasn't going to be kind to her. Forty was only six years down the road, and it was becoming a constant battle to maintain her looks and figure. It took a lot of money to stave off the years and age gracefully. That thought sparked an idea.

Helen's eyes widened. Gene had a significant life insurance policy. If he had, say, an accident, she would inherit everything. Or would she?

With the return of his so-called sister, Helen couldn't be sure about anything. There was no telling how far off the deep end Gene would go. Maybe that was why he'd brought up the subject of divorce? She knew that Arthur had a copy of Gene's will in his safe, but she had never actually read it. Then, she remembered that she still had keys to the office somewhere. Helen would bet that Arthur had never changed the safe's combination after she had quit working as his receptionist.

Her reflection in the mirror took on a thoughtful quality. What her dear, husband and his attorney didn't know wouldn't hurt them, she thought. Yes, she'd have to slip down to the law office one night and take a peek at the will.

Pleased with herself, Helen rose, walked to the head of the stairs and called for Lee to clean up the spare room. A quick shower would have to do, she decided. There were plans to make, people to see. Besides, shopping always helped her think better.

Instead of shopping, however, Helen drove straight to Craswell's office. Once inside, she barged past the receptionist, straight through the door to the inner office, and stopped in front of the startled attorney who was on the phone. She folded her arms, purse dangling from one elbow. "If you and Gene think I am going to stand by and let him give away five million dollars, you're both crazy!" she said very clearly and coldly.

Going rigid, Arthur muttered a quick, "I'll call you back," into the receiver and hung up the phone. "Helen, how dare you interrupt me!"

Helen took a step closer. "Mrs. Corbett to you! That girl waltzes into our lives, expecting to collect a fortune."

Behind his desk, Craswell stood and leaned over it. "I don't intend to just hand over, as you put it, that amount of money without making positive identification! Gene can insist all he wants, but I am the executor of his father's estate and as such, must abide by the will. If the DNA samples and fingerprints prove this Sarra Gray is who she claims to be, I cannot, nor will I refuse to release those funds. Indeed, I will be happy to do so!"

Helen stared back at him and then began pacing the floor. "Damn it! There has to be something. What precisely does the will say about that trust fund?" She stopped suddenly. "Has Gene made out a new will?"

Craswell glared at her. "That is privileged information, and you know it, Helen."

"I'm his wife! I'm entitled to know!"

"Actually, no, you're not!" Craswell recovered his poise. "You are entitled to see Gene's will only if he says you can. So, go ask him."

Unable to reply, Helen wanted to insist further, but clearly, he was not going to cooperate. "Bastard!" she said and stormed out of the office.

CHAPTER THIRTEEN

It was early when Jarrett and Caruso arrived at their desks. The first order of the day was two large cups of strong and steaming coffee. As they sat sipping the scalding brew, Jarrett tried unsuccessfully to reach Dr. Gene Corbett at the hospital and at his office to verify that he and Sarra were coming in to give statements.

Later as he poured over the Corbett file with Caruso, he reviewed the list of investigators, witnesses, and their original statements, as well as the reports assembled at the time of Angelique Corbett's murder.

"Well, from what is in this file, Captain Whitmore didn't have many leads twenty-three years ago. Everyone associated with the Corbett's had an alibi at the time of the murder," Jarrett finally said.

"Do we know how many people are still alive that we have to interview again?" Caruso retrieved his pocket notebook and a ballpoint pen.

Jarrett read off the names. "Mrs. Smith, the next door neighbor. Dr. Eugene Corbett, the son. The attorney, Arthur Craswell. His brother, Thomas Craswell, the woman, Thelma Joan Poole, and any of the doctors and nurses we can find that worked at the hospital at that time who established Dr. Howard Corbett's alibi."

"The doctors may still be in town, but, I consider it unlikely if many of the nurses are still working at Bay Memorial." Jarrett scanned the list of names for medical personnel. "I'll call and check with Human Resources at the hospital if you will interview Mrs. Smith."

"Thanks a lot!" Caruso grunted as he studied a fax that had been placed on his desk while he was out.

"Looks like I got a reply from the Maine Department of Motor Vehicles."

"Did they find a Thomas Craswell in Portland?"

"They have two. One is a ninety-year-old man, and the other is eighteen. No one with that name and date of birth resides in Portland, Maine at this time."

Jarrett grabbed the phone book and rifled through it until he found the phone number for Arthur Craswell. "Why don't we give the nice attorney a call right now and find out exactly where his brother lives."

The phone only rang three times before it was answered by the lawyer himself. "This is Arthur Craswell."

Jarrett identified himself and explained why he was calling.

"Why are you interested in my brother? " Arthur asked.

"He was at your house when Mrs. Corbett was found murdered. We would like to conduct an additional interview as that case has been reopened. How can we get in touch with him?"

"You can't. Thomas drowned in a boating accident four years ago."

"Is he buried in Half Moon Bay?"

"No. Unfortunately, my brother went sailing in the Gulf of Mexico, and neither he nor his boat was ever found. You may well recall Hurricane Dennis? My brother was foolish enough to take his boat out after the eye hit the Panhandle. He was never seen again."

Jarrett was silent for a moment. "I'm sorry for

your loss," he said and frowned at Caruso. Great, he thought, this case was becoming more puzzling by the minute. What man in his right mind would take a boat out with half of a hurricane still churning up the Gulf? "Thanks for your time. When could my partner and I stop by and review your prior statement concerning Mrs. Corbett's visit to your house?"

Arthur Craswell did not hesitate, "Any time this morning. What I told the police twenty-three years ago has not changed in any way. You can come to my office, or we can do this over the phone."

"It's nine-thirty now. How about ten o'clock this morning?" Jarrett said. "That would be fine. You have my office address?"

"Yes," Jarrett said and nodded at CJ. The attorney's office was ten minutes away. He hung up the receiver and turned to Caruso. "We have about fifteen minutes. What I can't figure out is why someone would want to murder Angelique Corbett?"

"Not all killings have a reason, a sane one that is." Caruso pointed out.

"Yes, I know, but. . ."

"But, what?"

Jarrett pointed at the paperwork in front of him. "From all these reports, this woman was a bereaved mother who had lost her child to a kidnapper. She was in the public eye as a popular campaigner for the underprivileged, and, apparently, she was a great wife and mother. Yet," he held up his hand to stop Caruso from interrupting, "a week after her daughter disappeared, she is found floating in the Bay. In all your experience with abductions, have you ever encountered a scenario similar to this one?"

"Not that I recall," Caruso agreed. "If a parent is murdered, it usually happens during the abduction because the parent discovered what is going on and fights back. Generally, it is the child's body that is found days, or years later, not that of the parent."

Jarrett glanced at his watch. "If we can figure out why the woman was murdered, I think we'll also find out who killed her. It's time to go talk to this attorney." He stood and grabbed his jacket off the back of the chair.

At Arthur Craswell's building, they found a directory and took the elevator to the Attorney's office suite. Once inside, Caruso looked around then whispered into Jarrett's ear. "The decor seems, well, a little too feminine."

Jarrett smothered a smile. "I agree, but everyone to their own tastes," he murmured just as Craswell met them at the main door to his suite.

The attorney barely glanced at their proffered IDs and ushered both men into his inner office, indicating the two chairs facing his ornate desk. After they were seated, he took his seat. "Now, gentlemen, how can I help you?"

"We would like to review the statement you gave the police about the night Angelique Corbett died," Jarrett said.

"Certainly, ask anything you like."

"Mr. Craswell, you stated that Mrs. Corbett came to your house around eight o'clock on the evening of August 19th, 1989?" Caruso said, taking the lead. Jarrett remained silent and watchful. Most times, he gleaned more from people's reaction to the questions than from their actual replies.

Yes." Craswell inclined his head.

"You also said that you asked her to come into your house, but she refused because she had to hurry back home because her son, Gene, was alone?" Caruso asked.

"That is correct." Arthur stared off into space for a second as if trying to remember the circumstances of the event, and then continued. "Yes, she came to see if I had gotten an estimate for my car. She had backed out of her driveway into my vehicle and wanted to pay for the repairs."

"When did that happen?"

"That accident?" Craswell said.

"Yes." What other accident would he be asking about, Caruso wondered?

"The accident had happened several days before. Mrs. Corbett had backed out of her driveway just after I left mine and smacked into me. She was on her way to the beach with the children, as I recall. I was driving some friends to the airport. Why do you ask?"

"I'm just trying to establish a sequence of prior events. How was Mrs. Corbett when she came to your house?"

Still watchful, Jarrett noted that this interview was almost a word for word match with the prior one he had given.

Craswell sat back and shrugged a little. "Angelique was her normal self. She told me to let her know when I took my car to a body shop, and she would write me a check for any work to be done. She didn't want me to file a claim with my auto insurance to prevent rate hikes, you understand. Anyway, that's what she told me. Such a kind, beautiful lady." Arthur was pensive for a moment, then shifted in his chair and glanced at the appointment calendar on his desk.

"I have a client arriving shortly. Is there anything else?" he said.

"Yes. Who is Thelma Joan Poole?"

"She was my clerk for several years."

"Why was she at your house that evening?"

Craswell smiled a little. "I often kept her working late, and then she would drop off papers for me to sign. That was why she was at my house that evening. When I finished, she returned them to the office to lock them away."

"Do you know where we can reach her?" Caruso pursued.

"I believe Thelma still lives here in town." Craswell shifted some papers on his desk, his disinterest becoming evident. "I think she has a condo on the beach somewhere. She's probably listed in the phone book."

"When did she quit working for you?"

"About five years ago. Thelma won some money in the lottery or something, and quit."

"Did either you or your brother walk Mrs. Corbett back to her house?" Caruso asked.

Craswell gazed at the detective, his expression became regretful. "No, sadly, we did not. It never occurred to us. Driftwood was such a safe neighborhood. She lived just next door, for God's sake." He paused for a moment and frowned unhappily. "I have had to live with the knowledge that I could have possibly prevented her death just by seeing her home, and I didn't," he said slowly. "How do you think I've felt all these years?" he added a little harshly.

Caruso grinned inwardly. He had found a crack in the attorney's reserve. "Do you recall hearing anything at all?"

"Like I told the police before, there was nothing unusual. Angelique left the entrance to my house, walked to the street, waved, and turned right, going in the direction of her front door. That was the last time I saw her." Craswell, his composure intact, stood, indicating the interview was over.

Jarrett and Caruso rose and followed him to the door. Jarrett took out a business card and handed it to the attorney. "If you think of anything, please give us a call."

Once out on the street, Caruso said, "I hate lawyers. They lie about everything. I'll bet you he lied."

Jarrett sighed. "I couldn't tell. He's slick, though. Besides, you can't judge all attorneys by the ones your ex-wives hired. You agreed to both settlements, so don't complain." Jarrett thought of his own lawyer, Lawrence Greenwald, and what a close family friend he always had been, and still was. Lawrence had been there for him when all his so-called friends and family had shut him out.

"What's next?" Caruso asked.

"Mrs. Smith."

"It's almost eleven. We should go back to the office and talk to Big John about his notes before giving Mrs. Smith a call." Caruso was beginning to sweat. The temperature had to be in the high eighties or low nineties. He wiped away the moisture from his forehead with his fingers and headed for the car and blessed air conditioning.

As soon as they were back at the office, Jarrett retrieved the case file from his desk and headed to Captain Whitmore's office. Caruso took off again, having agreed to drive to the Smith residence and conduct the interview with Mr. Smith's widow. With a sharp rap on the glass, Jarrett opened the door and walked in.

Big John looked up from the papers he was reading. "What can I do for you, Blackwell?"

"I wanted to talk to you about the notations you made on the people involved in the Corbett case."

"Take a seat. What can't you figure out? My handwriting?"

Jarrett grinned. "That, I can read. You kept tabs on these people all through the years, so I was wondering what the question mark next to Thelma Joan Poole's name means?"

Whitmore sat back and was silent for a few moments. "It was a 911, a battered wife case. In the process of intervening, I accidentally killed Thelma Joan Poole's abusive husband. I had the cuts on my face to prove it was self-defense." He elaborated briefly, describing the bruised and terrified woman he had rescued and how her enraged husband had attacked with his straight-edged razor, slashing Big John's face before a fist into the man's nose had ended the fight. The blow had killed him by sending bone fragments into his brain. "She started to sue the department and me but dropped the case. She went to work for her attorney after that. He's the other question mark on the list."

"Did you suspect them of being involved in the murder?" Jarrett knew that Big John disliked lawyers as much as Caruso.

"No. Their statements validated each other's alibis, plus the brothers. Thanks to me, Thelma became a single mother with a young daughter to raise by herself. I kept tabs on her to make sure she was all right. She passed her GED and worked as Craswell's receptionist. She made a success of her life." Whitmore frowned, pensive. "Yet there was always something about her that bugged me. She was a pretty girl, too pretty. Smart too, and, well ambitious."

Jarrett digested Big John's conservative assessment. "What about the attorney? Did you check out his background?" He hadn't been impressed by Arthur Craswell. The man was smooth and had a high opinion of himself, and it showed.

Whitmore leaned forward, "Blackwell, I looked into all their backgrounds. They were all clean. Didn't you read my reports?"

"Not yet," Jarrett admitted.

The Captain shook his head. "Well, read them! Anything else you need, Blackwell?"

"No, I was just curious about your notations. I'll review your reports on each person. Caruso and I will continue to dig into their backgrounds and see if anything new pops up," Jarrett said.

"Where is Caruso, anyway?"

"He's out interviewing Mrs. Smith."

"That will be a waste of time," Whitmore interjected.

Jarrett stood and turned to go. "That may be," he shrugged, "but we have to recheck everything. Maybe someone will remember something they had forgotten."

"You know I have little hopes of this case being solved, don't you?" Big John said.

"So I gathered."

"If you don't succeed, well, I know you'll have given it your best effort." With a nod of dismissal, Whitmore turned his attention back to his paperwork.

Frowning, Jarrett returned to his desk.

By the time Caruso returned, it was after one o'clock. He set about typing his notes on the interview into his laptop. He glanced up when Jarrett sat down at his desk.

"Any luck with Mrs. Smith?" Jarrett asked.

"No," Caruso said. "Her statement was essentially the same. Her husband was the one who noticed the sound of the boat. He woke her up. She really didn't hear anything."

"Have we heard from Dr. Corbett or his sister?" Jarrett asked.

"Not yet. Weren't they supposed to come in this morning?"

"I tried calling Corbett early this morning, but couldn't reach him. Interesting timing. . ." Jarrett added looking up to see Gene Corbett being escorted into the room. Both men stood as the doctor approached.

Gene nodded to each man, "Good afternoon, Detectives."

"Where's your sister?" Jarrett asked immediately, indicating an empty chair.

Gene glared back at him as he sat down. "I want you to stay away from her."

Jarrett sat down as well. "She is a vital part of this investigation and needs to give a statement," he countered firmly, scowling back. "What do you think I'm going to do? Attack her?"

"Now, children!" Caruso drawled. Jarrett shot him a dirty look.

Far too aware that Sarra Gray was deeply tangled up in his mother's murder, and just might hold the key to her own mother's death, Jarrett realized suddenly that he had accepted her as Gene's sister. Interesting.

Gene Corbett ignored Caruso's interruption and leaned toward Jarrett. "No. But, you wanted her to give a statement about what, my mother's murder or your mother's death?"

"Both," Jarrett said.

"I won't have you threatening her," Gene continued. "My attorney can come in with her. That way he can protect her from you."

Jarrett gave a dismissive wave of one hand. "Sarra doesn't need protection from me. I'm not threatening her," he said quietly. "All I'm after is any information she may remember about the night my mother died. Also, as you know, she was very young when she was kidnapped, but she just might remember something that will help us find her abductor. Now, would you please tell me where she is?"

Gene relaxed a little. "Hopefully, at home resting. Last night was difficult for her. I didn't feel it was necessary for her to be here for my statement, so I didn't pick her up. She's unaware of my visit here today."

Jarrett had to admit that he had been eager to see Sarra again. "We would like for you to recount the events of the evening your mother was murdered," he said, shifting himself away from the personal. Gene studied Jarrett's face for a moment. When he realized the other man was serious, he said, "You have my statement from that night, and it hasn't changed. I was asleep on the sofa. When Dad came home from the hospital, he woke me. We discovered Mom was not in the house, so he went looking for her. When he couldn't find her, he called the police."

Jarrett frowned and picked up a pencil to fiddle with it. "There has to be more to it than that. What happened that evening to make your mother go out and leave you alone?" He questioned, unable to believe that Angelique Corbett would have left her remaining child alone just after her daughter had been abducted. "What happened during the evening before your father left to go back to the hospital?"

"Not much. The police detectives and the FBI were gone that night, so Mom cooked dinner. Dad and I were watching TV, I think it was the news. Mom would pop into the room and watch for a few minutes while dinner was cooking. Then we ate dinner. Right afterward, the hospital called, and Dad left. He didn't want to go, but it was one of his longtime patients, so he felt obligated, and Mom encouraged him to go. I went back to watching TV while she cleaned up the kitchen."

"Then what happened?" Jarrett asked.

"Mom joined me. She was reading the newspaper, and suddenly she stood up. She went into the study, and I could hear her talking to someone on the phone. I don't know who. I always assumed it was our neighbor because she said she had to go ask Arthur a question." Gene stiffened and looked surprised. "I'd forgotten that she was reading the newspaper. I do remember her telling me to stay put, that she would be next door for only a moment. Mom took her house keys and locked me in. I fell asleep." He looked away then back at Jarrett. "That was the last time I saw my mother alive."

Caruso had been glancing through the file as he listened. Now he had the most peculiar feeling in his gut. Not once had he given a second thought to the date of death for Angelique Corbett and doubted if Jarrett had noticed the connection either. August nineteenth. Looking up, he asked, "Jarrett, what was the date of your mother's death?"

Surprised, Jarrett looked at him. "December 19, 2001, why?" He froze, eye widening as the realization hit him. "Damn! I should have caught that."

"What do you mean?" Gene asked, even more confused.

Jarrett looked at Gene. "The dates. Your mother and mine both died on the nineteenth of the month."

"Without meaning to be crass, so what?" Gene asked, even more confused.

Jarrett shot a knowing glance in Caruso's direction. "An odd coincidence." He changed his tone. "I want to thank you for coming in, Doctor. If there is anything else, I'll give you a call." Jarrett rose to his feet, indicating that the interview was over.

Rising, Gene did not offer his hand to the detective, just nodded and followed Caruso out of the office.

When the detective returned, he plopped down in the chair, leaned forward, placed his forearms on the desktop and stared at Jarrett. "How could we have missed that?"

"I've had my head up my ass over finding Sarra Gray, is my excuse! I don't have one for you!"

"You know that the date of both these murders could just be a coincidence, don't you?" Caruso said.

Jarrett nodded. "Yes and probably is. So let's not attach a lot of significance to it. Do you think we'll find the killer?"

Caruso shook his head and grimaced. "Honestly, I doubt it. I think too many years have passed. We might get lucky and find something. But, Big John Whitmore was a thorough investigator. He turned over every rock and twig, plus some. It's unlikely he missed anything." Caruso picked up the typed statement given by Thelma Joan Poole and began to read. "I think," he added slowly, "that we need to keep the matching dates information to ourselves."

"Hand me the statement given by Thomas Craswell," Jarrett said.

Neither report was very long. It corroborated the account given by Arthur Craswell stating Mrs. Poole was at his house waiting for him to sign some documents.

The Poole woman's original statement turned out to be a little different. She had refused to talk with the then Detective Whitmore. Citing her intense dislike for the man who she claimed had murdered her husband. She had insisted on being interviewed by Whitmore's partner, Herb Angst. She had confirmed that Thomas Craswell had answered the door and she had seen Mrs. Corbett standing on the front step. But, she did not know what had been said between the woman and Arthur Craswell. Shortly after Mrs. Corbett had walked away, Mrs. Poole stated she had also left the attorney's house. She had gone back to the office to place the signed documents in the safe as instructed. No, she had not seen any sign of the woman as she had driven away.

"I think we need to go interview Mrs. Poole again. Do we have her current home address?" Jarrett said.

"Big John has it noted here. It's on Beach Drive, downtown."

"Do we have a phone number?"

Caruso consulted the phone book white pages, and said, "Now we do. I'll call and see if we can go by and talk to her today." He glanced at his watch. It was now after three o'clock. He picked up the phone and dialed the number.

CHAPTER FOURTEEN

"God damn, son of a bitch!" Thelma Poole hissed venomously as she hung up the phone. Her old boss, Arthur Craswell had called to tell her that her daughter, Helen, had been in his office ranting like a crazy woman. A few minutes later, the phone rang again. Thelma listened as Helen announced that she was on her way over. Then the girl bitched on and on because Gene had just said he wanted a divorce. What did her daughter expect? Didn't she understand? You keep a wealthy husband happy. You don't continually upset him until he threatens to kick you out. But then, she thought, her son-in-law was in for a surprise. He was going to be the one to pack and leave, not Helen. She'd make sure of it.

Thelma Joan thought of all the years she had sacrificed. Ever since the night that cop had gotten rid of her abusive husband with one punch to his nose, her life had been one continual struggle to survive. The twenty thousand dollars from the life insurance policy had not lasted long. She had had no other money of her own. And, she had a brat to look after. What was a woman alone supposed to do? She had no particular skills, just her body, her good looks and the knowledge of how to use them. They had worked well for her, except with Charlie, her husband. He made it clear that she would never escape him. But she finally had, thanks to a cop's big fist.

After her money had run out, she had taken a job as a waitress at a downtown bar. The tips were good, but the hours were rough. She had hated the way the men thought she was just a piece of ass. She had learned fast just how to be nice, so she could use them. It had paid well, too.

It had been the cop who had seemed to genuinely care for her. But, this time, Thelma had decided she couldn't let her emotions get in the way. She had taken him up on his offer to pay for her night school. Thelma liked money and being in control too much to get attached to any one man. There were too many useful men out there. One had bought her a new wardrobe, and another had paid the rent on a beautiful apartment. And so on. Once she had gotten what she wanted from each, and before their attention wandered, she had dumped them.

After she passed her GED, then, she had met Arthur Craswell. He had been a fresh young attorney in town, setting up his office and looking for a receptionist, plus he was not interested in her body. Joan had quickly discovered that she and Arthur were both hungry for money. He was smart and knew all sorts of ways to succeed. Together, they had made a fortune. But, that had been years ago, and it took a lot of money to properly maintain her preferred lifestyle. She didn't know about Arthur, but she had spent most of what she had acquired.

Annoyed, Thelma thought about her daughter, of all the years of hard work she had put into the girl, and how the little bitch was about to blow it all. She wondered, not for the first time if her daughter had even one active brain cell in her head.

With trembling hands, she sloshed gin over ice cubes into a tall glass just as the doorbell rang. Then the phone rang as well.

"Damn it!" She swore again and grabbed the portable on the way to the front door. On the phone, a man identified himself as Police Detective Caruso Jones. She told him to hold and opened the door.

Helen stormed past her and headed straight to the bar to pour herself a drink. She turned to face her mother.

Thelma put her finger to her lips and pointed to the phone in her hand. "What can I do for you, Detective?" she asked gently. She listened to his request. "Why can't we do the interview now?" She held up her hand to keep Helen silent. Her daughter was shaking with rage. "Can we do this tomorrow?" she said trying to focus on the phone conversation instead of Helen. Finally, she said, "You can come by my condo at one, tomorrow afternoon. I hate tardiness, so don't be late. I have things to do." She ended the call, placed the portable phone in its cradle, then marched straight to her daughter and slapped her hard across the face. "Arthur called me. What in the hell is wrong with you? Why are you screwing up our lives?"

Stunned by the blow, Helen staggered back against the bar. "What do you mean? I'm not screwing up our lives."

"What don't you understand? As Gene Corbett's wife, you have everything. Without that, you will have nothing. Do you understand me? NOTHING!"

Helen rubbed her face, reddening from the shock of the blow. "I'll still have my position in the community, and I will be rich." She gulped down the Scotch and glared at her mother.

Thelma poured more gin in her glass and took a big swig, then pointed a forefinger at Helen. "You stupid girl! The moment you're divorced, it changes things. All the important social events, all the private parties we have attended in the past will become nonexistent to us. There will be no invitations. You will be ostracized. None of those doctor's wives will associate with you. Do you think those women will let you near their husbands? It's the Corbett name that means something, not yours! You will become persona non grata to the social community, and you will be forgotten. Deliberately!"

Helen shook her head and smiled. "That won't happen to me."

"Oh yes, it will! Helen, you're more of a fool than I thought! You can love a rich man a lot easier than a poor one. How many times do I have to tell you that before it sticks in that thick skull of yours?" Joan swept the room with her hand. "My money is almost gone. I paid for all your fancy education. Lest you forget, I took care of you so you could take care of me in my old age. Do you think I can continue to afford all this without the money you give me each month?"

The Beaches was a gated community with three fifteen-story buildings that lined the sandy beach around a narrow, protected inlet where residents could dock their boats and drive their cars back to their condo. The biggest apartment boasted twenty-five hundred square feet, and the smallest was a modest sixteen. A choice of two or three bedrooms with multiple baths was offered. The purchase price for a sixteen-hundred square foot condominium, with two bedrooms, was three hundred thousand dollars.

Thelma had paid two hundred and ninety-five thousand dollars for her fifteenth-floor apartment when she had retired five years ago. Even with a hefty down payment and a fixed rate, the monthly mortgage payment was still high. And now, its value had plummeted way below what she had paid. But she had wanted a beautiful place to live while she was still young enough to enjoy it. She had become accustomed to a luxurious lifestyle that she relished and was not about to lose it.

Time, hard work and the hot Florida sun had diminished her beauty. There were hard lines around her mouth, and there was not a beauty cream made that could soften the deepening wrinkles. She used an arsenal of all the latest products to maintain her looks. Dye helped to keep her thick long hair a dark auburn, and she had already had plastic surgery to tighten and lift her face.

Men her age looked for someone much younger to recapture their youth. A middle-aged woman could not compete. But money, however, was always a significant attraction.

Thelma had recently met a man who thought she was wealthy. Believing his own fortune was safe, he had been entertaining her in lavish style. Given that, there was no way she was going to let her daughter destroy the life it had taken her so many years to build.

Helen looked around at the lavish interior with suppressed hatred. Everything in the two-bedroom condominium was too flashy for her tastes. The wood furniture was too dark. The fabric of the sofa and chairs were dyed in various shades of blue. Even the walls were blue. She hated her mother's apartment and made it a point to visit as little as possible.

Her life was difficult enough just having to put up with Gene, and now his so-called sister. As her mother had pointed out, if she let Gene go through with the divorce, dear Mommy would definitely have to give up her view of the Bay.

Helen did not want to think about the things her mother had made her do. All those men! Back then, it had not mattered to Thelma Poole that her daughter was only a child, as long as she got the money out of it. Now, Helen decided, it didn't matter what her mother wanted. She would deal with Gene in her own way. Changing her expression to something more submissive, she asked meekly, "What do you want me to do, Mother?"

Joan studied her daughter for a moment. "I want you to make up with Gene," she said. "Act like a wife to him, even if you don't mean it. Our life is perfect right now, so don't be stupid and spoil it." She raised her glass in a pseudo toast. "Who knows how long a person is destined to live? Gene could have an accident."

Aware that she had had the same thought, Helen stared at her mother anyway. "You're saying it would be better to be a rich widow than a poor divorcee', right?"

"Obviously," Thelma snorted. "Now, go home and make your husband happy. I'll see what I can do on my end."

Helen finished her drink, gathered up her purse and started toward the door, then stopped and turned to look at her mother again. "Make sure that nothing leads back to you. Prison orange is not your color, and it doesn't look good on me either, Mother dear."

Thelma Joan smiled. "I don't take chances. Now, go away. I have a few phone calls to make."

As soon as the front door closed, she punched in a phone number. "We have a problem," she said.

CHAPTER FIFTEEN

June 9

The nightmare had not changed since he had turned eighteen. The same scenes unfolded precisely as they always did to torment him and drive him into a fury.

Back then when they were little, five or six, the days blurred together, because they never knew when she'd lash out at them. They never could figure out what they'd done to set her off. Her thick, shiny dark brown hair, unbound, tumbled in cascading waves down her back. Her pretty face and contorted ruby lips sneered at them, and her brown Italian eyes gleamed with dark intent. She hauled them out from under the kitchen table again, swung them, smacking them into things, then dragged them away. Her vice-grip on an upper arm, so hard the bone felt like it would break. She pulled them out the back doorway, across the yard, down the steps to the cellar, and then she shoved them through the entrance into the yawning mouth of the black hole.

Falling, they landed on things that were wet and filthy and stunk and scraped. They knew better than to scream or make any sound. She would get the big black belt with the shiny metal in the leather if they did. That was one type of pain, but it was not as horrible, or as terrifying as the hole. All they could do was cling to each other, listen to her scream curses at them and wait for the nameless dark horror to come.

"Bastards, that's what you are, nothing but little bastards," they heard her yell. "I hope they get you this time." And then she was gone, and they were locked in the dark.

He didn't know what terrified them more, their mother or the blackness. Their mother, they could see. But invisible creatures, monsters, lived in the dark. They knew about monsters. She had told them all about such things, their mother. The demons moved around them, brushing past, first touched, then bit, tearing away pieces of tender flesh.

And then the beasts were on him.

He screamed, gulped air and struggled to throw off the satin sheet as he sat up. His naked body glistened with sweat. Perspiration soaked his hair so that beads of the salty liquid ran down into the corners of his eyes. Trembling, he wiped them away and cursed.

"Damn bitch, why can't she leave me alone?" He clenched his hands into fists, hating the night. He continued to tremble uncontrollably. The dream still trapped him into such absolute terror, compelling him to hide, to curl up, to cover his eyes and wait for the creatures to come and tear at him.

He gasped, tried to catch his breath. It was only a memory, just a memory. But still so vivid, he could hear the sounds and feel the ripping, the agony of terror. He knew the pain wasn't real anymore, yet he pressed his fists against his forehead anyway and waited. The horror was centered deep in his mind, hurting, digging, and biting. Those cruel black things were always waiting in the darkest shadows, trying to get to him.

Then, one by one, they moved away. The pain faded, slowly transforming into a throbbing, hurtful, ache in his groin. His mother! He needed her now, wanted to touch her. He wanted to sit on her lap and be comforted, to love him as kissed her. And when he had tried to show her how much, she, instead, had taught him the pain of it.

He swallowed, forcing the knot in his throat down, as the anger began to build again, to tighten like a steel band around his chest and pulse in his head until it was hard to fill his lungs with air. Blood pounded through his veins, pooling down there, intensifying his need for release, for escape. It was the thing he had down there that she pulled on and twisted that was all wrong.

He stared in loathing at his crotch as his arousal grew harder until he could not bear the agony any longer. His release came suddenly, spurting in an ever-widening circle to run down between his legs. Revolted, he swung himself off the bed and jumped to his feet.

He could feel the rage welling up then, because it couldn't be his fault, because some part of him knew what she had done. He stared at the white satin sheet, now wet and stained. Fear slithered underneath his skin as the rage swelled because he had lost control.

"Bitch, fucking whore!" he swore.

Why wouldn't she leave him alone? Why did she have to keep coming back? How many times did he have to destroy her before she stayed dead? He ran his fingers through his hair and tried to smother the chaos of enraged terror as it turned into another kind of desperation. He would find her again. This time, she would have to leave him alone.

He ripped the fouled sheets from his bed, wadding the material into a ball, hurried to the kitchen and flipped the switch. Florescent light bounced off chrome and pristine, black, clutter-free counters, pure white cabinets, and gleaming appliances. He plucked a plastic garbage bag from a box in the storage closet, stuffed the soiled sheets into it and looped the top into a knot. Revolted, he crammed the plastic container into the trash compactor just outside the back door. Then, he took a small metal bucket from under the sink and donned rubber gloves. After filling the bucket with hot water and bleach, he returned to the bedroom.

Nothing remained on the bed except the plastic mattress cover. The man wiped down the bed from top to bottom, repeating the procedure until at last, he felt the mattress was clean. Only then, was the bed remade with fresh new linens before going to the bathroom to scrub his own body with disinfectant soap.

After his shower, he dressed meticulously in a crisp white shirt, gray tie and a black suit with matching socks and shoes. When he was dressed, he gathered his car keys and headed for the front door.

She had changed things, but he knew where she lived and the name she was using. No matter how hard she tried, she could not hide from him. He always found her.

CHAPTER SIXTEEN

Jarrett stopped the car at the security shack and flashed his ID. The guard inspected it closely then directed him to the correct building. After parking the car in a visitor's space, they walked up to the indicated high-rise to catch a young woman unlocking the security door to the building. Caruso flashed his badge and grabbed the door handle before it could close. They followed her through and entered the elevator to punch the fifteenth-floor button. Catching the woman's slight frown and look that wanted to know why they were there, Caruso flashed his Casanova smile in her direction and nodded.

Jarrett shook his head in amusement. When it came to women, he thought, the Irishman was an incorrigible flirt. They exited the elevator and walked along the balcony walkway to Thelma Poole's condominium. Caruso let out a low whistle as he surveyed the view. From north to south, the expanse of the city spread out inland from the bay. At night, with the city ablaze with lights, the view would be spectacular. It was in any case.

Jarrett rang the doorbell at twelve-fifteen. There was no answer. Caruso knocked. No response. Jarrett checked his watch. It was twelve fifty-nine. Thelma Poole had stated the appointment was to be precisely at one o'clock. Her sharp remark about punctuality had not suggested she planned to be elsewhere. Suddenly, he got one of those gut-wrenching bad feelings.

He pulled a pair of vinyl gloves from his inside pocket and put them on, then tried the doorknob.

Surprisingly, the door was unlocked. He glanced at
Caruso, who nodded, Jarrett pushed on it with a foot to
open it wider. A blast of hot, humid air hit him. He
stopped as soon as he saw the body sprawled in the
hallway, and motioned to Caruso. They both drew their
guns and hugged the wall as they entered the apartment.
Jarrett crouched down cautiously and checked for a pulse
on the fallen woman. There was none. She was lying
face up and was dressed in blue satin pajamas. Her eyes
were open, pupils fixed. There was the smell of urine,
and stains at the apex of her thighs. Jarrett gestured to his
partner to check the bedrooms while he cautiously
advanced down the hallway into the living room.
Nothing appeared to have been disturbed. It was hard to
breathe, he noted because it was so hot and stuffy. He let
go of the tension in his back and shoulders, pulled out his
cell phone, then quietly called the station.

     Caruso returned from checking both bedrooms
and shook his head as he loosened his tie and unbuttoned
the top button of his shirt. "It's empty," he said, reading
the look on Jarrett's face which confirmed that the
woman was dead. "Is that the Poole woman?"

     "Don't know. It's supposedly her condo. Do you
see a purse or photos or anything?"

     "Not yet," Caruso said looking around the room.
"Why the hell is it so hot in here?"

     "I think the AC's off. I called the station. The
Captain was there, and I told him what we found. He's
coming here, and Forensics is on its way. If this is
Thelma Poole, Big John will know. I'll look for the

manager of the complex and see what I can find out. You locate her purse.

The sales office was located in the next building. Jarrett judged the woman behind the reception desk to be in her mid-fifties. Her hair was cut short with curls softening the sharp planes of her face.

"Good afternoon, Ms. . ." Jarrett said as the woman stood to offer her hand.

She smiled. "Jennifer Carlson. I'm the sales representative. Are you interested in buying or renting?"

Her expression changed when he said, "Neither." He showed the woman his ID and badge. "I need information on the occupant of apartment fifteen twelve."

"In Ms. Poole's apartment? Is something wrong?"

"Yes. There has been an accident. I need to find the next of kin." Jarrett took out his notebook and waited while Mrs. Carlson examined a list of names on her computer.

"We keep records on all our occupants for emergency purposes." She told him, peering at the screen. "Her next of kin is a daughter, Helen Corbett, and her son in law, Dr. Gene Corbett."

"Damn!" Jarrett muttered, startled. Just his luck, another crime leading back to the Corbett's. Why? "Thank you," he said and left.

Captain Whitmore was already on scene when he returned to the apartment.

"It's Thelma Poole all right," Whitmore said, standing over the body, staring at the prone figure. He shook his head and murmured. "For some reason, I always knew she would end up like this."

When the forensics team arrived, Jarrett, Big John, and Caruso stayed outside the door to give them room to work. Detailed photographs of the body and hallway were taken as well as the other rooms. The body remained in place until the M.E. could check the victim.

Later, when he had finished, Harvey looked up at the three men watching him from the doorway. "She was strangled," he announced.

"Can you guess the time of death?" Big John asked.

Harvey clambered laboriously to his feet. "Rigor is setting in, so, sometime in the very early morning. I would guess before sunrise." He fanned his face ineffectively with one hand. "Feel how warm the apartment is? Someone turned the air off. That will speed up rigor. I'll be able to tell you more later."

Whitmore took charge. "Caruso, walk down to the guard shack and find out if anyone was on the late shift at the gate. We need to find the daughter. She married into the Corbett family."

Jarrett frowned at him. "You knew that and didn't say anything. Captain, I don't understand," Jarrett said.

Big John shrugged. "What bearing does it have on Angelique Corbett's murder? The daughter was only a child at the time."

"That may well be," Jarrett returned curtly. "But, given that you instigated reopening the case and dumped it in my lap, any detail is important. Now, this. Mrs. Corbett's mother has been murdered. Child or not, what if she saw something back then, and the killer is now trying to tie up a few loose ends. I think we need to have a talk with Dr. Corbett's wife, ASAP."

"Do what you have to do," Big John rumbled, and his shoulders slumped as he turned away.

Jarrett noticed the hunch of Whitmore's shoulders and the hesitation in the man's voice. "Captain, what is going on? Is there anything else about this woman and her daughter you should tell me?"

Whitmore glanced over his shoulder at him as he started toward the front door. "Wrap things up here. When you get back to your desk, come to my office. We need to talk about Thelma Poole." He continued toward the open door, then stopped and turned back to Jarrett and said, "I'm going back to the station now. I'll wait for you," and then walked out of the door and disappeared.

Frowning, Jarrett stared after the Captain. His boss couldn't be involved in the murder of Angelique Corbett, could he? Big John Whitmore? Yet, the man was uneasy about something.

Caruso's return interrupted his thoughts. "We lucked out," he said as Jarrett forced himself to shift focus. "The Security Guard on duty now, one Harry Taylor, is pulling a double. He came on at eleven last night. The day guard called in sick. According to him, no one came through the gate after two a.m. Before that, only three residents came in." Caruso pulled out several folded sheets of paper.

"If it wasn't a stranger, then it has to be a resident. What about someone coming in from the beach?" Jarrett asked

"I asked. Not possible, according to Harry. The

docks are just across the road from the gate so he would have heard the sound of a boat engine. Anyway, Harry says there are rip currents off the beach area. Anyone dropping an anchor offshore and trying to swim in would get caught in them and swept away. There are warning signs about that." Caruso unfolded the papers.

"What's that?" Jarrett asked.

"I went to the sales office and obtained a list of residents." Caruso continued, "This outfit has a lot of empty condos for sale. It is losing money big time. Since the drop in the real estate market, you can pick up one of these babies a lot cheaper than you could five years ago."

They moved out of the way so the Paramedics could wheel the body out on a stretcher. The M.E. walked past, paused and said, "I'll call you as soon as I finish my examination," then he left.

"Thanks," Jarrett called after him then turned back to Caruso. "CJ, is there a name listed that we might know?"

"None that I recognize. There are one hundred twenty units per building and approximately a hundred full-time residents in the two of the three buildings. Each building has about fifty seasonal snowbirds that come here only in the winter. In this building, we have fifty-two permanent residents." Caruso studied the list. "Maybe John will authorize overtime for a couple of the guys to help interview everyone on this floor. Maybe someone heard something."

Jarrett shook his head. "I doubt it. From the

looks of the scene, Thelma Poole was expecting her killer. I'd guess, she opened the door and was attacked immediately. She probably never even had a chance to make any noise." Jarrett closed the notebook where he had written the time of day, week, outside and inside temperatures, officers present, how many windows, doors in the condo, and a complete description of the victim, her clothing, her position, all information he would type into his preliminary report later and verify with the photos and video that was taken.

Jarrett knew the most important rules of investigating a scene were never to touch anything, and to write everything down and photograph each item no matter how small or insignificant it might seem to be. He knew plenty of cases that had been lost in court because there was a difference of opinion about a fact that had not been duly noted or photographed at the scene and was only brought into evidence much later.

"When we get back to the office, we can check to see if any of these people have a criminal record," he said.

"Do you want just the people in this building or the entire complex?" Caruso knew that checking all the names for a criminal background would take days.

"We can begin with the people on this floor, and later expand it to all the residents in the three buildings. Right now, we need to go back to the office and talk with Captain Whitmore. He wants to see me."

"Why?"

"I don't know, but I think he knows more about the murder of Angelique Corbett than he's telling," Jarrett said slowly, his eyes narrowing, his tone changed.

"Something stinks," he cut off the rest of it. He hated to think that Big John was involved somehow, but it seemed that he was. It was apparent the man was feeling guilty about something.

Caruso stared, shocked. "No way!" he gasped. "Jarrett, have you gone nuts? I've known the man way too long to believe he would be dirty."

Jarrett gave him a hard look. "No. Let's finish up here and get back to the station," he said brusquely.

Still taken aback, Caruso exhaled carefully. "I'll meet you there. I'm going to stop by the hospital and check on the girl. If she's awake, maybe she can describe her attacker."

Watching CJ leave, Jarrett knew he was pissed. CJ didn't idolize anyone, but he did have high regard for the Captain and certainly would not want to hear anything negative about his mentor.

Jarrett glanced at his watch as he headed to his car. It was two thirty. By the time he reached the station, it would be almost three. Maybe the Captain would be gone, and he could avoid the meeting. He doubted he would be that lucky. His weekend was shot.

When he arrived back at the station, Whitmore was in his office. Jarrett knocked on the glass door before entering. Big John motioned for him to come and once seated, he waited for Captain Whitmore to speak.

"I guess you're wondering what's so important that I'd have you meet me here on a Saturday." Big John looked down at a file on the desk in front of him. He flipped it open and stared at the contents for a moment, closed the folder and handed it to Jarrett. "This is the kidnapping file on Monique Corbett. I would like you to go over the information carefully. I believe the two cases are related. How I don't know. I have read and reread the reports over the years, and I haven't been able to find a connection, but I've never been able to shake that gut feeling."

"Is this what you wanted to talk to me about?" This information could have waited until Monday, Jarrett thought. Surely, Big John wouldn't have called him back to the office just for this. "What's going on, Captain?"

Whitmore frowned. "You've heard how I got these scars on my face?"

"Yes, you told me."

"That was in 1977, and the man was Thelma Joan Poole's husband," Whitmore reiterated.

"Yes," Jarrett said.

Whitmore straightened in his seat and met Jarrett's gaze. "What no one else knows is that I knew her before the confrontation with her husband. Every time he beat her up, she called me. I had tried to get her to leave him, but she refused. She claimed she was too afraid. After her husband's death, I tried to help her. Then," he shrugged, "we became involved. I fell in love with her, you see." He stared off into space for a moment. "She was the most beautiful woman I had ever seen.

"I know I'm an ugly son of a bitch, but she told me she loved me. Her hair was this gorgeous, deep auburn and her skin, so smooth. It was like touching white satin." He shook himself a little, freeing himself of the images. "Anyway, later on, I found out she had received twenty thousand dollars from a life insurance policy she had taken out on her deceased husband a couple of months before his death."

"That's not illegal. But, it does provide a motive. Why didn't you arrest the Poole woman?" Jarrett said.

"Timing. And for what?" Whitmore asked. "Her husband was beating her up that night. I was the one who killed him, not her. But, I did wonder if she set it up," he continued soberly. "I couldn't say anything to anyone, because it would look as if I had helped plan his death so she and I could be together. No one ever knew about our affair. In the seventies, a black man didn't get involved with a white woman if he wanted to keep on living, especially here in the South. Our affair ended when I found out she was prostituting herself to other men. She had been using me all along I discovered, just as she used other men. Probably even that husband of hers. Explains his rages, doesn't it? I could have arrested her for soliciting, but I didn't."

"Why not?"

"I was still in love with her. She was like a habit I couldn't kick. It took me several years and a lot of booze to break the hold she had on me. I knew she could have easily ended my career. I kept waiting for it to happen, hence the booze. Why she didn't, I never found out, but it's always been there, a sword of Damocles if you will. I'd like to delude myself and believe it was because she actually cared about me."

Now, Jarrett thought, he understood why the Captain had never married. The man had been as obsessed with the Poole woman as he had been with Sarra Gray.

"She went to night school, which I paid for," Big John continued. "I hoped she was going to straighten her life out and it seemed as if she had. A new attorney in town hired her as his receptionist. And, there was no more prostitution after that, at least, that I could find out about. I thought she had settled down to raise her daughter. But?"

Damn, why was there always a but? Jarrett thought

Big John paused and then expounded. "But, in a way, there was something wrong with her sudden success. I kept tabs on her. She seemed to have more money than her salary justified, a lot more. I never discovered anything illegal, but I was absolutely certain that she was into some type of scheme."

Jarrett stared, fascinated. "What about the lawyer she worked for? Was he involved?" he asked, carefully absorbing it all.

Whitmore sighed. "Not that I could find. Mostly, he handled trust accounts for clients, wrote wills, dealt with estate dispersals and so forth, and sometimes an adoption. That was about it. The man was clean. He earned every dollar he put in the bank. I kept a close watch on both of them. But, Thelma was a clever woman. She had never earned an honest dollar for long. Trouble was, I couldn't catch her at anything. And, believe me, I tried. She had to have had help from someone. Now, I guess that particular someone has killed her. And, somehow, all of it ties into the murder of Angelique Corbett."

Jarrett studied the other man, compressing several thoughts. "But, if you didn't find anything on the Poole woman during all these years, what makes you think she was involved in the Corbett murder?" He asked carefully. It didn't make sense.

Whitmore stiffened in his chair. His voice held an edge as he said, "Because Angelique Corbett called me the night she died!"

"What?" Jarrett stared. "That wasn't in the file!" He suddenly realized, "You never reported talking to her that night?"

"No, I didn't." Big John admitted. "Her conversation with me didn't make any sense. Mrs. Corbett called to say she had seen something in the paper, but she wasn't sure about what she had seen or read. Then she said she was going next door to a neighbor's house to discuss the car accident. Angelique was supposed to call me back. I waited, and when she didn't call, I drove by her house. All the lights were on, but I didn't go to the door. I went back to the office to see if she had called, but she never did. The next morning her body was discovered. If I had followed my instincts and knocked on her door that night, she might be alive today."

"How long did you wait for her to call?" Jarrett asked, busy mentally filing away details.

"About forty-five minutes. It was almost nine o'clock before I left the office. What's worse, I was close to being drunk that night."

Jarrett's eyebrows rose. "In the station? What

were you thinking?"

"In those days, I wasn't thinking too clearly." Whitmore's tone was full of self-condemnation. "I was still trying to get over my breakup with Thelma and was trying to solve the child's kidnapping at the same time. I screwed up royally. I sobered up fast when Angelique's body was found. I've been sober ever since," he added roughly.

Jarrett nodded. "From the autopsy report, she was already dead by then." He said after a pause. "You've been blaming yourself for her death all these years? Why? How were you supposed to know she never made it back home? Drunk or not, I doubt you could have saved her!" Curious, Jarrett thought. First the lawyer, now his boss. Each man blames himself for the death of the same woman.

"That doesn't matter," Big John was saying. "I should have gone up to the door anyway. Angelique called me for help." He sat back in his chair. He was retiring very soon, not by choice, but because his health had been corroded by too much stress and high blood pressure. As big and strong as he was, his heart had become weak. With proper rest, he might actually have a few more years. Only his immediate superior knew the real reason for his retirement. He looked steadily at Blackwell. "Find the killer, Jarrett." He said.

Jarrett was silent for a few moments. "Why did you tell me all this?" he asked finally. He was well aware that if it were discovered that his boss had been drunk on duty and had withheld information on a case, he would do far worse than write off his pension.

"Because, somehow, I believe the same man who

killed Angelique Corbett has now killed Thelma Poole as well. So, find him!" John stood and rounded his desk. "I have to get home and feed my dog," he added gruffly, holding out the file by way of dismissal.

"So do I," Jarrett said as he took it, then followed Whitmore out of the office. Reaching his own desk, he stopped to check voicemail on his cell phone. There was nothing from Caruso. He locked the file away in his desk and left. All he wanted now, he thought, was a Sunday of peace and quiet where the only calls were from birds. Jarrett had, he knew, a lot of thinking to do.

On his way out of the building, he tried to call Caruso again. Still, no answer. Instead of going home, Jarrett drove to Bay Memorial to see if the Irishman was there. They needed to have a long, quiet talk.

He found Caruso talking to a nurse outside the Intensive Care Unit.

"The girl is awake," Caruso said as Jarrett walked up to him. "She's still critical, but the nurse said we could come back tomorrow morning to see if the doctor will let us try and talk to her." Caruso hesitated then asked a little warily. "What did the Captain have to say?"

Editing carefully, Jarrett repeated the information Whitmore had conveyed to him.

Caruso was stunned. "You have got to be kidding me! He was at the Corbett house the night of the murder?"

Jarrett knew Caruso was startled by this new information about their boss. For that matter, Jarrett was having difficulty with Big John Whitmore's long-standing enthrallment with Thelma Joan Poole, which he had not mentioned. A man of the highest standards, the captain had always seemed too smart, too professional. The expose he had listened to had deflated that view into something unhappily human.

"After hearing all this, I need a beer," Caruso announced. "Let's get out of here." He turned and walked down the hall. Jarrett followed and caught up with him at the elevator.

Back at home, Jarrett fed Chance and let him out into the backyard. He settled at his desk in his home office and logged onto his laptop. After reviewing the files for an hour, he sat contemplating his relationship with Sarra or the lack thereof. Growing tired of all the unanswered questions, he phoned Caruso and arranged to meet him at the office on Sunday to go over the evidence again.

CHAPTER SEVENTEEN

June 10

Sarra had fought with her conscience all weekend about the right thing to do. Late that afternoon, and without letting Gene know, she drove to the police station. She had trouble finding a parking space in front of the building and ended up parking a block away. It was a short walk, but the heat was suffocating. By the time she walked through the tall glass doors, her white blouse was damp, and the large leather bag containing the envelopes and DVD discs felt like a thirty-pound cement block in her left hand. The refrigerated air inside the building sent ripples of blessed relief against her skin.

Focused, barely aware of the people around her, Sarra walked toward a raised counter walled in by glass. A young male officer was busy answering a phone and another, older gray-haired man, was trying to conduct business through one of the small openings cut in the glass.

The red-haired man on the phone talked briefly then hung up. He turned to motion to a tall, dark-haired man standing in the doorway of a room behind the counter. The man came forward, and Sarra heard the officer say. "Hey, McCabe, I have to leave. Can you give the Sergeant a hand with these phones for a few minutes?"

Sarra clutched her oversized handbag tighter and stepped up to the counter.

The older man gruffly asked. "Can I help you?"

"I would like to speak with Detective Blackwell," Sarra told him, then heard Jarrett's voice behind her. She spun around to face him as he approached.

Jarrett's surprise was briefly visible. "Good morning Miss Gray. I thought you were coming in with your brother and his attorney?"

"Gene doesn't know I'm here. I want to get this over with. Besides, he has a tendency to be overprotective where I'm concerned." Then, "Where is your partner?"

"He had to go down to the hospital this morning."

"Nothing serious, I hope."

Jarrett shook his head. "No."

Sarra glanced at her surroundings. Various people were waiting to be helped. Two men in business suits were using public phones and speaking loudly enough to be overheard. A woman and a young boy sat huddled together on a bench against one wall, conversing in hushed whispers. Another man in what looked like biker leathers leaned against one wall. They all looked as if their lives were on hold. It was strange, she thought, that she hadn't noticed them before. Her attention had been so focused on the glass cage.

"I'd rather not talk here at the police station," Sarra looked at Jarrett again. "I have a lot to discuss, and I'd like some privacy. Is it possible for us to go somewhere else?"

Jarrett inclined his head. "Sure. There's a diner down the street on the next corner. We can walk there and have some coffee."

"That would be fine," she said and began walking

with him toward the door.

They left the building, and as Jarrett led the way, walking slightly ahead of her, Sarra stole a glance at his profile. He was still as handsome as she remembered. The smooth, boyish look had strengthened into maturity. There were crinkle lines at the corners of his eyes now and slight creases by the corners of his mouth. She wondered if he spent a lot of time in the sun. His face had the healthy tan of most Florida residents. There was a touch of early gray at his temples. If anything, she thought, he had become better looking. He moved with a smooth stride, too. She could see by the way his brown jacket hugged his shoulders and narrowed to a trim waist that he was physically fit. His trousers were not tight, but, she thought, they did fit well. His long legs ate up the sidewalk, and she had to work to keep up with him. When he noticed her struggling, he slowed.

"Sorry," he said. "I'm used to being in a hurry."

The diner looked like a long aluminum railroad car that had been parked on a siding and forgotten. Inside, it had a counter and a few booths and was an established eatery for the police department for years. The food was inexpensive, and the coffee was hot and tasty.

They slid into a booth and sat self-consciously facing each other, both eerily feeling as if they were being transported back to that night in New York.

Jarrett finally broke the silence. "I never forgot you," he half whispered. "One minute you were there, then the next time I saw you, you were running from the house with your clothes half ripped off." He inhaled and glanced down. "And my father was responsible," he added bitterly. "He told me everything that happened that night."

He tried not to stare at her, but he couldn't seem to look away. She was even more beautiful than he remembered, he thought, feeling startled by it, more fragile looking as well, as though her experiences had refined her. She was a survivor though, he sensed, a quality he admired. Thinking metaphorically, he decided that she had grown from a budding rose into full blossom. It occurred to him then that the older woman, Pearl Ann, must have been the gardener for this flower.

"I looked for you for years," he continued after a short pause, his eyes glued to her face. "Not only because I wanted answers about that night, but because of what had occurred between us."

"I never forgot you either," Sarra hesitated, then admitted. "Honestly, I didn't want to forget you. You were the one good moment out of my whole life in New York." She looked down. Their fingers were inches apart, yet she was afraid to reach out, to touch him. She moved her hand out of his possible reach and looked up again. "If you had known what I was about to do that night, you would have hated me."

Jarrett breathed deeply. "I did," he said truthfully. "Hate you, that is. My feelings were quite a cocktail. Add furious, hurt, disappointed, disillusioned, as well as confused. Now, I'm fighting hard to understand it all. I still don't know why everything happened." He paused a moment. "The one thing being a cop has taught me is that nothing is what it seems. It has changed the way I look at things. I've seen what people do to each other. For some it is greed, for others, it's a need for power, for control. And then there are those who have a deep rage burning inside that erupts, and that rage is beyond control. And that's just the tip of the iceberg."

Sarra caught a glimpse of awful things in his eyes, the kind of knowledge no one else would want.

"For me, the worst are the crimes committed against children," he continued. "I've seen tykes, no more than three or four, abused and molested by grown men or women, who do know better. There are a lot of gray areas in life too. I realize now that someone was controlling you that night. That's the person I want to find."

Sarra nodded, somewhat relieved by what he had just said. "I want to explain about that night." She continued to meet his gaze, fighting to deal with this moment, still unsure of his opinion of her. "I want you to believe me when I tell you, I didn't have any choice. I was forced to do what I did. If I had refused, Homer would have had me killed. Like, as I found out, he did with other girls," she added.

Looking perplexed Jarrett didn't respond at once. "I realized you didn't have a choice," he said after he had absorbed her last remark. "My father told me he raped you. Last night, you said some other man did it." He went silent as a waitress approached and took their order of coffee. He offered to spring for breakfast, but Sarra refused. She was too queasy from anxiety.

After the waitress left, Jarrett continued, "I know

my father's version of what happened. I'd like to hear your account of the events."

He took out a small tape recorder. When Sarra's eyes widened, he quickly explained. "This is so I have a record of your memory of that night. That way, I can compare it to what's in the original file." When she nodded, he placed it flat on the table and set it to record.

Sarra eyed the small instrument but understood his need to document what she had to tell him, so said nothing. His eyes were now focused on her face. She could see that now, he was all cop and ready for business. It was disconcerting, the abrupt change in his manner. Perhaps she should have waited for Gene, she thought. She remained silent as the waitress returned with their coffee and watched as Jarrett swallowed a mouthful, studying her in turn.

"Is there something wrong?" he asked.

"Your cop's face scares me." She told him, feeling her stomach begin to knot.

He nodded. "Sarra, I am a cop," he said. "If I don't distance myself from the emotional turmoil of that night, I could miss a vital piece of information. A lot of time has passed since then. All I actually have to go on is the New York police files and your memory. My mother lost her life that night. My father was accused of her murder. Believing he did it, he killed himself. The uproar was horrendous." He leaned back and gazed at her for a second. "I don't think you realize how important you are to me. I don't want to scare you. I do want to help you in any way I can." Jarrett clasped his fingers together and rested his arms on the table. "But, you are the key to everything. You have to tell me what you know. You can't leave anything out. So, please, will you help me?"

Her insides quivering with dread, she studied his face for a second. "You want to know in detail what happened in New York."

"Yes."

"All right," she said slowly. "I'll tell you everything I can remember. I must warn you though, it may not be what you want to hear, but it will be the complete truth." Then, each word an effort, she began.

"It goes back further than eleven years." Sarra kept watching him closely as she recounted her early memories of life with the abusive drunk, Harry Gray. With clipped, short descriptions that managed to reveal a great deal, she progressed through being sold to Homer James, her life, and training after that. And included her deluded, naive affection for Homer. She saw Jarrett wince a time or two, his expression growing stark as she described becoming Homer's mistress at thirteen, still grateful.

And then, she had turned sixteen, and Homer put her to work.

Sarra shifted uncomfortably in the booth, trying to relax, as she continued, "Anyway, that night on Long Island, I was told to use the name, Candace James. I was supposed to be a rich debutante, going to my first ball with the elite of Long Island. I was so naive. I wanted to believe it was the magic of Christmas, and I was some sort of Cinderella. The truth of the matter was that I went out of a sense of obligation. I didn't learn until later that

I had no choice. Still, I felt I owed Homer for rescuing me from Harry. Also, I was curious to see how the rich really lived." Sarra saw Jarrett grimace as she went on. "A limousine picked me up precisely at seven-thirty. I was so easily impressed even by my escort, George. I thought because he was impeccably dressed in a black tux, he was one of the wealthy members of society. He wasn't unattractive, but his eyes were hard, opaque, you know what I mean? He stared at me, and kept staring at me." Sarra shivered, remembering. "God, he made me nervous.

"I knew better than to ask any questions. That was a big rule of Homer's. No questions, ever. George wore gold cufflinks, and they flashed every time he raised his arm to draw on the cigarette he was smoking. I decided that I was going to enjoy the evening, regardless. No one there knew who I was or what why I was there. Just some pictures with an older guy called Blackwell, like the ones Homer liked to take," she shrugged. "When we arrived at the house, going up the steps, I slipped on the ice and fell into your arms." She looked away briefly. "That moment changed my life."

Sarra stopped speaking, and looked at Jarrett, unable to decipher his expression. He didn't look at her but continued to stare at his hands instead, his right hand fiddling with his coffee spoon. He did not look up as she continued, sidestepping their extraordinary encounter, to relate how she had been taken upstairs by George, beaten and raped. Now thoroughly cowed, she had just laid there when Mr. Blackwell came in. With camera flashing, and later, how George had hauled her away and burned her breast.

And then, still believing she was Homer's girl, she had turned to him for help only to have every carefully nurtured illusion utterly shattered. Sarra fell silent at last, whatever else she could relate congealed in her throat. Across the table, Jarrett stared grimly into his coffee cup.

Looking up with a little jerk, Jarrett could see she was waiting for him to say something. He swallowed. Her story disturbed him profoundly, bringing it all back vividly enough to reopen his own hard-won scars. All of it was compounded by his attempt to absorb her experiences of that time. He realized he no longer had a clear idea about his true feelings for this woman. His obsessive fixation with her had been balanced on a beam of very particular and contradictory convictions that were now all skewed to Hell. How could he hold her responsible for the death of his parents? It was clear now that she had been used as bait in a trap. Ignorant bait at that. A trap sprung on both his parents by someone else with very definite plans, which, given that they were both now deceased had apparently succeeded.

Who? Why? Those questions remained unanswered. All these years he had blamed Sarra when none of it had been her fault. She had been a tool, victimized through her own ignorance. Jarrett forced himself to concentrate on his coffee cup to give himself time to compose his thoughts and feelings. Only after his control returned did he dare look up at Sarra's anxious face. He smiled in an attempt to put her at ease. She relaxed fractionally and attempted a small smile in return.

"Would you like more coffee?" he asked, retreating from the issue, needing a moment's relief from the overwhelming load of information she had given him. He motioned for the waitress to refill their cups. When she left, he cleared his throat and said, "I'd like to go over a few points if you don't mind?"

Sarra squared her shoulders and lifted her chin, ready to face his questions. "All right."

"You said Homer had been hired by someone to set my father up? Did he ever say why or mention anyone's name?"

"No," she said. "All I could guess was that it was someone very wealthy."

"Why do you say that?"

"Because, Homer's services did not come cheap," she stated firmly. "He required a lot of money up front before he would send a girl out on a job. So, with what Homer charged, they would have to have a lot of money."

"You have no idea who this George character was?"

"All I know about him is that he is the owner of the Lowell Art Gallery in New York City. The reason I found out that much is that, without my knowledge, Pearl Ann submitted one of my paintings to a competition in New York several months ago. The Lowell Gallery was sponsoring the event. Anyway, we received a letter from the manager saying my work was to be the main selection." She paused to take a sip of coffee. "I explained to Pearl Ann that I knew the man who'd raped me owned an art gallery and we should leave Kentucky because he would come after me. She thought we'd be safe. I knew better. We should have left immediately, but we didn't. It cost us."

Jarrett frowned. "Why didn't you?"

"I thought we had time to prepare. My daughter's school year ended the last of May. We planned to leave immediately afterward. We began closing up the house and had even packed the car, and then suddenly, the painting was returned. We knew then our time had run out. It was all terribly hard on Pearl Ann. She wanted one more night in her home before going on the run with me. That proved to be one night too long. George had sent two men after me. They came that night. The only reason we escaped was because of our dog Skipper." Sarra blinked hard as she thought of the dog. "He saved us. He attacked one of the men and got shot for it."

Jarrett was silent for a moment. "I know about your house being blown up," he told her. "A missing person report was issued by the Madison, Kentucky Police Department with your photographs, and the story of Pearl Ann's house being blown up was on the news. They contributed it to a gas leak, and that you and Mrs. Burke were on vacation somewhere. I even went to Madison looking for you." He could see amazement spread quickly across her face.

"You were still trying to find me?"

"Yes." Jarrett shifted uneasily. "I never gave up. And now you're here." He changed direction. "The Kentucky Police never connected the deaths of the two strangers." But he had suspected that they were. He almost grinned as he asked, "How did you manage to out drive-two professional killers?" And she had because the two men were found dead in their car after having gone over the side of one of the mountains.

"Strictly luck," she said. "There's an old road outside Madison that has a lot of horseshoe curves. We were used to that road. I had driven it many times in Pearl Ann's old Cadillac. That night, they were right behind us, shooting at us. They missed a curve and went through the guardrail and over the side. I knew George would send others to take their place, so we headed south and ended up here."

Jarrett paused and then nodded. "I'll have the gallery, and the owner checked out by the NYPD," he said and wrote the name of the gallery down on his napkin and shoved it in his shirt pocket.

Sarra frowned. "I know George also made Homer sweat. Not literally either. Homer was afraid of him. I found out later that Homer didn't know that George had escorted me to the party. Your father knew George too." That bit of information she had almost forgotten.

Jarrett looked startled. It was as if she had dropped a bomb. "How?"

"I don't know." Sarra moved her shoulders trying to relieve the tense muscles. "When George introduced me to your father, they acted like they were old friends." She touched the large handbag on the seat beside her. "When I ran from New York, I cleaned out Homer's safe." She pulled out the envelopes and the encased video discs and several old cassettes, then carefully placed them on the table in front of Jarrett.

"What is this?" he asked, staring at the items.

"I have no idea. I've never viewed any of the discs, opened an envelope or listened to one of the cassettes. I never wanted to know what all these contained, but now I do. I want you to examine it all, on the condition that I'm there when you do." Scared but determined, Sarra continued. "I want to know why George wants me dead. Will you agree to let me be there when you go through them?" Possessively, she kept her hand on top of the pile of discs and tapes.

Jarrett had to admire her resolve. She wanted answers as much as he did. "What if I refuse?" he asked, testing her.

"Oh, you could physically take this from me." She gestured to the stack, "But, I would refuse to help you in any way from this point on. I think my brother's lawyer would be able to block any attempt by the police to force my assistance." She returned his gaze evenly.

Jarrett grinned, "Well, in that case, how could I refuse your offer to help? Should we go back to my office?"

She was bluffing, and he knew it. However, a voluntary statement by a witness was more valuable in court than one obtained by legal force. He motioned to the waitress for the check.

"No! Not at the police department. I'm afraid of what might be on those video discs," she said, roughly and lowered her gaze, deeply embarrassed. "Homer was a strange man. He liked to see himself perform. He used to record us in bed."

The smile evaporated from Jarrett's face. He felt a surge of revulsion. He certainly didn't want to view her in the arms of another man. "Where do you suggest we go? Your house?"

Sarra read the change in expression. He was all withdrawn and businesslike again. Jarrett's blue eyes revealed nothing of his feelings. But she knew he had to be repulsed.

"We can't go to my home. My daughter and Pearl Ann are there. Do you have a private office somewhere we can go? I don't want anyone else to see these." Bluntly she added, "I can't change that I was intimate with him, but I'll be damned if I'll let the world see me in the act!" She stared straight at Jarrett, daring him to reveal some sort of reaction. Not even a flicker crossed his features.

Jarrett thought for a moment, hesitating before he said, "The only other place I would feel secure in viewing that evidence is the office at my home. We'll have complete privacy if you don't mind going there?" When she didn't answer right away, he offered. "I can call my partner to meet us there if you don't want to be alone with me. I promise you have nothing to fear."

"No! Don't call your partner," Sarra said at once. "I'll only let you view the discs for now." She shuddered a little. "If there is one showing Homer and me in his bedroom, promise me you'll erase it."

"I can't promise that until I've looked at everything. But, I do promise to keep any recording of you from being seen by anyone else," Jarrett told her. "I'll do everything I can to protect you. But you have to understand, I can't withhold evidence if it's on these discs. Is that agreeable with you?"

Sarra nodded. "It will have to be," she agreed heavily. "I appreciate anything you can do. Thank you.

Now, can we go? I want to get this over with." She shoved the envelopes and video cases back into the bag and stood.

Jarrett rose and picked up the check, paid the cashier, then held the door open for Sarra. Outside, he gave her his address and saw her surprise when she discovered how few streets separated their homes.

CHAPTER EIGHTEEN

It was a short, fifteen-minute drive south to Jarrett's house. Sarra parked behind him in the driveway and followed him up the walk. The sun was hanging low in the late sky, but the heat had not cooled in the least. There was a heavy floral scent in the air which burned her nose and made her blink her eyes. The odor was almost too overpowering, burning the inside of her nose. She glanced around, wondering what flower could produce such a fragrance.

The house was the complete opposite of the mansion on Long Island and not at all what she expected. It was white masonry with blue trim and a white tiled roof. A thick green lawn led up to a small porch. There were no flower beds to brighten the landscape, just a trimmed boxwood hedge along the front of the house. The only other greenery was a poor man's orchid tree in the middle of the yard.

All along the street, the other houses were of similar design and construction. Landscaped foliage graced most of the yards, giving the appearance of a well-cared for neighborhood. The cheerful bright pinks, white and red impatiens in the yard across the street made Jarrett's house look desperate for a touch of color. He did not seem to notice.

Key in hand, he walked to the front door and stopped, then turned to her and asked, "Are you afraid of dogs?"

"No, not at all, why do you ask?"

He pointed to the large window to her right.

Through the glass she could see a large tan dog,

head cocked to one side, his ears standing straight up, and his brown eyes staring straight at her. He would have made three of Skipper. "Well," she ventured. "I hope he doesn't bite."

"No. He's friendly as long as I'm with you, but Chance is a good guard dog." He opened the door, went in and grabbed the dog's collar. "It's safe to come in. Just let me put him in the backyard."

Sarra heard the clicking of the dog's toenails on the tile floor, and the opening and closing of a door. She entered further and found herself in the living room.

It was a small room and spartanly furnished for comfort with a recliner, bookshelves, and a television. But, Sarra found it was the blank walls that made an impact. She thought of the homey atmosphere of Pearl Ann's Kentucky house with all its crocheted afghans, pictures and a lifetime's worth of mementos.

This room gave the impression that Jarrett's life was on hold and this was just a house, not a home. That he was a transient waiting to get on with his life. Sad, Sarra thought. This was clearly a lonely place for a lonely man. Not even a single photograph. Only a few leather-bound books that looked well used. She looked toward the kitchen counter where Jarrett stood checking the messages on his answering machine.

Finished, Jarrett turned to face her. "I can offer you a Pepsi or a glass of water. If you prefer, I can make a pot of coffee. What would you like?"

"Ice water would be fine," she said, looking around the immaculate kitchen and dining room. She doubted if any of the appliances saw much use. Even the dining room table and chairs were isolated artifacts in an otherwise empty room. She realized he was staring at her.

"I've been remodeling the house since I bought it." Seeing things in her expression, Jarrett became a little defensive. "I keep it furnished with just enough to keep me comfortable. I eat out most of the time, so I don't need much." Why, he wondered, was he explaining all this to her? As he looked around, he realized how unlived in the place looked.

Feeling embarrassed, he dumped cubes in a glass, grateful that at least there was ice in the fridge. Filling the glass with bottled water, he turned, gave Sarra the glass then leaned back against the counter. In an effort to redirect her attention, he asked, "Where did you go after New York?"

"West." Sarra sipped the cold water. "I had a friend, one of Homer's girls, Rose Ann. She had made me promise, if I succeeded in getting away, I was to go and find her mother. That's how I ended up in Kentucky. When the bus stopped in Madison, I got off and stayed."

"That's where you met Pearl Ann." He made it a statement.

Sarra smiled. "First, I rented an apartment from her, but I've never told her about Rose Ann, or how she died. The police from New York had notified her of her daughter's death. She didn't need to know the sordid details," she paused. "Pearl Ann was the first person I ever met who was kind to me. I owe everything I am to her." She remained silent for a moment. "I had a dream of becoming an artist. Pearl Ann made that dream come true. High school and college were out of the question because Homer always hired tutors for us, so we never attended school. Being a retired school teacher, Pearl Ann solved that problem. She taught me for four years until I could pass my GED. Then I spent the next four years at Madison College and graduated with a degree in Fine Art."

"She sounds like a remarkable woman." He had been correct in his metaphor, Jarrett thought, about Pearl Ann being the gardener for this flower.

"She is," Sarra affirmed quietly. "If it wasn't for Pearl Ann, I don't know where I would be today. Probably dead. I was a sixteen-year-old girl who didn't know who she was, where she was going, or how to survive." Sarra began to fidget. She was far too aware of Jarrett leaning against the counter looking too handsome and too male, so like the enchanting young man he had been. She was talking too much, she thought, yet was unable to stop. "Rose Ann was the street-smart one," she continued. "Homer kept tight control of me. I was his special girl. I wasn't supposed to be allowed out, and I wasn't allowed to ask questions. But Rose Ann and I used to sneak out when we knew Homer would be gone for a few hours.

"After a couple of months in Kentucky, I discovered I was pregnant. Talk about terrified! There I was, a child myself, alone, ignorant, and in a town filled with extremely conservative people. Pearl Ann stepped in and took care of that problem too. She claimed me as a distant relative. She is the mother I never had, and I owe her my life. That's why I'm here today." Taking a drink of water, she lowered the glass and looked Jarrett squarely in the eyes. "I may not want to let you see these tapes, but to protect my family and end this madness, I'll do whatever it takes to keep my daughter and Pearl Ann safe."

Jarrett nodded. He understood and remembered how alone he had been through his own, dreadful time. It was pointless now to regret the past, he thought. It could not be changed. Pointing down the hall, he said, "My office is in the spare room. Bring your bag, and I'll get you settled in a chair."

Sarra was amazed by the office. This, she realized, was where he really lived. Just inside the door, a computer and printer occupied a large white wooden desk along with numerous piles of papers. Bookshelves, lining one wall were crammed with manuals and textbooks on forensic science, and other subjects, while stacks of file folders were used as bookends. On another wall, an oversized bulletin board was buried under the weight of thumb tacks holding photographs and notes.

As she moved closer to examine the photos, he stopped her. "I wouldn't look at those too closely if I were you. They're from unsolved cases I've worked on. Most are extremely graphic shots of murder victims." Sarra quickly looked away and took a seat in the chair at the desk with her back to the photographs.

Jarrett pushed aside papers and placed the glass of ice water on a coaster within arm's reach. He left and returned carrying one of the kitchen chairs. "When you're ready, we can examine those DVDs and papers."

Her stomach flipped as she saw the television and

numerous other pieces of electronic equipment filling the open shelves of an entertainment center. She looked up at Jarrett and said. "I have to tell you that I'm scared."

He nodded that he understood. "Don't be. You're doing the right thing. From what you've told me, and since the news that you are Dr. Corbett's sister has been spread over the wire services, chances are this George character will come after you. I think it's safe to assume he's afraid of something you have, and it has to be here."

"Yes," Sarra whispered. No, George wouldn't stop until he killed her and probably Amanda and even Pearl Ann. Opening her bag, she removed three discs, a box of ten old style cassette tapes, along with three large sealed envelopes and handed it all to Jarrett. "Please open the envelopes first."

Jarrett did as requested and broke the tape on the first envelope. It was filled with eight-by-ten color photographs. "Good God!" His face blanched as he shuffled through the pictures. They were of men in active intercourse with boys and girls. He judged the ages of the children ranged from ten to twelve, although some might have been as young as seven. It was also clear the children were unwilling participants. Their contorted expressions said it all. Jarrett's whole body knotted with fury as he replaced the photos in the envelope. When Sarra reached out to take it from him, he jerked it out of reach.

"No!" he gritted. "You don't want to see these either. They're pictures of pedophiles." He inhaled raggedly and didn't elaborate further. "It makes me sick, and I've been a cop for nine years." Collecting himself, Jarrett placed the packet on the shelf next to him before opening the next one. It was filled with the same thing, but with different men. The third held papers filled with what looked like financial records. There were two thin black ledger books. One had page after page of numbers mixed with letters and dollar amounts written beside dates. The other had columns listing the same type of letters and numbers, but the dollar amount was subtracted from a running total. Jarrett handed everything to Sarra. "Do you have any idea what these are?"

She flipped through the pages and shook her head. "It's some sort of accounting system of Homer's. He never trusted banks. I have no idea what it all means." She handed the ledgers back to him.

She watched unhappily as he picked up one of the video discs. Sarra wanted to run but knew she had to face this and hoped Jarrett had an understanding attitude. So far, he seemed to.

Before he placed the disc in the DVD player, Jarrett turned to Sarra, "I don't know what's on this, but after seeing what was in the envelopes, I believe it might be more of the same. Maybe I was wrong not to let you see the pictures if only to prepare you."

Sarra nodded grimly, braced for humiliation. "Thank you for warning me. I'll let you know when I can't handle it."

Jarrett placed the disc in the machine and pushed the play button, then returned to his chair with a remote control in his hand. There was a blank lead, and then the camera focused on a bed. The sight of the young girl, wearing white lace bikini underpants, a white garter belt, white stockings, and a lace bra, stunned Sarra.

"My God, it's Rose Ann," she whispered, appalled.

Jarrett aimed the remote and stopped the machine at once. "You don't have to watch this. Why don't you leave everything here, I'll look at it and let you know what each contains."

Sarra shook her head. "No. I can't do that. I have to know."

Jarrett didn't press the issue. Instead, he pressed play on the remote and waited for the video to restart. When the images appeared once again, he pointed to the girl on the screen. "Tell me about her."

Her eyes glistening, Sarra did so. "She was the only friend I had in New York. She taught me how to drive a car. We were more like sisters in some ways." She twisted the flower ring on her little finger then raised her hand to show Jarrett. "She gave me this ring so I wouldn't forget her." Sarra swallowed hard and blinked. "Like I ever could. Anyway, like me, she lived with Homer, but off and on. More off than on. He would send her away for days. I never asked where.

"I remember this one time, she had a fight with Homer. She refused to go with some man. That same day, she was taken away. The next day she was dead. Her body was found in the river. I never knew how she died, until I read about a girl's body being found. There was a photograph of her. I always knew Homer had something to do with it. When I tried to find out, he told me to mind my own business and keep my mouth shut.

So I did." She swallowed hard. "Rose was two years older than me. I think she made the mistake of defying Homer and died for it. Hard not to understand that lesson, but look where it got me. I've been running for years."

Jarrett nodded. "I think we will make sure your problems will be over soon." He tried to sound positive.

We? Sarra thought.

As the scene on the disc continued, a naked man appeared with his back to the camera. There was no sound. In the silence, the girl rose from the bed and began a slow strip, swaying and grinding her slender hips in an erotic dance.

The man seized her and pushed her back onto the white spread. Suddenly he ripped off her underwear and dragged her across the bed. Like a kitten facing a Doberman, she tried to scurry backward out of his reach. But he caught her ankles and hauled her to him.

Sarra, unable to prevent the tears from rolling down her face, could not look away. It was like memory viewed from another angle. She desperately wanted a glimpse of the man's face. Because of the camera's angle, most of his features were in shadow. Yet, she was positive she knew him.

She flinched as the man slammed his open palm against the side of Rose's face. Her head snapped to the side then back. Then she went limp, lying still and terrified. Sarra turned away unable to watch the rape she knew would follow. "Oh God!" she whispered.

Jarrett pushed the pause button. "You don't have to watch this. I'll fast forward until I find a shot of this guy's face."

"No. I have to." Sarra got out roughly. Her stomach churned with revulsion, but she couldn't not watch. "That's my friend," she said, "I have to know what happened and who killed her."

Jarrett frowned. "Are you sure?"

"Yes," she said grimly and visibly stiffened.

"Okay." Jarrett pushed the play button once again.

Rose Ann became wild and struggled against the man's forceful thrusts as, with one blow after another, he beat her into submission. He punched her in the face and head until her features were battered beyond recognition. Then, when she lay still, he held her hips and pummeled her, repeatedly driving into her until he shuddered and climaxed, throwing back his head to reveal a partial view of his face.

"Oh, God!" Sarra cried out. "Stop it. Please, stop it." She swiveled. "I think that's George," she gasped and let the tears flow unchecked.

Jarrett swore under his breath, stopped the disc, and then went to Sarra. He felt both helpless and disgusted. Without waiting to wonder if she would recoil from his touch, Jarrett gathered her into his arms. "My God, Sarra!" he whispered.

She didn't say anything, but clung, wrapping her arms around him and burying her face in his shirt. Between ragged sobs, she raged against his chest. "He killed her. She was the only friend I ever had, and he killed her."

Jarrett swallowed hard and rubbed her back,

appalled to realize the same thing had been done to her. The same night. The night they had danced, long ago. It seemed so right to be holding her again now. He swallowed knots of feeling, and when she lifted tear-filled eyes to look at him, he brushed the hair back from her face and lowered his mouth to hers. He had expected her lips to be soft and warm but was unprepared for the shock of feelings that raced through him. He jerked. Struggled. Stepped back. Then swallowed as she just kept looking at him, her eyes large, too moist. "I've wanted to do that since the first time I saw you," he got out.

Sarra nodded a little. "Yes," she whispered, then came forward, back into his arms. This time, she met his mouth with a fire of her own. He felt her trembling, just as he was. And then it was as though all the intervening years had suddenly evaporated and they had finished that magical dance.

Jarrett reeled with the impact's pure conflagration, it was more than sensation. It was an extraordinary melding and then, holding her, feeling her pliant and real, he kissed her eyes, her brow, her throat as she pressed against him, holding him tightly by turn.

The telephone's ring was abrasive. They jerked apart, neither functioning properly as they stood facing each other, their gazes locked, breathing hard. The phone jangled again.

"Damn it!" Jarrett swore and marched into the kitchen to rip the receiver off the hook.

CHAPTER NINETEEN

"Yeah," Jarrett growled into the phone.

"Jarrett? Thank God." It was Caruso. "We have a problem, and Big John will not like this development."

"What's up, CJ?"

"I'm at Sarra Gray's house. All hell has broken loose here."

Feeling like he had just crash landed, Jarrett frowned and looked at Sarra, who had followed him to the kitchen. "Well?"

"Someone broke in and assaulted the old lady. She's in a bad way. Somehow, she was able to get to the phone and dial 911. When the operator couldn't get a response, she sent a squad car to check it out. I came here looking for you."

"I'll be right there."

"Jarrett?" Caruso said

"Yeah?"

"Sarra and the little girl are missing."

"Sarra's with me. We're on our way." He replaced the receiver and turned to Sarra.

"What?" Sarra began.

"Grab your purse. We have to go to your house."

"Oh my God! What's happened?" Sarra felt the blood drain from her face as terror fisted in her stomach. "Tell me what's happened," she demanded.

"Your friend, the older lady," his voice faded, unable to continue.

"Pearl Ann," she whispered, clutching her throat.

"She's alive. She's been hurt. Someone broke in," Jarrett said immediately. "That was Caruso. Let's go." He wrapped an arm around her.

Sarra pulled free. "Where's my daughter, where's Amanda? Is she safe?" Fear grabbed her, filling her mind with terror. Was it George? Had he broken in and hurt Pearl Ann? Did he now have her daughter? Sarra did not doubt for a second that he'd kill Amanda without hesitation.

"Caruso didn't mention your daughter being injured. We'll find her, Sarra. Come on, I'll drive."

A small glimmer of hope dug into her fear. "You can't," she called over her shoulder. "We have to take my car. I'm blocking you in the driveway." She hurried ahead of him out of the house and unlocked the driver's side and climbed in. As Jarrett slid into the passenger seat, she hardly gave him time to slam the door before she was backing out of the driveway. She rolled through the stop sign at Ninth Street and shot north through the yellow light at Sixty-second Avenue.

It was a four-minute trip to her driveway. Reaching it, Sarra slammed on the brakes, skidded to a stop within a fraction of an inch from the rear bumper of the police car parked in front of her neighbor's house. The jarring stop threw her forward, and she struck her head on the rearview mirror.

She blinked, hardly noticing the flash of pain that shot from above her right eye to the back of her head. Instead, all she saw, as she scrambled out of the car, was the bright red Fire Rescue truck parked at the curb and the ambulance parked in her driveway. Jarrett forgotten all she could focus on was getting to Pearl Ann and

Amanda.

Two men in blue uniforms jumped out of the truck. One, carrying a large black rectangular box, dashed up the driveway. God, please, Sarra prayed, as she reached the front door just behind the two men. Suddenly, the huge form of Caruso blocked her way. She opened her mouth, but, he grabbed her elbow and spun her back toward Jarrett.

"Let those men do their job," he said. "Your friend has been hurt and needs their help."

"How bad?" Sarra tried to pull free. "Where's my daughter?" He didn't answer. "I have to see Pearl Ann!" Pearl Ann would know where Amanda was. Again she tried to pull away from him, but Caruso tightened his grip, then let go. She jerked back as Jarrett put a hand on her shoulder.

"She'll stay here with me until the EMTs," he began and started to link his arm with Sarra's.

"No! I've got to find my daughter." She ducked away, rammed past Caruso into the house.

Sarra came to a dead stop a few feet inside. Ahead at the kitchen doorway, EMTs were bent over Pearl Ann's still form sprawled out on the tiled floor. Her face was bruised and battered, and blood ran from a nasty gash on her forehead. The portable phone was still clutched in her hand.

One man was checking her eyes with a penlight while the other swabbed her arm with an alcohol pad. He didn't even look up when Sarra skidded up and dropped to her knees. His partner just motioned for her to move aside while he busied himself with the job of inserting a needle in a vein to set up an IV drip.

"Oh God, Pearl Ann?" Sarra' voice cracked. This was all her fault. If she had left Madison alone, this would not have happened. If.

The EMT picked up a microphone from the large metal box on the floor beside him and began speaking into it. "This is Fire Rescue at" he gave the address and waited. The two way radio beside him crackled as a voice at a distant location acknowledged his call.

"We have a white female, approximately sixty-five years of age, with a head injury." He turned away to listen closer to the responding question, which Sarra could not make out. She was in their way, she thought and scrambled to her feet.

Amanda? Where was Amanda? Fear welling, Sarra turned and hurried from room to room, searching everywhere the child could be hiding, checking closets and under the beds. She was nowhere to be found. Raw panic made everything seem both clear and strange. Where was she? Amanda had to be safe. Of course, she was. Pearl Ann would have kept her safe. Where was she?

She charged across the living room, and Jarrett grabbed her before she could rush out of the front door, locking his arms around her and bringing her to a stop. "We'll find her, Sarra," he told her.

"No!" She yelled at him, wild-eyed as she struggled to free herself. "Amanda's safe. She has to be!"

"Jarrett, can you and Sarra come here for a minute," Caruso interrupted from just outside the front door. "I may have found the child."

Sarra tore loose and charged through the door ahead of Jarrett. She followed Caruso to the curb where a uniformed police officer now pointed to the neighbor's house.

Caruso turned to face them. "A call came into the Station a few minutes ago from a neighbor trying to locate you." He looked at Sarra. "Do you know someone named Barbara Toller?"

"Yes, she lives next door," Sarra gasped.

Caruso nodded. "Your daughter is there. Your neighbor wouldn't let her come home with all the ruckus going on over here."

"Thank God!" Sarra cried and took off before he finished, running down the pavement to Barbara's drive. She could see her neighbor and Amanda standing together inside the screened porch.

Upon seeing her mother, Amanda careened out of the door and rushed into her Sarra's arms.

Shaking all over with relief, Sarra held her tight, afraid to let go for fear she would crumble and frighten Amanda more than she already was. The relief of physically holding her child washed through her.

"You're squishing me!" Amanda complained.

Sarra forced herself to loosen her hold and began to check her over for injuries. "Are you all right?" she managed.

Amanda pulled away. "Mommy, what happened to Gran? I was over here playing with Allison and started to come home. These men were coming out of the house.

They didn't look like very nice men."

"My God!" Again panic washed through her as Sarra asked, "Did they see you?"

"No. I was going to cut through the hedge. When I saw them, I hid. They scared me, Mom. One of them looked so mean and kept beating his hands together as if he were punching someone. I ran back here to tell Mrs. Toller what was happening." The child was shaking with fright.

Her neighbor, Barbara, walked up, "By the time I understood what she was talking about, there was a patrol car next door," she said, having overheard Amanda. "I waited and called the police to let them know she was here. I tried to phone your house, but the line was busy."

Sarra found a watery smile. "Thank you for keeping her safe." She hugged Amanda again. "I have to go. Pearl Ann's been hurt. The ambulance," she left the sentence unfinished. Then, keeping a tight grip on Amanda's hand, she walked down the driveway to where Jarrett waited by the ambulance while the two paramedics collected a stretcher. It was surprising how quickly they moved into the house and back out with Pearl Ann strapped securely on the gurney. They had her loaded and anchored in the back of the vehicle within a few minutes.

Jarrett stayed close to Amanda and Sarra while Caruso prowled around conducting the preliminary investigation. It appeared Pearl Ann had been surprised near the front door and then had been assaulted. She had made it to the kitchen and the phone before being knocked out. He'd find out more from CJ later. The blast of the ambulance siren sent Sarra and Amanda hurrying away to her car.

Bolting after her, Jarrett caught her just as she reached for the car door. "I'm driving this time," he said.

Sarra didn't attempt to argue, just tossed him the car keys. She was too strung out to drive anyway. It was crowded in the front seat as Amanda, still clinging to her mother, squeezed close to Sarra.

"Is Gran going to be all right?" she whispered in a small voice.

"I don't know, sweetheart." She had never lied to the child, and she wasn't going to now. "She may be hurt pretty bad. We'll have to wait until we get to the hospital to find out."

"Mommy, who were those men? And why did they hurt Gran?" Her eyes filled with tears, "Like Kentucky?" she whispered. Her face puckered and she began to cry.

Sarra said nothing and hugged her close, caressing her daughter's silky hair. She wanted desperately to reassure Amanda but she couldn't. Planting a kiss on the top of Amanda's head, she hugged her tighter and fought to stay rational.

Jarrett stayed on the bumper of the ambulance as the driver accelerated past cars and trucks attempting to get out of the way.

As the driver pulled the ambulance up to the doors of the hospital emergency entrance, Jarrett parked the car in a slot reserved for the police. He opened the door for Sarra, and they followed the paramedics wheeling Pearl Ann into the building.

As they rushed in, Sarra saw Gene dressed in green scrubs coming toward them. He met her at the door to the trauma room where the paramedics had taken Pearl Ann. He was issuing orders like a military commanding officer.

He paused long enough to give her a quick pat on the shoulder. "I can't stop," he said. "I promise to do everything I can, Sarra. I have to go." An instant later, Gene pushed through the doors and vanished into the trauma room.

They all followed his orders. Jarrett pulled Amanda away toward the nurse's lounge as Sarra went to the Registration station. Addie wasn't working, and she didn't recognize a couple of the girls at the counter but knew the evening Coordinator on duty. They had all heard the stories floating around the ER and knew Sarra was Dr. Corbett's sister. No one said a word to her when she sat down at the computer to register Pearl Ann and print a chart.

Within five minutes, she joined Jarrett and Amanda in the lounge. It was a large room equipped only with the necessities, a sofa, a long table with magazines on it, comfortable chairs and a television mounted on the wall. There was a sink with a counter and a microwave oven. The two most essential items in the room were the coffee pot and the wall phone. Nurses, clerks, doctors, and on-duty police officers could help themselves to a cup of hot brew anytime they could get a break and still be at a moment's call if needed.

Jarrett had a Styrofoam cup of fresh hot coffee waiting for her and had supplied Amanda with a coke. They sat at the table in silence just waiting.

After thirty excruciating minutes, Sarra stood and began to pace. Each time she passed the table, she lightly touched her daughter's shoulder to offer more reassurance.

Watching her, Jarrett felt helpless. All he wanted was to take Sarra in his arms and hold on to her. And, Jarrett knew he had fallen in love with her all over again. Or, he'd never fallen out of love with her. He'd just relaxed inside somehow and let it settle where it belonged as part of him. Because she was real again, more real, if anything, not just some elusive Will o' the Wisp always wafting just out of reach. Touching her had made her real, and the impact of that still stunned him. This time, however, he would be there for her through thick, thin and anything else, he thought. He got to his feet and walked around the table to where she stood behind Amanda. Coming up close beside her, he pulled her gently into his arms and drew her head against his chest.

"You need someone to lean on too, Sarra," he said softly.

Sarra didn't resist, but turned into him, glad for the warmth and gentleness he offered. Jarrett Blackwell, who, somehow, never had been a stranger. It undid her. With a gulp, she pressed her face against his shirt, trying to hide her sudden tears. It felt far too good to be held by him and comforted. She was thoroughly overwhelmed. She slipped her arms around his waist to cling, relaxed, against his chest, and cried.

"She's the only one who ever tried to help me and love me," she said unevenly into his shirt. "She can't die,

Jarrett."

Gene entered the room to hear the last. He looked doubtfully at Jarrett then, as Jarrett gently set her back, he touched Sarra's shoulder. "She's not going to die, Sarra," he said as she swiveled to face him. "I told you I would do everything in my power, didn't I? Well, I'm a damned good doctor, and I'm not about to lose that dear lady."

"Where is she?" Sarra whispered. "Can we see her?"

"She's stable and on her way to have a CAT scan of her head. Then, I'm sending her up to Intensive Care. She may have a skull fracture. I'll know shortly. Our major concern is possible bleeding into the brain. If that happens, we may have to go in and relieve the pressure." He shot another look at Jarrett, who was half-glued to his sister. He wanted to do the big brother thing and hold her, but the hovering policeman somehow made that impossible. He swallowed his feelings and gave her a reassuring smile instead, and patted her shoulder. "I'll take good care of her, Sis. I promise. Now, I want you and Amanda to go to my house. I think you'll be safer there."

"That's not a good idea," Jarrett pointed out at once. "The papers have had this story about you and your sister for two, three days now. If her home address were that easy to find, yours would be even more so. I'm taking them home with me. They'll be far safer with me and," he didn't get to finish.

"I'm not going anywhere," Sarra interrupted, "until I know for a fact that Pearl Ann will be all right."

"Which might not be until morning," Gene countered firmly. "Your daughter needs to be taken somewhere decent where she can get some sleep. So do you, for that matter. You won't do any good here."

Sarra had to admit he was right. Amanda was looking hollow-eyed. Supper, she thought. Amanda had to eat.

"As for going to Blackwell's house," Gene was still speaking, shifting to address Jarrett. "I have a suggestion that might solve this problem of your safety. I don't want my sister and my niece in some dingy hotel, or at what you people call a safe house. My father's house is sitting unoccupied over in Driftwood. It should be perfect. Wait here. I'll get the keys from my locker, and you can stay there."

"Now what makes you think the Driftwood house is safer than mine?" Jarrett asked, irrationally perturbed by Gene's take charge attitude.

Gene stared back at him. "It's isolated, surrounded with a privacy hedge, and it also has an excellent security system. Not to mention that no one will wonder what you're doing there. I use it as a guest house when friends come to town. I'm not about to send my sister anywhere I don't consider safe. There is a dock out back on the Bayou. Have a police officer winch the sailboat into the water and stay on board. The house is large enough for you and your partner or even a couple of other officers if you want." He cocked an eyebrow at the detective.

Jarrett nodded. "I have to agree, it sounds good. Okay, we'll give it a shot."

Gene hurried away and returned shortly with a set

of keys. "You might have to stop at the store for food. The house was just cleaned and fresh linens put on the beds, but the fridge will be empty." He handed the keys to Jarrett, gave him directions and instructions on how to disarm the security alarm. "I have to get back. I want to be there while they do the CAT scan. I'll call you at the house and give you the results." He hesitated and made a mental note to also tell Helen, when he finally heard from her, to pack her shit from their house and move to a hotel.

"Oh, God!" Jarrett said with weird timing, "In all the excitement over Pearl Ann, I almost forgot. Where is your wife, Doctor?"

About to leave, Gene stared for a moment. "I have no idea. We haven't spoken since Friday morning. Why?"

"The police have been trying to locate her since Saturday and need to find her," Jarrett said. "I hate to have to notify you like this, but I have bad news. Your mother-in-law, Thelma Joan Poole, has been killed."

Shock rode across Gene's face. "What? How?"

"It appears she was murdered early Saturday morning at her home. We don't know all the particulars yet." Jarrett hated delivering this type of news.

In sudden disarray, Gene knitted his brow as he collected himself. He pulled out his cell phone and dialed his home number. After a brief conversation with the houseman, flipped the phone shut and shoved it in his pocket. "Lee says he has not seen or heard from my wife. I left word for her to call me here, or to call the Police Department. That's all I can do for her right now. Thelma and I were never close." he didn't finish, but shook his head, still off balance, and turned back to Sarra.

"Sis, that house in Driftwood is as much yours as it is mine," he told her. "That's where we all used to live."

What a great idea, Gene thought suddenly. Giving the house to Sarra would keep the property out of his wife's clutches. Easy enough to call Arthur and have a Quit Claim Deed made out. He gave his sister a quick, urgent kiss on the cheek, and without saying anything to Jarrett, walked out of the room.

The kiss was unexpected and surprised Sarra. Gene had slipped into his role as big brother with such ease it was scary. Equally frightening was how quickly and naturally she had accepted him as such. Would the house seem familiar, she wondered? It was unlikely. After all, she had been three or four when she had been taken.

And Jarrett? She turned to look up at him. His concern was there, almost tangible in his eyes. Given her past close experiences with men, Gene and Jarrett were a startling contrast, both examples of the very best qualities a man should have. Looking at the detective, Sarra could still feel the lovely magnetic, earthquake quality of his touch. Did she dare trust him, she wondered, feeling her own history tugging in the other direction.

Jarrett wondered why Sarra was studying him so intently, his thoughts scrambling in several directions. Fear for her, of course. That was paramount. What if she had been home? Would she be the one lying in that hospital bed with her skull caved in, or would all three of them be dead now? And, losing her? The realization of the depth of his feelings didn't surprise him, but it was disconcerting to discover how they had been waiting to spring to life again

Stuffing all that into an internal box, Jarrett refocused. It was up to him and Caruso to keep them all safe and to find Pearl Ann's attacker. It had to be this George what's his name, Jarrett thought. He had found her just as he had. Probably due to the news on the TV about the Corbett's.

Amanda was still sitting silently at the table looking pale and drawn.

"Sweetheart," Sarra said, placing her hand on Amanda's cheek, turning her face so that she could meet her eyes. The unhappy nervousness reflected there made Sarra inhale sharply. She sat down in the chair next to her daughter. "Are you all right?"

"Mom, is it my fault Gran is hurt?" Amanda whispered. "Is she going to die?"

"No! No! She is not going to die." Sarra leaned closer. "The doctors will take good care of her. Now, tell me, why you think it's your fault?"

"Because I went next door to play with Allison. I wasn't there."

Sarra gathered the child to her and hugged her close. "Amanda, baby, none of this is your fault. Don't ever think that. Gran was hurt because of something that happened a long time ago before you were born. Those men would have hurt you too if you had been in the house. I'm just thankful you were next door." Sarra released the child and ran the back of her fingers along her cheek. "I love you, Amanda, and so does Gran." She looked up at Jarrett and pleaded silently.

Standing close to Sarra, he rested his hand lightly

on her shoulder, crouched down in front of her and, smiled at the little girl. "Your mother's right, Amanda, and, guess what? I promise I will catch the men who did this to your Gran. Okay?" he said gently.

He was trying not to let it show, but he felt awkward with children. Normal children that is. Most of the youngsters he came in contact with were crime victims or criminals. Amanda was neither. She was a bright little thing, yet vulnerable, and blaming herself for what happened. That thought struck home. He looked at Sarra and recalled again how she had been just a child herself at sixteen. A woman child, granted, but still a child with no control over what she had been forced to do.

Jarrett stood and glanced at his watch. It was growing late. He felt suddenly and violently hungry. He cleared his throat. "I say, girls, err, ladies. I'm starving. How about dinner?"

She looked at Jarrett. "You know the way to Gene's house?"

"It's not far from here. I'll have Caruso meet us there later. He should be about finished for the night. He can lock up your house for you."

Sarra nodded. "Just have him lock the bottom locks from the inside. That will do for now. We'll need clothes and toiletries if we're going to be gone for any length of time."

"I'll see to it," he said, ushering them out of the building and to the car.

CHAPTER TWENTY

Jarrett had no trouble finding the Driftwood house. It was in a beautiful, old Floridian style section in the southern part of Half Moon Bay, on a narrow road canopied by giant oak trees. All the homes faced the street with the back lawns sloping into the Bay. Most were two stories homes in varying styles, some Spanish, with an occasional ranch style thrown in. Others had the appearance of a colonial style and were set well back from the road. All were surrounded by high, dense foliage.

Negotiating the brick driveway leading to the house was not unlike trying to drive through the Brazilian rain forest, Jarrett thought, swearing when he scraped a wheel against the raised curb. "That was fun," he said sarcastically as he stopped by the front door. "This is the hairiest driveway I've ever come across! I hate to think of trying to back out of here in the dark."

Instead of forming a circle, the drive curved in toward the house and ended with enough space to park two cars, but not large enough to turn around in.

"Now I know what Gene meant when he said his mother hated this driveway," Sarra said, getting out of the car. Amanda scooted across the seat after her, and the three walked up to the front door.

The house was a large, two-story white stucco, Spanish-style building with a red tile roof. Giant oaks, and a variety of other trees, Sarra didn't recognize, shaded the entire front yard, darkening it considerably, the branches from one extending over the roof on the right side.

Sarra was nervous as Jarrett unlocked the door. There was nothing about the place that seemed familiar. She relaxed a little as they entered a foyer that seemed darker than it should be this early in the evening.

Jarrett fumbled for a light, found and flipped the switch, then hurried to shut off the alarm. As they entered the room to the right of the entrance, he saw the reason for the darkness. Heavy drapes covered the windows at each end of the room. Swiftly, he pulled them open.

The entrance faced the stairway, and to the right was the living room. Sarra wasn't sure what she had expected, opulence, definitely. After all, this was the home of a prominent physician, one who had amassed a fortune with his skills. She wasn't prepared however for the sheer wealth of the room. Slipping off her shoes at the door, Amanda's hand in hers, she padded barefoot across the thick carpet and sat down on the sofa. Round-eyed, Amanda also stared around the room.

The tables were carved from rich dark mahogany and topped with glass. The sofa was covered with a bright peacock brocade that was thoroughly elegant. A fireplace graced the wall next to the staircase, and a peacock designed, brass fire screen stood guard to block erratic embers from reaching the plush cream carpet. On each end of the mantelpiece, knights on horseback, carved from black polished wood, held thick white candles as if brandishing raised swords. Guarded by the knights, and mounted on the wall above the fireplace, was a painting. Sarra shifted to study the family portrait of a man, woman and two children, a young boy and small girl with long dark hair. She couldn't see them clearly from where she sat but knew it had to be Gene's mother, father, and sister. Or, should she say, herself? There would be time later to examine the portrait.

Sarra continued to take in the details of the room. Books cluttered the coffee table, and on the wall behind the sofa, a mirror etched with white peacocks was held in place by a half inch brass frame. At the far end of the room, was an oversized cobalt blue chair with an ottoman covered in a matching fabric. Wooden stack tables sat nearby, available to hold a drink or tray. Low bookshelves, topped with a thin layer of marble tiles, lined the wall from one corner of the room to the other. An array of porcelain figurines and wood carvings were artfully displayed on the top.

The room was tasteful and filled with color. It was a place you either loved or hated. Sarra loved it. The different colors worked together to form a refreshing palette of bright blues and vivid emerald. She felt herself begin to relax.

Next to her, Amanda breathed a reverent "Wow!"

"Wow is an understatement," Jarrett said coming through the doorway. "I'm almost afraid to go in there." He smiled at Amanda.

Running her hand over the rich material of the sofa, Sarra looked at them both. "Gene said to make ourselves at home, but my word, what a home!" She gazed in wonder around the room. "Can you imagine what the rest of this house must look like?"

Jarrett sighed. "Some other time I'd be happy to imagine anything you'd like. Right now, I have to contact Caruso and set up security around you and Amanda."

He strode away through the long room and turned left. Behind the wall flanking the stairway was a large dining room with a table and chairs of the same dark mahogany. To the left, created to form a giant U shape, was the kitchen. He flipped on the wall switch and headed for the refrigerator. Just as Gene had said, it was empty except for a couple of bottles of wine and a six-pack of Coke.

He returned to the living room where Sarra and Amanda still sat on the sofa. "Is there anything, in particular, you two want for dinner?" he asked. "I'll have Caruso pick up a meal, and we can lay in groceries later." He looked from one to the other.

Together they said, "Chinese."

Jarrett nodded and removed his cellular phone from his jacket pocket and began punching a number.

After two rings, Caruso's smooth voice answered. "It's about time you called me, Jarrett. And, this had better be you on the other end of this phone!"

"It's me all right."

"Well, Laddie, where are you and what's going on?"

Jarrett drifted out of the living room. "I have Sarra and Amanda with me. Pearl Ann is in ICU at the hospital. Sarra's brother is the attending. I need you here. We have guard duty."

"Where is here, and what do you need me to do?"

Jarrett gave him directions and told him to stop by

the Chinese restaurant on Thirty-Fourth Street and pick up an assortment of food. He continued his conversation with CJ as he resumed his inspection of the house.

"The victim didn't make it, Jarrett," Caruso stated. "She slipped away quietly and suddenly. There is no word on the DNA of her attacker. Nothing. Like the others," Caruso told him.

"Damn!" Jarrett swore. "I was hoping she'd survive. I don't suppose we were able to identify her?"

"Not yet. We will eventually."

"What's happening out at the Poole apartment?" Jarrett asked. They had been forced to leave two other officers to conduct the interviews with the neighbors.

"I don't like the report so far."

"Why?" Jarrett frowned. "What's going on?"

"The next door neighbor heard a man shouting at Joan Poole. The man was so loud he woke her up."

"Did she see what he looked like?"

"No, but she heard every word. The man had a rough voice, she said and kept demanding to know why Joan had rejected him. The neighbor says he kept screaming it over and over. Then suddenly everything was quiet. She was too afraid to go next door."

"Why didn't she call the police?" Jarrett asked.

"How many witnesses do we dig up who don't want to get involved?" Caruso countered sourly.

Jarrett was silent for a few moments. "Caruso," he said quietly. "Find out where Big John was at the time of the attack. Don't tell him why you're asking. Something is going on with him, but I don't know what. Get here as soon as you can. But, hold on for a moment. I need to check something out."

"Will do," Caruso said.

Jarrett crossed to a small hall off the living room and saw two doors he hadn't noticed before. One led to a bathroom. The other, positioned behind the mirrored wall, was the doctor's office. The desk was piled high with clutter. Boxes sat around on the floor, or on what looked like extra chairs to the dining room set. The room looked dusty and neglected.

Out of earshot of Sarra and her daughter, he told Caruso to go to his house and collect Chance. He also told him to bring all the materials Sarra had given him. "Leave the video disc there," he added, aware of his promise. They had viewed only one so far.

After ending his call, Jarrett walked back into the living room. Amanda was curled up on the sofa with her head in her mother's lap. Sarra was leaning back with her eyes closed, her breathing regular and even.

Jarrett checked the front door to make sure it was locked, then decided to explore the rest of the house. Upstairs, to the left of the landing, he found a large master bedroom with a private bath and a screened porch. There was another bathroom midway down the hall, a bedroom next to it, and then two smaller bedrooms on the Bay side of the house, one with a small balcony shaded by thick limbs and branches from one of the trees. While everything was quiet and all the rooms were empty, he made another quick call on his cell phone.

He returned downstairs to finish his search. Off the dining room, in the back, was a large family room with another sofa, recliner, and tables. From there another door led to a back patio. Behind the house, the lawn stretched away to the dock, where he could see the sailboat Gene had mentioned, now winched above the water next to the dock. It was large enough to sleep more than one person.

A tall hedge ran almost to the water's edge on either side of the property. That wasn't good, Jarrett thought. Someone could come in from the Bay with a boat. A man would have to be stationed at the back of the house. He flipped out his cell phone again and dialed the department. As soon as the phone was answered, he gave his name and was put on hold.

A sudden, booming voice made Jarrett wince. "Okay, Blackwell, this is Captain Whitmore. Why haven't I heard from you and Caruso?"

Jarrett took a deep breath and then filled Big John in on all that had happened.

"Good," Whitmore said in a milder tone. "I'll send over Jankowicz and Hershey. They can watch from the sailboat. You keep in touch with me daily. Is that understood? Whatever else you need, just call it in. It'll be sent over. Is there any news on the young rape victim at the hospital? Have they identified her yet?"

"She didn't make it, and we still haven't identified her," Jarrett told him. "We've contacted the Center for Missing Children." He hesitated, "Sir, I would rather not draw too much attention to our being at the house. If you don't mind, I'll decline Jankowicz and Hershey. With Caruso and an old friend of mine, McCabe, we should be able to handle it. McCabe can stay on the boat. Nothing will get past him. Also, Caruso is picking up my dog. He's a good guard dog. I'd also suggest that we set a twenty-four-hour guard at the hospital on Mrs. Burke until she's able to join us at the house."

"That's fine. As I said, whatever you need. You call McCabe and give him directions. I'll notify him from this end. Jankowicz and Hershey can stake out the front of the house. They can park a short distance down the street and call you if they see anything. Anything else?" Captain Whitmore asked.

"There was a witness at the Poole murder," Jarrett said and added the few specifies he had.

Whitmore was quiet for a moment. "Did she see anything?"

"No, just heard the shouting."

There was a sigh on the other end of the phone. "Well, keep me informed about what you find."

"Yes Sir, I will."

"Who are you talking to?" The voice behind Jarrett made him jump and spin around. Sarra stood in the dining room doorway.

"My boss," he mouthed, and turned back to catch what else the Captain was saying, "Don't forget what I told you about reporting in." There was a click on the other end.

Jarrett folded the phone and replaced it in his pocket. He swung around to face Sarra. "Do you feel better? I know you didn't doze long. That's why I came in here. I didn't want to disturb you. Is Amanda awake?"

"No. Let her sleep. Is your partner coming?"

"He should be here any time." He hesitated

before saying, "I told Caruso to go by my house and pick up everything you gave me except the videos. As I promised, no one will see them except you and me."

Her eyes widened in disbelief. "You're going to bring that filth here where my daughter might see it?" She spun away from him and went into the kitchen.

He followed her, a little miffed that she hadn't given him the benefit of the doubt. He stopped in the doorway. He wanted to explain that they needed those ledgers and papers. "Look," he began, but she cut him off.

"I don't want to hear it. I'm sure you think your reasons are good, but I don't. Not with Amanda here."

"She will never see those pictures. I'll seal them in an envelope. All I want to do is go through the ledger and papers to see what we can find. If we have to look at the photos, I'll make sure Caruso takes Amanda to another room." Exasperated, he ran his fingers through his hair.

Sarra stared grimly back at him. He was only trying to do his job, she reminded herself. "All right," she conceded. "But if she gets even one peek at that trash, I'll punch your lights out."

Jarrett struggled against a sudden grin, then gave in to it. "You can punch me all you want!" he said happily.

Sarra glared, her face flushing. "You wouldn't be the first man I've hit! I broke the last guy's nose."

Jarrett beamed. "I'll watch my step," he told her.

She changed the subject. "When do we eat? I'm starved."

Jarrett's smile faded. "Caruso should be here

shortly. If you'll make a list of the foods you and Amanda like, either Caruso or I will go to the supermarket."

"Fine! I'll do that. Thanks," she added still miffed, and then left him standing alone in the kitchen, returning to the living room to find her purse, a pen, and paper.

As she entered the room, Amanda was just sitting up and rubbing her eyes. "Mommy, I'm hungry."

Sarra sat down beside her. "Food's on its way, Sweetie."

The doorbell rang. Sarra flinched, then watched as Jarrett came into the room. "Stay put," he said. "You don't answer any doors or phones. That's my job. Okay?" He looked steadily at her. She nodded meekly.

A minute later, Caruso came traipsing into the room, his arms loaded down with bags. "Who in the hell?" he stopped himself. "Who designed that damn driveway? You can total a set of tires on those curbs!"

"Tell me about it," Jarrett said, relieving him of several bags and leading the way to the kitchen. Glancing over his shoulder, he called to Sarra and Amanda, "Dinner will be served in the dining room, ladies."

Out of the hearing of mother and child, he asked, "Where's my dog? You were supposed to bring him with you."

"Couldn't," Caruso said. "I went by your house first and picked up everything you asked. Then, as I was planning on going to both the store and restaurant for our dinner, I had to leave Chance behind. It was too hot for him to be in the car while I went shopping. I'll stop by and pick him up tomorrow. And yes, I fed him."

"Okay. I don't expect anything to happen tonight," Jarrett said. "In the meantime, let's serve this up. The kid is right, I'm starved, too."

After Jarrett and Caruso disappeared into the kitchen, Amanda whispered to her mother, "He seems like a nice man," she pointed at Jarrett. "Is he one of the good guys?"

"Yes, Amanda, Mr. Blackwell is a policeman. Detective Jones is also. They're here to protect us. I think Jarrett is very nice, and he wants to cheer us up," Sarra whispered back. "We could let him think he's succeeding." She raised her eyebrows and gave her daughter a questioning look.

Amanda nodded. "Is the doctor sure Gran will be all right?" she asked then.

"Dr. Corbett said she'll be okay. Now if he said so, and he is an excellent doctor, then we must believe him, right? Gran will be fine." Sarra tried to smile but could only manage a slight grin.

She pulled Amanda up off the sofa, and they entered the dining room arm in arm. Amanda went to sit at the end of the table. Sarra stood in the kitchen doorway and watched Jarrett search the cupboards for dishes. "Look to the right of the sink," she said without thinking. Jarrett froze for a moment, then opened the cabinet door and reached for the dinner plates.

"That was a good guess," he said slowly, turning to stare at Sarra for a second. He sat the plates on the counter and walked over to her.

She looked up at him with a sudden realization. "Jarrett, it wasn't a guess about the dishes," she whispered. "I knew where they were."

Jarrett nodded and took her hands. "So I gathered."

Sarra shivered. "That's just it. I know which drawer the silverware is in too, and I can tell you which cabinet you'll find the glasses in." She looked into his eyes, her own widening. "Gene is telling the truth. I am his sister."

Jarrett went still and continued to stare at her for a moment longer. "Yes," he murmured, then, "Well, first things first," he said crisply, releasing her. "Let's eat dinner. Then, I think we should explore the house and see what other memories we might jog out of the dark recesses of your mind." He gave her a warm smile. "I don't know about you, but I could eat a cow."

Sarra felt as though she could fold up like an accordion. "You're right. Here," she said taking the plates off the counter. "I'll set the table. You two bring in the food."

By the time Caruso and Jarrett opened the containers of oriental food, Sarra had a cloth on the table with placemats. Amanda sat glued to her chosen seat, looking hungry and anxious. Sitting down on her right, Caruso grinned at her. A moment later, he served her a heaping plate.

Too hungry for conversation, the four concentrated on eating, savoring each bite, demolishing everything. After the meal, Caruso took Amanda's hand in his big one. She eyed him suspiciously, giving her mother a worried glance. Sarra smiled and gave her a reassuring nod. The child relaxed and stared up at the big Irishman.

"Ye know," he said, amplifying his slight brogue, "I've always fancied a wee lassie of me own. Could I perhaps be talkin' ye into pretendin' fer a bit, that ye'll be me own sweet little girl and have ye come inta the t'other room wi' me to watch a bit o' the telly while them two clear the table and," he added, giving her a wink, "do them dishes?"

Amanda gave a giggle. "You're funny. Come on." She jumped up and headed into the family room. "Let's go find something funny to watch."

"Go on, you two," Sarra approved, getting up and gathering the rest of the plates and silverware.

Jarrett finished clearing the table then leaned back against the counter while Sarra began loading the dishwasher.

"Your friend is good with children," she handed him a plate to rinse.

Jarrett turned on the faucet. "Caruso is very good with kids. He has two boys, but he always said he'd love to have a daughter. So watch out, he'll steal her away. Um," he hesitated.

"Um what?" she asked.

Jarrett shrugged. "It's just that he's been divorced twice. As much as he loves children, it makes it difficult with his kids." He placed another plate in the rack.

She digested this. "Yes, it would."

"It's a pity he never found the right woman," Jarrett said a little gruffly, fussing with the sink.

Sarra stopped what she was doing. "And you? Have you found the right woman?"

Jarrett turned to look her in the eyes. "Yes. I found her a long time ago at a Christmas party. I lost her for a while, though." He smiled suddenly aware that he was enjoying this homey feeling, helping her in the kitchen, just the two of them sharing chores after dinner. It felt normal and good.

"Oh," Sarra said, flushing a little as she looked down and busied herself with rinsing another plate. That was as direct as you could ask for, she thought, and she had asked.

She felt? She wasn't sure what she was feeling. Not lightheaded or giddy, just immensely pleased that he still cared. But, there were obstacles in the way. Nasty, dangerous barriers that must be dealt with. "Do you think George will come here?" she ventured.

Jarrett inhaled sharply. "I don't know. He might," he said, sorry that the moment had ended. "He won't get to you or Amanda. That's another promise I mean to keep."

He placed the last glass in the rack and closed the door to the dishwasher.

In the television room, Caruso eased his large frame onto the sofa. Amanda stood staring at him. Remote in one hand, he studied the child. "Whatever you want to ask me, don't be shy. I don't bite."

"Can I sit next to you?"

"Certainly," he said, shifting to make a place for her. She settled next to him, snuggling close.

"I don't have a daddy," she stated in a matter of fact manner. "I'm a bastard." Shyly she looked up at him. "Will you like me even if I'm a bastard?"

"I'd like you no matter what," Caruso told her, thoroughly surprised by her statement.

"Do you know what a bastard is?" Amanda asked.

Where did you hear that word?" Caruso inquired, a little shocked by her statement.

"Charlene called me that."

"Who's Charlene?" he probed. Amanda did not seem upset over the word but replied as if she was talking about someone else.

"She lived next door to our house in Kentucky."

"You're not a bastard."

"Yes, I am. I looked it up in the dictionary. It says I'm also ill . . . ," she stumbled over the pronunciation, "illegitimate. I don't have a daddy." Amanda tilted her head to one side and asked, "Will you be my daddy?"

Profoundly moved, Caruso hugged her close and said, "I can't be your daddy, but I can be your uncle like your Mommy's brother. Is that all right?"

She nodded solemnly and hugged him back. "I wish you had been there when those bad men blew up our house and killed my dog, Skipper. Now my Gran is hurt. Will they kill her too?"

"No one is going to hurt you or your mother, or your Gran ever again. I promise." He kissed the top of her head as she leaned against him. Above the child, Caruso inhaled controlled fury. When he got his hands on the sons of bitches who wanted to hurt this child and who had killed her dog, they'd pay dearly for what they had done.

"Come on," he urged, "let's find something funny to watch on this TV." He was rewarded with a glad smile as he pressed the 'on' button.

CHAPTER TWENTY-ONE

In the living room, Sarra stuffed a pillow behind her back, slipped off her shoes and settled into the corner of the sofa, suddenly aware of every tired muscle in her body.

Jarrett sat down next to her, suddenly aware of how her shoulders drooped and the smudge of dark circles under her eyes.

The tension between them was gone, replaced by the intriguing sense of being old friends reunited after a long separation, and in a way, picking up where they had left off. Renewing the short relationship would take time, but it would happen. They could both feel it. The kiss at Jarrett's house proved they were as drawn to each other as they had been in New York.

Now, there were new currents in the air. In the few moments she had spent with Jarrett, all those years ago, Sarra had somehow understood he was a sincerely kind, caring person. It felt natural now for her to lean against him and nestle into the curve of his arm when he slipped it around her shoulders. She looked up at him. Their eyes met.

"I want to kiss you again, but I don't think I had better. Kissing you is not all I want to do," he said softly.

She laid her head on his chest and relaxed against him. "I know. I feel the same way. This is not the place." Then said, slowly. "I feel safe with you, Jarrett." She used his given name for the first time. "Do you know what it's like to always be afraid, every waking moment, and sometimes even in your dreams? To have fear control your life?"

"No, I've never experienced anything like that." His life had been easy and safe until that night. Jarrett tucked his chin against the top of her head. "I was afraid for my father, but that was different," he told her gently, glad that she was opening herself up to him.

"Well, that's what my life has been like," Sarra continued. "For all the good, there's always been this underlying fear hanging over me. It made me feel perpetually neurotic. Now, tonight, for the first time in my life, I feel safe." Safe was feeling Jarrett's warm breath against her cheek, his arm holding her, Sarra thought. "At least for now, until George finds me. I know he will. I feel it. I don't know how. He found me before and he will again." She snuggled closer.

Listening, Jarrett swallowed and moved his free hand to touch her hair.

"It has to come to an end, Jarrett. I've been running away from someone most of my life. First, it was my so-called father, Harry Gray. Then I was trying to get away from Homer. Then I was running from George. If it were just me, it wouldn't matter. But there's my daughter and Pearl Ann. I won't have them hurt more than they have been. Pearl Ann and I have been through a lot together, mostly my growing pains. And I haven't done such a good job of protecting her. It's my fault she was hurt. I didn't think George would find me this quickly." In a tired voice, she finished. "But he did."

Jarrett squeezed her a little, hugging her closer with both arms now. "She won't die. Your brother knows what he's doing. And stop beating yourself up, Sarra. There are enough people in this world who will put you down without you doing it to yourself. Mrs. Burke didn't get hurt because of you, damn it! That was this SOB George's doing! The sadistic son of a bitch, beating on a woman your Gran's age! You know what I don't understand?" he continued, "Why is George still after you? After all this time, why is he so determined to find and dispose of you? Surely, he has to believe that you've been to the police?"

"Which I haven't until now," Sarra interrupted.

Jarrett ignored that. "Why is he still around? Why isn't he on the run?"

"You didn't see his face or his eyes like I did," Sarra told him. "You saw what he did to Rose." Jarrett gently squeezed her arm in acknowledgment. "The night he beat and raped me, he was the same." Sarra continued her cheek against his chest. "He loved it. He delights in hurting people. It's like a sort of high."

"Power," Jarrett cut in quietly above her head. "It's all about power. He hurt Pearl Ann to get at you. It was a message. He's saying, he can find you anywhere and at any time. None of it makes sense, though. Why does he continue to believe you're a threat?"

"I've always believed he's after the stuff from Homer's safe." Sarra began, moving back to sit up and look at him.

Jarrett lowered his arms. "No, I don't think it's that. After the recent publicity and the attack on Pearl Ann, I'm certain he now knows you've come to the police. I'm sure he has enough money to leave the country, or disappear. No, there's something more we're missing." He yawned before he could stop it. "Sorry. You're not boring company. Truthfully, I'm whacked. The food did me in, too. Guess I need more coffee. Would you mind making a pot? My coffee is lousy, and it's going to be a long night. McCabe is a big coffee drinker, too. He'll want a few mugs."

"You mean he's here?"

A smile played at the corners of his mouth. "He's been here on the boat keeping watch since shortly after I talked to my boss."

"That poor man! And you didn't even take him dinner," she admonished, giving him a light punch in the ribs.

"Ouch!" He protested and then grinned. "He hates Chinese food from a restaurant. Besides, he told me he'd bring his own. He's rather picky about what he eats."

They both stood up, and Jarrett followed her into the kitchen to watch while Sarra put a pot of coffee on to brew.

"I want to prepare you," he said. "We will have to watch all those videos. Also, I do want Caruso to see them." He waited for her to explode. She didn't.

Sarra just nodded and looked at him. "I know," she said quietly. "I realize you'll have to review all the evidence. It's just that I'm terribly embarrassed for you or anyone to see me if I'm in them. I'm not a prostitute, Jarrett. I never was. I was just trained for it. I've been with only one man, by choice, and he was a big mistake. I tried to make him a substitute for you." She told him about the brief affair she had had with a man in Kentucky. "It was a disaster. Remember I told you I punched a man in the nose?" she said.

Jarrett smiled, picturing it. "I know you're not a prostitute," he told her sincerely.

Sarra nodded, going to perch on the high kitchen stool. "I told you about my one and only trick." She looked away. "When I met you, well, you looked at me as if I was a real person, not a commodity. You treated me as if I really was special. As if you could see me, who I was. It was quite a shock, actually. Because at that point, I had no clear idea of who I was."

Jarrett, remembering every detail, couldn't utter a sound.

"I wanted to tell you, yes," Sarra continued huskily. "Yes, I'd marry you that very night. I could see you too, you see, and what I felt for you in that short time was so strong, I panicked. I believed that as soon as you found out what I was, you would see me differently. So, I ran away from you and did what I had been sent to do." She inhaled raggedly. "Well, I don't belong to that world anymore. I'm a good person and a good mother. I love my child and Pearl Ann. They are my family." She looked at him again. "I'll do whatever I must to stop George, even if it means allowing Caruso, or whomever you say, to view those videos and any evidence I've given you. I'm just so sorry I can't give your parents and your life back to you." She fell silent.

Jarrett didn't say anything at first. He saw how she watched him, trying to judge his reaction. Her face was haggard now. Then, he held out his arms. "Come here, you," he said gruffly, sweetly.

Sarra went to him, and as he wrapped his arms around her, she slid her own around his waist.

Jarrett hugged her to him, feeling how right it was. They both had lost so much, including each other. "My parents," he began slowly, speaking into her hair, "gave me every advantage that anyone could possibly have. I went to the best schools, ate the best food, and wore the best clothes. I had everything I wanted. I had it all. My father taught me to be responsible, and my mother taught me about loving and caring. None of that prepared me for the experience of losing them both so horribly, or so close together. Death is never easy for those left behind. But who's to say which is better, a quick death or a long lingering slow one? My mother wasn't given a choice, but my father was. He chose not to live.

"In my job, I've seen many types of death, none even remotely pretty. With a quick death, the initial shock is disbelief. It didn't happen. It's a dream. Worse, a nightmare. You think you'll wake up and it will all have been just that, a dream. The person or people you've lost will be as whole as ever. The trouble is that it's not a dream. They really are dead, and there is a hole in you that can't be filled."

"Pearl Ann told me about how her husband suffered from cancer," Sarra said, her voice a little muffled against his shirt. "His was dying by inches and in terrible pain. She told me how helpless she felt, unable to stop it. She blamed herself for being a coward too, refusing to help him die. But, she isn't a coward. She's the bravest person I know. From what she's taught me, it isn't a matter of choice or blame. However it happens, we die when it's our time."

"Maybe," Jarrett said, sounding skeptical. "At first, I blamed it all on you." Sarra tried to pull away, but he held her fast. "Then, in my mind, I kept seeing the terror in your eyes when you ran out the door that night. It's taken me a long time to realize that you were another victim of that mess.

"I searched for you for years. I didn't know what I expected if I found you. But, I desperately wanted to find you. Now that I have, I don't intend to lose you ever again." He held her tighter, moving a hand to lift her face and lower his mouth to hers. Gently he savored her mouth tasting sweetness as she parted her lips.

Sarra only knew one way to kiss this man, giving herself up fully to the sheer intensity of feeling that surged through her from the electric touch of his mouth on hers. She slid her arms up around his neck and pulled him closer, loving the flavor of him. It was the second time they had kissed, and it wasn't what she had expected. The other kiss had been stunning, high voltage, filled with fire. This was different; it was everything gentle, pure sweetness. Intoxicating. Currents rippled along every nerve. She swayed, weak-kneed, against him, nothing else existed except Jarrett. She had a sudden, nearly overpowering, urge to rip off his clothes and attack him right there on the floor. She pulled back instead and stared into his eyes. She could see his desire reflected there, felt it in his body's response against her. No other man had ever set her insides quivering like this. No other man had ever made her feel weak and delicious all over. It was all so strange, so new.

Was this what real love was like, a burning hunger to be consumed into the very essence of another person? If so, she would gladly surrender to this great need inside her which only Jarrett could satisfy.

Jarrett shuddered from the pleasure of the kiss. It was as he knew it would be, powerful, mind-bending. It was enough to make him forget for the moment that someone was out to kill her. He did not try to hide his desire. He wanted her to realize the effect she had on him. He wanted her to share his need and welcome her own, visible in the glitter of her eyes. He could see that she had never known what lovemaking could be like with the right kind of man. He had to show her that his feelings were not based on lust alone. God yes, he was filled with lust for her, but his feelings were so much more. He wanted her and needed her to complete him, and the physical was only part of it. He had loved her since the moment she had climbed those icy steps and fallen into his arms, and this time, he would proceed with due care, because he wasn't going to lose her again.

He moved a hand to caress her cheek and smile wryly. "It's bad timing, isn't it? At least all this will give us a chance to get to know each other. Hopefully, you won't run away from me this time."

Looking up at him, her eyes deep pools, Sarra shook her head. "No Jarrett, I'm not running from you anymore, or George, or anyone ever again." Her voice softened. "And no, that kiss wasn't bad timing. It was beautiful." His eyes were so vibrant, like blue flames, she thought as he looked down at her and brushed the hair back from her face.

"Beautiful," he repeated softly. "Yes, it was. You take my breath away when I look at you. I ache with wanting you." He drew back, releasing her. "But unfortunately, this is not the time or the place. I have to keep my head clear and you and Amanda safe."

She reached up and kissed him quickly on the lips. "Thank you for being the sensible one."

He skimmed his fingers along her cheek in another caress and dived in. "I love you, Sarra. I told you that before, and I still mean it." A little embarrassed by both the declaration and depth of his feelings, he added, "I just want you to know how I feel."

Sarra's eyes glowed with her response.

He smiled and set his hands on her shoulders. "There's no rush. We have time to get to know each other better." He inhaled deeply. "Now I think we should go and put Amanda to bed. Then tomorrow, you, Caruso and I need to go over that ledger book of Homer's. I think it ties in with my parents' death somehow, and I'd like to know how and why."

Sarra stared at his mouth as he spoke, wanting him to kiss her again, to feel the deliciousness of his lips and immerse herself in the man. He was glorious, strong, virile, capable and self-confident. He made her feel safe. But, protecting her also put him in harm's way, and that frightened her. "Okay," she nodded. "Okay," she said again, taking his hand.

Outside the sun had set and the muffled sounds of the night could be heard in the television room. Amanda was curled up next to Caruso on the long sofa, sound asleep with her arm around his waist. He sat comfortably motionless so as not to disturb her. As Jarrett and Sarra entered the room, he grinned, put a finger to his lips then pointed at the sleeping child. In a low whisper, he said, "Show me where you want her to sleep, and I'll carry her upstairs."

Sarra looked at Jarrett. "We'll have to explore. We haven't been upstairs yet." She was surprised when he replied.

"There are three bedrooms upstairs. Sarra can sleep in the master bedroom, and the little girl can occupy one down the hall. Caruso, you take the room next to Amanda. We'll set the alarm. I'll pull up a chair outside Sarra's bedroom."

Amanda's assigned bedroom was definitely a boy's room with football banners on the wall, a patterned bedspread and model airplanes suspended from the ceiling. A desk sat next to French doors leading to a small balcony. Caruso laid the child on the bed and then turned to test the doors to be sure they were locked.

Sarra didn't want to take the chance of waking Amanda, so she didn't bother to undress her. She covered her with a blanket, and quietly left the room, leaving the door open. The burly Irishman went into the adjoining room and stretched out on the bed fully clothed. He would hear any noise out of the ordinary. He was a light sleeper.

It was a lovely bedroom that Sarra and Jarrett entered, all cream satin and lace with lots of bed pillows accenting bold splashes of color from the peacock blue-green carpet. The same colors as the living room, only reversed, yet the color scheme, repeated in the paintings and vases of silk flowers, tied it all together and carried over to the adjoining master bathroom and a huge walk-in closet.

Like Caruso and Amanda, Sarra was too tired to undress, so she lay down across the bed while Jarrett checked the outside doors. When he grabbed a pillow from the bed and headed for the hallway, she stopped him. "You might as well stay in here. I would feel safer, and you would rest better." She patted the bed beside her. "Come and lie down."

Holding the pillow, he looked at her. "You know this isn't a good idea, don't you?"

"I'm sleeping in my clothes, Jarrett, and so can you. For tonight anyway," she added. "We're both too tired for anything else."

"Yeah, right!" he muttered and walked wearily across the room. He stretched out beside Sarra, put the pillow between them and tucked one arm under his head. "If you stay on your side of the bed you might be safe."

"Go to sleep, Jarrett," Sarra yawned, turned on her side, her back to him and closed her eyes, her mind racing with worry over Pearl Ann. Gene had promised to call and hadn't. Maybe he was tied up with other patients. Due to the late hour, she would make sure to call him the first thing in the morning. Moments later, her eyelids heavy, she drifted asleep.

Jarrett lay awake, far too conscious of her next to him, of each sound and movement she made in her sleep. Then he felt Sarra grow restless. He recognized when the nightmare began. She fought the air once, suddenly crying out. He moved closer, pulling her to him and held her to feel the torment that invaded her sleep. How long had she had nightmares? He wondered, appalled. Her entire life? Wasn't she even allowed peace during her rest? He whispered softly to her, "I love you, Sarra," repeating it in a song of sorts until, finally, she relaxed and settled against him, nestling into him as regular sleep claimed her.

CHAPTER TWENTY-TWO

June 12

Monday passed into Tuesday morning without incident. Sarra awoke still cradled in Jarrett's arms. He was snoring softly. She smiled at that and extracted herself carefully, leaving him asleep. She eased off the bed and paused to look down at him. Unconscious, he appeared so young, she thought and slipped out of the room.

By the time he came stumbling into the kitchen looking for her, hopping mad, she had breakfast ready.

"You are not to be out of my sight for one minute!" He stormed, looking delightfully rumpled.

Sarra beamed. "Well, I was awake, and you needed to sleep. Besides, nothing happened."

"That is not the point!" He fumed. "What if someone got past McCabe, broke into the house and was waiting for you down here?"

"Jarrett, no one did. I'm all right. Speaking of McCabe, go bring him in for breakfast."

"No. I don't want him off that boat," Jarrett huffed. "He has his cell phone with him. I'll call him and tell him I'm bringing it out to him. Will that make you happy?"

"Yes," she gave him a beautiful smile. "Then you can go wake up your partner and my daughter. I want to call Gene at the hospital and check on Pearl Ann. Now go." Intrigued by how much she was enjoying his display of temper, Sarra watched him stalk off.

Feeling like an idiot, Jarrett climbed the stairs.

Still, she was right. The night had passed without incident. Maybe this George character had left the country. No, he believed, that would be too easy. Pearl Ann wouldn't be in a hospital if George were planning to leave. He was out there somewhere, in the vicinity, waiting. The question was where and when would he strike again? On his way to Caruso's room, he dialed McCabe.

While Jarrett was upstairs, Sarra called Gene at home. He answered the phone after the first ring sounding groggy and half asleep. "Yes," he mumbled into the receiver.

"Gene, it's Sarra. I'm sorry to wake you, but I wanted to find out how Pearl Ann is doing."

"Oh. Hi Sis." She heard him moving about. His voice became clearer and not as sleepy. "Uggh! I'm awake now. What was the question?"

"How is Pearl Ann?"

"Hairline fracture with minor swelling. Slight concussion. She'll be fine, but I'm keeping her in the hospital for a few days. I want to be certain I didn't miss anything."

Sarra frowned. "You said you would call."

"I pretty much keeled over," Gene admitted. "How are you doing in the house?" he managed, half listening and rubbing his eyes. He glanced at the clock, seven-thirty. Four hours rest was not enough. Of Helen, there was still no sign. Another long day, he thought. A vacation was what he needed.

"Strange," she replied. Then, "Gene, did you ever

climb the trees in the yard?" she asked, realizing that she just acknowledged him as her brother.

Gene blinked eyes that did not want to be open. "You remembered something, didn't you?"

"Yes, but it doesn't make any sense. I'll tell you about it some other time. I put Amanda in your room last night. The one with all the airplanes, right?"

"That's it."

"I also called to say thank you for all your help, and for being there for me."

"That's what family's all about," he said gently. "You're my sister. We stand by each other." He paused for a moment, "Look, I have to get a shower and find Helen, then go to the hospital. I'll see Pearl Ann first thing, and I will call you. You stay safe. You tell that cop I'll have his head if he anything happens to you."

"Jarrett will keep me safe, Gene. You're as bad as he is. I have plenty of protection. Call me as soon as you can," she said.

"I will," Gene said. As he started to replace the receiver, he thought he heard a click. But when he listened, there was only silence.

Amanda came running into the kitchen and grabbed her mother around the waist. "What's for breakfast? I'm starved." Caruso and Jarrett followed close behind.

"As you always are. Toast and cold cereal, no hotcakes this morning," Sarra said, giving her daughter a quick kiss. "Go sit at the table, and I'll bring it to you."

"You're beautiful, and you cook?" Caruso stared at her in admiration. "If I go buy what you need, will you make pancakes for us tomorrow?"

Sarra had to grin back at him. The big man was almost drooling. "Certainly. I even have a special recipe Pearl Ann showed me. Now, would you please take a tray out to Officer McCabe for me?"

"That, I will do," he said, not bothering to correct her assumption that McCabe was a cop, and waited while she fixed a tray with a bowl of dry cereal, a banana, a pitcher of milk, hot buttered toast and a thermos of black coffee.

Jarrett made a beeline for the coffee pot. "Ask him if he wants to be relieved for a while. I can call in Parker if need be. Gabe can be counted on to lend a hand if we need him," he said.

Caruso nodded and picked up the tray. Throwing a big smile over his shoulder at Amanda, he said, "Now, sweetheart, make sure you eat all your breakfast because I plan on beating you at those video games we found last night."

The child giggled, ducked her head and glanced at her mother. "I didn't hurt anything, Mommy. They have all these TV games. I didn't think you'd mind if I showed Mr. Jones how to play."

"That's all right. Don't look so guilty. You haven't done anything wrong. Now finish your breakfast. I'm sure Mr. Jones will be eager to play as soon as he gets back."

Later, Sarra returned to the kitchen and busied herself cleaning the dishes and straightening the counters.

Jarrett stayed propped against the door frame sipping his coffee. He enjoyed watching her work. She glowed with energy this morning as she removed the dishes from the dishwasher and put them away, and then wiped down the counters. Every few seconds, she'd glance his way to catch him staring at her. Finally, she stopped bustling about.

"Okay, what gives? You keep staring at me," she demanded.

Jarrett grinned. "I love to watch a woman work."

"Rat!" She stepped closer to swing a dish towel at him.

"And I'm staring because you're beautiful and I adore you." He pulled her close, pinning her arms to her sides so she couldn't swing at him again. "Do you have any idea how much trouble I'd be in if my Captain knew how I felt about you? He'd pull me off this case faster than I can say, Big John."

"He can't do that. I need you here. I don't trust anyone else to protect us. Why do you think I've been so happy this morning?" She gazed up at him.

"We just have to be careful, that's all. When we're alone, that's one thing. Caruso knows how I feel about you, of course, but. . ."

Sarra nodded. "Whatever you say, Jarrett."

As the day wore on, Sarra found herself getting antsy. Lunch had consisted of cold sandwiches and dinner was going to be pizza, per Amanda and Caruso. She sat at the dinner table rifling through Homer's ledgers trying once more to make sense of them. Jarrett sat across from her, while in the TV room, Caruso tried to keep Amanda involved in yet another video game.

"All these numbers and letters? Homer was not a dummy," she mused aloud. "He didn't use banks, so I'm sure this has to be some sort of record of his transactions. He used to pore over these books when he didn't think I was around. Look at this page," she turned the book so Jarrett could have a better view.

He peered at the combination of letters and numbers and then dates with dollar amounts beside each date.

5672a77T2207 Dec 14 $50,000.00
1234B85M4516 Dec 14 completed Dec 21

She pointed to one heading. "Look at this date, December fourteenth. That was the week before your mother was murdered." She moved her finger to rest on the numbers and dates directly underneath. "Here. That's the date of your mother's death."

Jarrett frowned. "I know. I wish I knew what those other numbers meant. I keep thinking that they look like account numbers, 1234B85M4516. But account numbers don't contain letters."

"From what I knew of Homer, those numbers told him exactly who was paying him, and the dollar column shows how much," Sarra said, studying the page for a moment. "For what, though?"

There was one page with the number 4517LA82C3813 as the only heading, followed by one date and, this time, listing the year. Then they found the same date, but different years listed subsequently on page after page.

Jarrett's eyes widened suddenly. "This is a

blackmail ledger," he said. "It has to be. Look at this first date, March 30, 1990. Whoever this person was, they paid him each year on the same date. And this guy was paying through the nose. Wonder what goods Homer had on him?"

"Why would it have to be a man? Couldn't it have been a woman?" Sarra asked.

"Figure of speech. Either way, Homer James was collecting money, big time."

"What was that date again? Show me," Sarra said, and Jarrett showed her the number and the date. Her brow puckered. "That was barely three months after I came to live with him. Weird." She looked up from that particular page, sat back and stared at Jarrett for a second. "Why do I get the feeling that all that money has something to do with me?"

Intrigued, Jarrett looked down at the pages again. "I have no idea." He responded, slowly. "Do the numbers look familiar to you?"

Sarra shook her head, her features relaxing. "No, it's just a feeling. I remember shortly after Harry sold me, he came by to see Homer. Boy was Homer mad. We were living in a different apartment then, not the one on Central Park West.

"Homer made me hide in the bedroom. I was glad because I never wanted to see my fa," she caught herself, "Harry Gray again. I don't know what he wanted, but I remember that Homer shouted a lot." She paused, digging around in her mind for something deeply buried. "I remember Homer came into the bedroom, made a quick trip to the closet and went back into the living room. He must have been hiding this stuff in the closet even then. "Anyway, that was the last time I ever saw Harry. After that, we moved to the nicer apartment. That's why I feel that date has something to do with me."

Jarrett nodded and began to open one of the thick envelopes. Sarra shot a look toward the room where Amanda was still engrossed in a game with Caruso.

Seeing the direction of her glance, Jarrett set the envelope down. "No, I'm not taking them out of the envelope. I'm looking at the back to see if anything is written on them, hopefully, the same numbers from the ledger. If we can match up one of those numbers with one of these photographs and identify the man, maybe, just maybe, we can figure out what those numbers mean."

"All right, but you be careful." There was a threat in her low voice as she looked in her daughter's direction again.

Jarrett kept the photos face down and slipped one out about three inches, arching the paper to look inside at the back of the rest of the pictures. Across the middle of each, in ink, were indeed written the same type of numbers as in the ledger. "Bingo! The numbers are there." He shoved the photos back in the envelope, closed the flap and secured it. "Caruso!" he called out.

His partner patted Amanda's cheek as he stood up. "I won't be long, darlin'. You keep playing. Don't get too far ahead of me now." Entering the room and coming to the table, Caruso took a seat across from Sarra and glanced at her. "That child's a whiz at those games," he told her cheerfully. "She beats me every time."

Sarra gave him a pleased smile. "She's quick to

learn."

Still focused, Jarrett ignored the exchange. "CJ, you do the cryptograms in the paper all the time, don't you?" he asked.

Caruso shifted gears and tone. "That I do. And I must say they're getting too easy these days. It takes no time at all to work one. It's a matter of finding that first common letter."

Jarrett cut him off. "Explain how to do them some other time," he said and shoved the envelope across to Caruso, with a definitive nod. "Look inside and see if you can decipher what those numbers and letters might mean."

"Well, now, let's have a look." Caruso opened the envelope and peeked inside. He looked up abruptly. "Sarra, me girl, might you have a pen and paper handy so I can doodle a bit with these numbers?"

"I'll see if I can find something." Giving Jarrett a frown, she rose from her chair and went out of the room.

Caruso shifted his chair closer to Jarrett. "She's seen what's in these envelopes?" he half whispered. "Such bloody filth, it is."

"She's seen them," Jarrett cut him off tightly.

Caruso stared at him.

"Purely by accident," Jarrett added.

Caruso raised his eyebrows.

Sarra returned and handed him a writing tablet and a ballpoint pen.

"Thank you," Caruso said solemnly, taking the items from her. "Sarra, won't you go sit with Amanda. I'm going to be busy for a time. Have you?" he said and pointed toward the envelopes leaving his sentence unfinished.

"Yes. And that was too much." She said emphatically, glanced again at Jarrett, and went to join Amanda in the family room.

While Caruso played around with the envelope and its contents, Jarrett pulled out his cell phone and called Big John at his office. "Captain, this is Blackwell. I wanted to touch base with you this morning and request a few items."

"What do you need?"

"Caruso ordered some records faxed, or FedEx'd to us from New York regarding a corresponding case. Can you see that the file is sent over with the one on Angelique Corbett as soon as it arrives? Also, Sarra Gray gave me the name of a gallery in New York, The Lowell Gallery. Would you have the NYPD check it out for us? We need a report on the owner and his whereabouts. Any background information they can dig up will help as well." Jarrett knew that, as department head, if Big John put in the request, he would get quicker results.

"I'll send the file over with Jankowicz," Whitmore's curiosity was audible. "Anything else?"

"Not now. We're keeping a low profile here. McCabe is watching the back of the house. He's arranged for an unmarked patrol boat to cruise the Bayou. They'll anchor off the dock at night for added security. I'm considering calling Gabe Parker and have him keep surveillance at the front of the house. With CJ and me inside, that will make six or seven of us, depending on how many we have at the back of the boats."

The silence lingered before Whitmore finally said, "I hope you catch this killer soon," he grumbled, and then asked, "Jarrett, what's happening on the Poole case?"

"Dr. Corbett was notified and will tell his wife and."

Whitmore cut him off. "The murders look like they're tied together."

"I think so too," Jarrett agreed. "I don't know how yet, but I intend to find out." He had no doubts that Thelma Joan Poole was killed to shut her up because she knew something. The Captain probably felt the same way.

Whitmore sighed. "If you need it, order it. Hang the cost! I'll back you."

Sarra and Amanda spent the rest of the afternoon watching television while Jarrett and Caruso stayed at the dining room table trying to break Homer's coded ledger.

Around one in the afternoon, and then again at three, Sarra called the hospital to check on Pearl Ann. The first time, she talked to a nurse in ICU to learn that Pearl Ann was now stable and improving. The second time, she spoke with Gene, who told her he still hadn't been able to locate his wife.

She hated not being able to go to the hospital to visit but knew it wasn't safe. Safe? What was safe? She wondered. For that matter, would Jarrett be able to keep her safe from George? George was cold, evil, and devious. He had slipped in on Homer without his knowledge. Could he do the same here, even with all these men to protect her? Suddenly, a thought struck her. How had George known beforehand that she would be going to that particular party, in that limo, on that night?

Stunned, she realized that it was a question she had never asked before. She left Amanda watching a movie and joined the two men at the table in the dining room.

"Jarrett," she said, "something just dawned on me. How did George know I was going to that party?"

Clearly preoccupied, he looked up and considered the question. "Because, George arranged for you to be sent to Long Island, that's how," he said. "George set the whole thing up. My question is why?" As Sarra raised her eyebrows, he rubbed his eyes. "I'm getting cross-eyed from staring at these wretched numbers for so long! I need a break." Caruso didn't even glance up as Jarrett stood and stretched his back. At the same instant, the front doorbell rang. Jarrett swiveled and smoothly reached behind his back. A revolver appeared in his hand.

Seeing the gun, Sarra started visibly, her eyes going wide.

All business, Jarrett gave a brisk nod. "Stay put while I check the door. Caruso, get the child." Having risen from his seat almost at the same moment, Caruso rushed into the other room, scooped up Amanda and carried her back to set her down beside Sarra. He then positioned himself in front of them while Jarrett went to the door.

They all exhaled when Jarrett called out. "Everything is fine. It's Jankowicz."

Wiping the sweat from his round face with a damp handkerchief, a sullen, heavy-set man in a wrinkled tan suit followed Jarrett into the dining room and handed him a thick manila folder and a Fed-X package. "Big John sent these over," he said roughly, running his fingers through his thinning hair. "Anything else I can do for you?" he growled, his hostility evident.

"You got a problem Jankowicz?" Jarrett eyed the man coldly.

Jankowicz glared back. "This was supposed to be my case. Guess I don't like that the old man took it away from me." He waved the hand holding the handkerchief at Sarra and Amanda. "Hell, I'm too busy to be babysitting anyway!"

"Watch it!" Jarrett glanced toward Amanda hovering with Sarra and Caruso near the kitchen doorway.

The other man hesitated, then gave an apologetic nod toward Sarra. "Sorry, Miss. I meant no disrespect," he said gruffly.

"Apology accepted," Sarra said, then ushered Amanda back to the TV room to get her child out of the way.

Caruso stepped toward the thickset man, "Jankowicz, can you stick around?"

"Yeah. Sure. But not for long," Jankowicz said reluctantly.

"Long enough for me to pick up a change of clothes for myself and Jarrett," Caruso told him. "We'll be getting a bit ripe by this evening." A big grin spread across the big man's face. "I don't want my little charge to wrinkle her nose at me."

Jankowicz gave him a strange look. "I'll give you an hour. That's all I can spare."

Tossing his house keys to Caruso, Jarrett said,

"You'd better bring enough clothes for two or three days. Make it casual, we're supposed to look like visitors, remember, the family type."

"I'll make it quick," Caruso said and slipped the keys in his pocket. "Do you want me to bring Chance?"

Jarrett thought about the expensive cream colored carpet and shook his head. "Better not. Let him out, feed and water him and tell my next door neighbor, Mrs. Dolly, that I'll be gone for a few days. She'll take care of him for me."

"Will do," Caruso said and was out of the door and on his way to his car before Jarrett had a chance to add anything.

Jankowicz stayed, planting himself in a recliner, while Amanda watched television nearby. Surreptitiously, he watched as well but did not attempt any further conversation.

In the other room, Sarra and Jarrett continued to pore over the ledgers.

"Well, this is definitely not anything like a cryptogram. Caruso established that. Trying to make letters out of the numbers and vice versa doesn't work." The frustration Jarrett was feeling showed in the set of his jaw and the way he tapped the pen on the table. "I can't explain why, but I feel this ledger holds a lot of information that will help us. I think we need to look at it differently."

He reached and picked up the Fed-X package and ripped it open. He had intended to wait until Caruso came back, but needed to change gears.

This was a packet he really didn't want to review, he thought, feeling the old wounds becoming tender again.

"Maybe we're making it more difficult than it is," Sarra said, without looking up. "Homer wasn't stupid, but he didn't have the brains to make up a complicated code to hide all his dealings." She picked up the pen Caruso had left on the table. "Let's take out all the letters and see what we have." She wrote down one line of numbers without the letters and stared at them in disgust. "That leaves ten numbers which don't mean squat to me."

Jarrett watched her for a moment. "Why don't we both take a break?" he said. "I want to go through the file on my parents, and I need your help."

Sarra stared back at him. "Shouldn't you wait for Caruso?" she said, adding, "I don't want to look at that file, Jarrett."

"You don't have to, I do. All you have to do is remember as much about that night as you can."

"I've already told you everything."

"No, there has to be more, something else tucked away in your memory. Something that you might not have considered important. So please tell it to me again."

He had on what she now thought of as his cop face, withdrawn and impersonal. Sarra stiffened, resisting. "You're going to make me relive all that, aren't you?" God, she didn't want to do this.

He nodded. "I need to know everything. All the details. Don't try to spare me. My father told me he had sex with you. He thought he was the one who raped you."

Her face flamed. She glanced through to the other

room at Amanda. "My daughter knows nothing about her father," she gritted out softly. "She thinks he was killed before we got married."

"He may well have been," Jarrett said bitterly in a low voice.

In a whisper, Sarra snapped back. "You don't know that Amanda is the result of your father and me."

Jarrett finished it. "Your daughter could be my sister."

"No!"

"There is that possibility. George raped you, yes. But you were also intimate with my father the same evening. The only sure proof, one way or the other, is through DNA testing."

"No way!" Sarra shook her head and glanced into the family room to see if Amada was listening. The child was focused on the television. She turned back to Jarrett and sliced the air with her hand. "You can forget it. I will never subject my child to being tested to determine her paternity. Amanda is my child! That and only that matters!" She exhaled violently. "If you value me, as you claim, if you value how we feel about each other, don't ever broach that subject again!"

Jarrett held his hands up in surrender. "I won't mention it again, Sarra. Besides, it hardly matters now. Nor is it the point. I do not doubt that I will love your child," he emphasized, "as if she were my own."

Sarra stared at him, slowly relaxing. "Okay," she conceded.

Jarrett had to regroup. "Let's start from the

beginning. What happened after you ran from the house?"

"I got into the limo, and we drove back to town."

"What do you mean, we?" Jarrett started jotting notes on the paper. "As close as you can, give me every detail of who, what and when went on after you climbed into that limo."

"Good grief, Jarrett! How do you expect me to remember the exact details of something that happened over eleven years ago?" Sarra protested, folding her arms across her chest glaring at him.

"What I'm asking is not as hard as you think." He tapped his forehead. "It's all stored in your memory. All we have to do is unlock the door."

"All right," she growled wearily. "I'll try."

"First, take a couple of deep breaths." He waited while she did so. "Now, close your eyes and visualize that night." Jarrett lowered his voice, keeping the tone even and relaxed. "Remember how cold it gets in New York in December. It was snowing, and the wind was bitter. You run from the house, your dress is torn, you climb into the car, then what happened?"

It all came roaring back, a collage of details she had no wish to pull out of the blurred quagmire of that abominable night. "The man who had been taking the pictures was just getting into the car when I got there. He threw my coat over me. I was shivering, I was so scared. And, I hurt. I don't remember the cold. Then George was there. I sat facing the two of them in the limo. He slapped me when I called him a bastard." She reflexively rubbed the scar on her upper left breast from the old cigarette burn. "He burned me with his cigarette, told me to say nothing. All I wanted was to get back to Homer."

Jarrett interrupted very quietly, "Where exactly was George when you got into the limo?"

She stared at him blankly for a moment. "In the car," she began, her brow furrowing in concentration, her eye half closed. "No. No," she frowned. "He got into the car just before we went out the gate." She opened her eyes. It all came out in jerky, staccato phrases. Details she had blurred together in her mind to smother them, now jumped into focus one by one. "I could hardly move. I hurt all over. Mr. Blackwell collapsed on top of me. He had passed out or something. The photographer guy kept flashing, more pictures. George wasn't there. I got him off me. The photographer guy said something and then left. All I could think of was that George wasn't there and I had to get away. So I ran for the car," her voice died away.

Recovering somewhat, Sarra watched Jarrett make another notation, then open the folder in front of him. "You believe he killed your mother, don't you?" she whispered.

Jarrett began sifting through the reports that filled the folder. "Yes," he said without looking up. He found his mother's autopsy report and reading quickly, paled in sickened disbelief as he learned things he had not known before.

His mother had been savagely assaulted. There had not been a mark on her face that he could remember. Just the strangulation marks around her neck. Her torso, he now learned, had been covered with welts and bruises.

She had repeatedly been struck in the stomach and ribs, several of which had been broken, and sexually assaulted, as well as slowly strangled. He had always known about the listed cause of death by strangulation. Why had he never been informed about the rest of it? "My God," he whispered, both stunned and appalled. "Why were we never told about this?"

Also enclosed were the results of blood tests and various hair samples taken from different parts of his mother's and his father's bodies. There were hairs found on his mother that did not match his father's, yet that information had not been used to clear his father of the crime. All the evidence had been discounted, as his father had taken his own life too quickly. That fact had convinced the police of his father's guilt.

Distressed, Jarrett sat back and continued to stare at the papers in his hand. "Yes. George did it," he repeated.

Had Lawrence seen this report? Jarrett doubted it. Otherwise, his father would never have been charged. When had it been typed and filed? He checked the date. Too late to save his father, the day of the report was December the twenty-ninth, the same day his father had committed suicide.

Sarra watched the intense play of emotions cross Jarrett's ashen face as he read several sheets of paper from the folder. Disbelief and shock most of all were reflected in his eyes. Sarra didn't move when he finally looked at her.

"It says here that my mother was sexually assaulted and was damaged inside," he said awkwardly. He shook his head, "My father would never hurt my mother at all, let alone like that. They were devoted to each other. Besides, my father was a kind man who never hurt anyone." He picked up one of the documents to flap it briefly. "This says my father tested positive for drugs. He didn't touch drugs."

Sarra said nothing, still coping with details she had buried, one of which recalled that Blackwell had been high on something.

"Why was all this done to my parents?" Jarrett asked helplessly. "Perhaps my father didn't kill himself. Who's to say someone didn't slip into his study and shoot him?" He flung the papers down and yelled, "WHY! Who hated us so much as to plan out and execute this kind of destruction of my family?"

Sarra swallowed hard. "George would be vicious enough," she said. "Remember? I told you that your father knew George."

Jarrett stared at her, then reached for her hand to clasp it desperately. He frowned suddenly. "G.T. Lowell!" he exclaimed. "I remember. That's who my dad said introduced you to him. Lowell. It has to be the same man who owns the art gallery. Why?"

"I don't know, Jarrett," Sarra said, gripping his hand in sympathy. She could feel his pain. Both his parents lost to such ugly violence. Then it hit her. Her mother had been murdered, and she had only recently learned that her father had died in a car crash. True, she did not remember her parents except in vague, dreamlike scraps. And Jarrett was sitting there in agony.

"Jarrett, going through that folder is not helping

you. If anything, it's making things worse. I think you should let Caruso review that file. He can be more objective than you."

Jarrett slowly released Sarra's hand and, closing the folder, nodded meekly. "Yes. You're right. I'll let CJ do it." He rubbed his eyes, suddenly drained. God, he was tired, he thought and glanced at his watch. It was barely five-thirty. "He should be back any time."

As if on cue, Jankowicz rose from his place in front of the television and came into the dining room. "Okay, Blackwell, it's been over an hour. I have to check into the office if you want me to stay longer."

"Thanks," Jarrett nodded. "CJ is due back any minute." At that same moment, Caruso came bursting through the front door, a suitcase in each hand. He was followed by Gene Corbett.

Caruso nodded to the doctor and glanced at Sarra. "Your brother is here. I'm taking the suitcases upstairs," he announced and disappeared again. He thumped away up the stairs, taking them two at a time.

Gene appeared at the door to the kitchen to see Sarra and Jarrett seated at the dining room table, a heap of files and papers between them. "Sarra, I just stopped by to tell you that I'm filing for divorce." He held up a hand as Sarra's eyes widened. "It has nothing to do with you. I never should have married the witch in the first place!" He smiled briefly, a sketch of his own relief at the decision. "I have to find her, though. I feel I should be the one to tell her that her mother is dead. Trouble is, I've no idea where she's gone off to. By the way, Arthur called, the fingerprints are a match." He smiled fully then, half provoked into it by Sarra's round-eyed gape.

"I've got to get back to the hospital." He waved toward the untidy pile of paperwork. "I'm glad to see you two are having fun!"

"Not really!" Sarra countered sharply as he spun on a heel and headed out of the front door.

CHAPTER TWENTY-THREE

"Where the hell have you been?" Gene demanded, rather startled when Helen came through the front door. "I've been calling all over creation trying to find you."

"I drove to Ellington to do some shopping," Helen lied.

Gene exhaled carefully. "You should have let me know."

"I didn't think you cared."

"That's not the point, Helen. Besides, there's something you need to know. Your mother is dead."

"Dead?" Helen's surprise was audible.

"It's a terrible shock, I know, but she was," Gene didn't get a chance to finish before she burst out.

"Good!" Helen interrupted, hissing. "At last the old hag is finally out of my life!"

Killed, Gene finished silently, shocked and revolted by the venom he could hear. "My God! Helen, she was your mother!" he said.

"So what? She never gave a hoot about me, you moron. All my life she used me. First, with those damn kids she adopted out then with her male clients. I'm glad. Now I'm free of her."

Gene didn't want to hear the rest of it, then sighed and said. "Shut up, Helen! I want you to pack your shit and get out of the house today," he clipped out. "I am filing for a divorce. Remember, I've already warned you that if you mess with me, you won't get a penny. I'll see that it happens too!" Gene felt sick to his stomach. How had he lived with and loved this woman for over three years and never suspected that she was as cold and mercenary as she had turned out to be? What kind of chump had he become?

A big one, he thought in disgust, having just discovered she had withdrawn thousands from their joint savings account a couple of days ago. He had promptly moved the remaining funds into a new account. It was something, at least, to realize that it was to his advantage the marriage had been under five years.

"You son of a bitch!" Helen stormed, picked up a blue vase and threw it across the room. It hit the wall and left an indentation in the plaster. She knew how to stop Gene. She scooped up her purse, hotel keys, and car keys then hurried out of the house. Everything else she had come back to collect was already in the car. The houseboy had wisely made himself scarce.

Helen slammed the door to the BMW and settled herself behind the steering wheel. Her hands suddenly shaking, she fumbled with the key ring and finally inserted the right key in the ignition. Once the engine began to purr, she punched the AC button, and a blast of frigid air fought with the hot, stuffy interior.

"Dead?" Helen whispered aloud, absorbing it fully, shocked anyway because she felt like a puppet whose strings had suddenly been cut. Her mother had ruled her life, and now, she was free, Helen realized. Free! The old whore was gone. It felt strange.

She was furious with her husband. Hell, no! How dare he threaten her! No way would she lose this house! This house, and the one in Driftwood. They belonged to her. She would see that bitch sister dead before she would let him sign over a Quit Claim Deed to her.

"Damn him," Helen fumed aloud. "Thinks he's so smart! I'll show him!" She shifted into reverse and backed out of the driveway. It was almost eight p.m. She pushed the accelerator hard, and the car roared down the street toward downtown. "That son of a bitch doesn't know who he's dealing with!" she muttered.

She had been busy the last couple of days since she had left her mother's. She had found a nice, obscure motel, cashed out most of the joint savings account. Now she was faced with a problem. She wasn't sure how to handle Gene yet. Her mother was supposed to have taken care of that little detail, but had managed to screw that up. Surely she could find someone to handle the job. In today's economic situation, some people were willing to do anything for the right price. She'd make a beautiful grieving widow, she thought, patting her hair into place.

The people they socialized with knew her as a loving wife. She'd made sure she had cultivated that image over the last three years. All those horrible committees, all the tedious fundraisers, plus the miserable professional parties she had been required to attend. She had performed through it all for one reason. To show everyone what a kind, loving person Gene had married. Hell, he'd fallen for it easily enough, just like the rest of them. He'd been a piece of cake to seduce.

God, she couldn't stand him. She needed a man, not some neurotic wuss blinded by guilt and worshipping a long lost sister. Sucker! This Sarra Gray must have been planning this for a long time. Well, she was in for a surprise. She'd put a stop to her ever getting her hands on that trust fund. And soon, very soon.

Helen had worked hard to develop business skills only to find herself trapped by her mother and festering in dead-end jobs that didn't pay diddlysquat. She had no intentions of going back to more of the same, especially now that dearest Mommy was out of the picture.

The day Gene Corbett had walked into Arthur Craswell's office, she had recognized an opportunity to get what she wanted. He had reeked of money and position. He also had been an easy mark. Three months later, they had been married.

She'd have to get rid of Gene's fake sister first. Then Gene would inherit all that lovely money he was so determined to give away and, once he was out of the way, she could live the way she was meant to live.

Thinking about it was relaxing, Helen found as she whipped the BMW through the evening traffic, not caring how close she came to cutting off other cars. Now, it was vital that she get to Arthur's office and get Gene's will from the safe.

She parked a block away and walked the short distance to the attorney's building. Without hesitation, she removed the duplicate office keys she had made long ago from her purse and opened the door. She slipped inside, locking it behind her.

The interior reception area was dim, but there was enough daylight left to show the security alarm was still turned off. That puzzled Helen. Arthur was very careful about securing his office. Concerned, she rechecked the door, not wanting unexpected company.

Her footsteps silent on the thick plush carpet, she hurried toward Arthur's inner office, then came to a sudden stop near the door. A crack of light showed as a thin streak up the side of the door and under the frame. Someone was in there, she realized, even as she heard the muffled voices.

Ready to bolt, and ever so gently, using one finger, she pushed on the door. There was the faintest squeaking of hinges. She froze, hearing two voices, but still muffled. Again, she pushed, fractionally. The conversation continued, but now she could make out scraps of it.

"I followed her. . . they're at. . .saw. . .and he's there, too."

"The son. . . ?

". . . do them all. . ."

". . . make sure. . ."

Helen didn't recognize either voice. Where was Arthur? Who were these men in the attorney's office she wondered, recognizing the vernacular 'do them'? Who were they planning to kill? Why? She caught another something that included 'Caymans' and now, eager to get out of the office without being seen, Helen pulled gently against the door to close it.

She'd have to come back later, she thought and, slipping away, she tiptoed toward the front door. She almost made it. A faint blur flipped in front of her face. There was no time to scream as the blur became a noose around her neck, cutting off her air. Helen flailed wildly, stunned to realize that someone was actually trying to . . .

And then everything disappeared.

CHAPTER TWENTY-FOUR

At the Driftwood house, a mellower Jankowicz was ready to leave. Jarrett had arranged for him and his partner, Hershey, to return around eleven p.m. They were to park down the street beyond the impossible driveway all night and watch the front entrance. Even with the late afternoon passing quietly, time weighed heavily on each of them. Dinner was a silent affair. Even Amanda was withdrawn and had little to say. There was nothing left to do but to settle in and watch a movie on television. Still restless, Sarra prowled about and peeked out of the back patio window in the family room. She could see nothing but a faint light at the end of the dock. Other than that, the rest of the yard appeared a solid, impenetrable wall of night blackened foliage. The thick darkness sent apprehension shivering through her. The sound of Caruso's laugh at something on TV was jarring. The night seemed too quiet. Outside, not even the sound of insects broke the stillness.

Sarra gave up and retreated to her seat on the sofa next to Amanda to watch the movie, but it was impossible to concentrate. Things were going too well. Pearl Ann was healing, Jarrett and Caruso and company were keeping them safe. There was not a ripple in their surface of safety, and that frightened the daylights out of her.

She knew George was out there somewhere, and it scared her to pieces wondering what he was planning. Jarrett was right, she thought. It was revenge on

George's mind. God help them when he came.

After the movie, they all climbed the stairs. Caruso carried Amanda to her bed and went to his own, leaving both their doors open. Sarra, Jarrett, and Caruso decided to sleep in workout shorts and shirts for comfort.

As Sarra climbed into bed, Jarrett hovered at the foot of it, gazing at her, as if trying to come to a decision. "You remember I proposed to you that night, and you ran away from me?" he asked.

Afraid of what was coming, she answered, "Yes."

"Well, tonight, you can't run away from me, and I know all about you. So, once again, I'm asking you to marry me. Will you say yes?"

"Can't we talk about it after all this is over?"

"No, I want an answer tonight. I want to dream about our future together and to do that, I need a definite yes or no."

Sarra was hesitant but forced herself to answer. "I'm scared, Jarrett. You know the type of men in my life; they were hardly the devoted and commitment kind."

"I don't care. That's done with." Jarrett made a dismissive gesture. "You think you don't know what love is, Sarra. Don't you think it's time you found out?" His face was earnest and curiously young. "I have loved you ever since that night. I will continue to love you even if you say 'no' to my proposal. It's a condition I'm stuck with." A wry look crossed his face. "You know, there's a sort of umbilical connection between us. I want the chance to show you how good a real relationship between a man and a woman can be. Give me that chance."

Umbilical? Interesting choice of word, Sarra thought. Apt, though. She could feel it in her insides, a visceral certainty that had been there ever since they had first met. She did love Jarrett. Of that, she was sure. They each deserved a chance for happiness too. And then she thought of all Pearl Ann had taught her. Taking a deep breath as though about to dive underwater, she said, "Yes, Jarrett, I'll marry you."

He gave her a big, radiant grin, catapulted himself onto the bed and gathered her in his arms. "Sweet dreams tonight! We're limited here, but once I get you alone, oh Baby, I have such wonderful plans for us!" He kissed her long and hard, melding passion and joy, then nestled into the bedding to gently cuddle her in his arms. "Go to sleep, love. This mess will be over soon, and we can begin our life together."

It seemed to Sarra that she had just closed her eyes when a hand clamped over her mouth jerked her into full wakefulness. Jarrett's voice whispering fiercely into her ear was all that kept her from going ballistic.

"I heard something," he hissed. "Don't make a sound. Stay here, I'm going to make sure Caruso is up." He eased out of bed and grabbed his gun from the nightstand.

Only the dim light from the hall bathroom diluted the darkness. Frozen, Sarra watched the faint shadow of Jarrett move across the floor, then slip out of the bedroom.

With his back against the wall, Jarrett stole silently down the hallway to Caruso's room. The big Irishman was already at his open doorway.

He pointed toward the other bedroom and

mouthed to Jarrett, "The kid's room." They dropped to a crouch and peered around the door. Amanda was sleeping soundly. Caruso crawled through the entrance to the side of the bed.

Jarrett, gun ready, stood to the side of the doorway, his nerves on edge, ready for anything that could go wrong before CJ could get the little girl out safely.

That would finish him and Sarra if he let something happen to her daughter. How did they get past Jankowicz and Hershey? What had happened to the security alarm? And where in the hell was McCabe?

Caruso hurriedly scooped Amanda up in his arms, holding her mouth to keep her quiet. He had barely whisked her out of the room when the balcony door creaked and slowly began to open. The alarms going off to made an ear-splitting din.

With Caruso and Amanda now out of the way, Jarrett settled back into the shadows and waited. He hadn't been able to see the intruder in the pitch black interior of the room. Ready to pounce, he wanted him to come through the door.

He caught the shuffling whispered sounds of footsteps on the carpet. His gut told Jarrett it was Sarra's monster, George. When Jarrett judged the man was near the foot of the bed, he bent his free arm around the door frame and slid his hand along the wall reaching for the light switch. There was a sudden flash of light, a pop, and a bullet whizzed past the door frame, narrowly missing his head.

Jarrett dropped to the floor and yelled, "Police!" as he aimed his pistol. A second shot ripped into the floor beside him. He returned the fire. There was a loud grunt, and the assailant stumbled back toward the balcony.

There was a crash of shattering glass and a distant thud as if someone had landed on the ground outside. Jarrett got to his feet and called out, "He's gone over the balcony! CJ, stay here! Take care of Sarra and Amanda."

He bolted down the stairs and out of the front door, cursing when he stubbed his toe on the curb in the dark. Almost tripping, he ignored the pain and ran around the side of the house. Suddenly, the backyard was flooded with light, and nearby shouts told him McCabe was racing down the dock to block any escape in that direction.

As he charged around the dark foliage obscured corner, Jarrett was unaware of the shadow that glided silently from behind the thick black trunk of the biggest big oak tree and paused at the open front door.

Galvanized by the shrill whine of the alarm and the sound of gunshots, Sarra catapulted out of bed and froze. She began flipping on lights as soon as she heard Jarrett thump down the stairs. In the distance, the crackle of McCabe's radio could be heard, and there were shouts between several men. Thinking only of Amanda, she paused at the door, then slipped into the hall to stop suddenly at the top of the stairs as a hand clamped onto her shoulder.

"Hold it!" Caruso said, grabbing her as he pushed Amanda into his room and shut the door. Then he released Sarra and started to say, "Stay here." He never finished. There was a sudden, loud pop, and he twisted around to fall backward onto the landing with a hard thump.

Sarra screamed, then froze at the sight of the figure in dark clothing and a ski mask halfway up the stairs. He was holding a gun pointed directly at her.

"Quiet!" the intruder snarled. "Get down here. Now!"

Sarra blinked, still frozen like a hypnotized rabbit, then heard the click of the door latch and a wavering, "Mom?"

"Now!" the masked intruder rasped. There was another pop, and something whizzed past her ear to smash into the wood behind her.

Amanda screamed.

"No!"

Pure reflex sent Sarra tearing down the stairs directly in front of the raised gun, intending to smash into it, into him. But the man dodged forward and to one side. A black arm came up and locked around her neck, throwing her off balance. Then she felt the gun bore ram into the side of her head. "Not a sound," he hissed, and then he hauled her down the rest of the stairs and out through the front door.

He wouldn't hesitate to kill her, Sarra knew. Off balance and half choked, she struggled anyway as her abductor dragged her across an uneven, motley patch of light from the house and the black shadowed swatches of front yard, behind a huge tree, and through a narrow gap in a large hedge. Where were the men Jarrett had posted out front? Sarra wondered frantically, clawing at branches to kick out wildly. An instant later something smashed into the back of her head, and everything went black.

Jarrett entered the house to switch off the alarm, eager to tell Sarra that the intruder was dead, only to hear the muffled sound of crying echo down the stairs. He whipped out his gun again and glided quickly upwards, taking the stairs two at a time, to come to a shocked halt at the top.

An ashen-faced and sobbing Amanda was clinging to Caruso who was sprawled across the landing, a bloody streak creasing the right side of his forehead. He was moaning and twitching, but coming around.

"He had a gun," Amanda got out, hiccoughing around the words as Caruso groaned and levered himself up onto one elbow.

Jarrett froze. "Who?"

Amanda straightened as Caruso sat up, and rested a hand on her shoulder. "The black man with the gun," she said through gulps of air. "He took Mommy."

"Black mask, silencer, I saw. . ." Caruso muttered, got to one knee and wobbled.

Jarrett didn't wait. He spun around and plunged down the stairs, yelling for McCabe and the other men. A frantic search of the grounds and street and offered nothing, until they found the still figures of Jankowicz and Hershey slumped in their car. Both men were dead from a gunshot to the head.

Raw, infuriated and jumpy, Jarrett returned to the house, waking up Big John with his call, and then brusquely reporting what had happened. He paced restlessly around the dining room table while, upstairs, Caruso did his best to calm a terrified Amanda.

Ten minutes later, there was a callback. Jarrett clamped the phone to his ear and barked a harsh "Yeah?" into the receiver. Listening intently, he planted himself on a chair in the dining room and scribbled furiously on the notepad left the table. At one point, he froze for a few seconds, his face, already haggard, going white with shock. He did not look up when Caruso came into the room.

"When can we expect the rest of the team?" he asked roughly. "Time is short." He nodded at the reply, turned off the phone and set it on the table.

"CJ," Jarrett bit out looking up. "Jankowicz and Hershey are dead. Backup is on its way." And in the distance, the sound of sirens could be heard, growing closer with each second. His partner, clutching a bloody washcloth to his head, sat down heavily. "That was Whitmore. You need to go to the hospital."

"I'm fine," Caruso growled. "The little girl's in there." He waved a hand toward the family room. "Couldn't leave her up there by herself."

His face still drawn, Jarrett nodded and glanced over at Amanda curled up on the sofa staring in their direction. "We got a report from New York PD on George," he said, fighting for control, terrified for Sarra.

"Well?" Caruso demanded, pressing the bloody cloth harder to stop the bleeding.

Time, no time to waste, Jarrett thought and collected himself to summarize in rapid minimal phrases. "NYPD went to the Lowell Gallery. They tracked down the former manager, one Margaret Newgate. Per Ms. Newgate, George Lowell could be here in Half Moon Bay. Apparently, he visits here frequently. Relatives," Jarrett swallowed and continued. "DMV traced him through his driver's license. He was born in Portland, Maine. Get this, Caruso. He's a twin."

Caruso stared. "You mean there are two of those bastards on the loose?"

Jarrett got up from his chair to prowl restlessly. "Fraternal, not identical. It gets complicated. There was a big scandal back in 1956. NYPD tracked down a couple of people who remembered, although it was all hushed up at the time. The boys' mother was one Gabriella Pasquale. She was a kid, fourteen, fifteen, maybe, worked as a maid for, get this, Ada Thornton!" The name came out in an uneven rasp. Watching, Caruso frowned. "She was raped by her employer's husband, one Lowell C. Thornton." Jarrett glanced down at his notes, hardly seeing them. He didn't need to.

"The girl turned up pregnant, with twins, no less. Thornton paid off the girl's father so he wouldn't press charges. There was no abortion, but, Thornton's wife got rid of the girl as soon as she found out. The girl stayed in the area and had the boys." Jarrett's voice roughened. "Apparently, she was pretty abusive and, when they were about seven or eight, she dumped the boys on Thornton's doorstep. Ada Thornton wouldn't have them, and they were packed off to a succession of foster homes. They were in and out of trouble until, when they were fourteen, old men Thornton sent them to a military school."

Jarrett paused to scrape the fingers of both hands through his hair. "They settled down after that. Got college degrees." He continued unevenly. "One became a lawyer. The other went into business. They both left the area and disappeared." Jarrett stopped pacing to look at Caruso. "At the time they vanished, their mother's home was burned down. Her body was found outside of town. She had been beaten and strangled. The Portland Police couldn't prove anything, but the brothers were the prime suspects. But, they couldn't find them."

Jarrett paused, his eyes hollow. "Here's the clincher, Caruso," he said slowly. "Their names, George Thomas Lowell and Lewis Arthur Craswell. Their father was Lowell Craswell Thornton, my grandfather. These men are my uncles, CJ!"

"Jaysus H. Christ!" Caruso swore breathlessly, his eyes wide and round.

Just then, McCabe burst into the room. "The troops are here," he announced.

Sarra first became aware that she was lying on a bed, and secondly that she couldn't move, or lower her arms. She squirmed uncomfortably and opened her eyes to discover that her wrists were securely tied to something, a headboard and that her ankles were also bound. Panic slithered through her, and she blinked against the glare of a single light bulb in the ceiling of a small room. There was a regular creaking sound beside her, and she turned her head, trying to lift it a bit to see over her own extended upper arm. A man in black clothing sat beside the bed next to her rocking back and forth.

"You can scream if you like," he said pleasantly. "The room is quite soundproof."

Sarra gasped awkwardly. It was the attorney, Gene's attorney, Arthur Craswell.

Amanda, she thought with a surge of terror, then remembered, Caruso down, her daughter's scream behind her.

Behind her, yes, she had gotten in the way. Made sure she was out of the way.

Craswell leaned forward, his eyes glittering, face stark and eerie with shadows in the uneven light. "It didn't take you long to wake up," he smiled. "I've got you tied down quite securely. That big cop friend of yours is dead, you know. Good shot, if I say so myself." Sarra cringed as he got to his feet, the chair creaking, rocking as he left it. He turned and moved a few steps to the single window in the small, bare room. There was thick black material hanging from a curtain rod covering the window. He peered carefully out through a small gap in one side of the heavy drape. "Quite the madhouse over there," he said in the same cordial tone, dropping the material to return to the chair.

Sarra shuddered as he sat down again, fear a palpable, creature thing, trying to take over. The back of her head throbbed in time with it.

The rocking of the chair made spastic, repetitious creaking noises that only made it worse as he continued talking in the same hideously benign tones. "It's a shame to have to do this to Gene again, but. . . He's been such a good client. He never got over you being snatched away the first time, you know."

He's mad, Sarra thought. Stark, raving. "Me?" she half squeaked.

"Oh, it's not about you," and added as if an afterthought, "although, now it is, I suppose." He went on, rocking back and forth, looking at the gun he held, then set it down on the small table beside him, which she hadn't noticed before. "The first time, your kidnapping was a fluke. A mistake. Harry was on the lookout for a dark-haired little girl for a couple up North. He scooped you up right off the beach. Trouble was, you were a high profile kid. Didn't take kids like that, you see. Too many complications. I realized who you were, and the Corbett's were so well known. Couldn't let you go, of course, so, we kept you here in this room until it was safe to ship you out. Harry was stuck with you after that.

"Pity about your mother," he continued in the same, atrociously pleasant, confiding voice. "I really liked Angelique. She wasn't at all like ours." Something in his face shifted strangely. "George had to kill her, though."

Sarra swallowed knots. "George?" she got out hoarsely.

He nodded and frowned, lifting his hands to study the black leather gloves he wore as if had not been aware of them before. "Your mother shouldn't have come over to the house, you see."

Sarra listened, appalled and feeling half mad herself as he chattered on to describe how, on the day she had been stolen, Angelique Corbett had backed into his car and had seen Thelma and Harry with one of their kids in the back seat.

The chair kept creaking, rocking back and forth, back and forth.

How Angelique Corbett had come to his house a week later and brought up the business of car repairs. She had seen Thelma Poole and had mentioned an article in the newspaper about a missing child. She had been on the verge of making the connection. "She heard you screaming and wailing upstairs in the other room. The sedative had worn off." He shrugged. "So, of course, George had to kill her. Thelma hit her with an umbrella before she could get out of the house, then George finished things.

"He was right, you see. Angelique had just figured it out. He got rid of her, too. Got you out that night as well and gave you to Harry at the airport."

George, Sarra thought. George was responsible for the pain and mess of her entire life.

"George should be here by now," he said fretfully.

Now what? Jarrett thought desperately as, with both his and Caruso's flashlights beaming down on the intruder's body, he studied the corpse. McCabe and one other officer had been left in the house to guard and hopefully reassure Amanda while he and Caruso went to secure the scene. The men knew what they were doing, and seeing the bodies of Jankowicz and Hershey, both with gunshot wounds to the head, still sitting in their car parked just down the street from the driveway, was even more upsetting for their comrades. They were all seasoned cops. How had the two been persuaded to roll down their windows, and expose themselves, to be disposed of so quickly? And without a sound? The gun had to have had a silencer, of course.

Sarra, he thought, with a surge of terror. Near his feet, the intruder's body lay like a tumbled rag doll. Jarrett's bullet, amazingly, had caught him in the chest. Not fatally, but the man's backward fall from the tree-shaded balcony had finished him, breaking his neck. He watched as Caruso knelt and carefully removed the dead man's ski mask without changing his position to expose a face that was not young at all. Sarra's nemesis, George? Jarrett wondered. But there had been two of them. George?

George Thomas Lowell and?

"CJ?" he rasped as Caruso straightened. Then, unable to finish, he swung back around the house to go back inside. He reached for his cell and began punching in Captain Whitmore's number.

Her hands were going numb, Sarra realized vaguely. The loss of feeling was of relatively little importance compared to her defenselessness, and the abrasive pendulum rocking of the chair and the monologue of the lunatic swinging himself back and forth in it.

"George wants you, you see," he continued. "You've got something of his. You shouldn't have cleaned out that safe in New York. And now, you've gotten mixed up with that Blackwell boy. Who'd have thought he'd turn up here as a cop? We lost track of him.

He's our nephew, you know. The only one left. We got rid of the rest of them. Or, George did, mostly. Only fair." He kept fiddling with his black gloves. "I remember you, though. I took the pictures, not when George was fucking you, but after. George likes them young. He wants your girl, too. I told him you'd give us everything you took if we got your girl as well." He shook his head, something inside him began to change.

Was it possible to be more terrorized than she was already? Sarra wondered, feeling as if she was being twisted into nothing more than a relentless, endless scream.

"It's not like that for me, you see," he said, his tone altered, his face morphing. "I love George. Do anything for George. Couldn't let Mom hurt him. Not like she did me. Keeps doing. . . had to keep Arthur safe for George, too." His voice broke off abruptly, and one gloved hand shot forward to clamp over Sarra's mouth, very nearly covering her nostrils as well.

Sarra went even more rigid, then heard it too, a distant banging, like someone thumping on a door. A shout she couldn't make out filtering up through the window. Equally distant, a doorbell chimed. And then again.

Then, nothing.

"The old lady was asleep and didn't hear or see anything," the officer reported, pointing in the direction of the house on the left. "We tried the other one too. But there was no one home. The garage was open. No cars. There are some broken branches in a narrow gap in the hedge."

"This is my house, damn it!" came thundering through from the living room. "BLACKWELL!" reverberated into the dining room just as Gene Corbett, and one of the new police officers in tow, erupted into the room.

"It's all right," Jarrett told the officer. "He's Ms. Gray's brother."

"What's going on?" Gene demanded. "There are police cars and cops all over the place."

Jarrett flinched, barely noticing that Caruso moved to stand next to him. "There's been a break in. Two men. One's dead. The other took Sarra," he bit out. "They killed two of our men."

Gene Corbett went sheet white, groped for, then collapsed onto a chair. "Sarra? No."

"The child is safe," Caruso inserted with smoother professional equilibrium. "We're doing everything we can."

"No," Gene whispered again and stared up at Jarrett. "You're supposed to be protecting her."

"Yes!" Jarrett snarled. "Well, it turns out that this. . . George has a brother, Lewis, who lives in Half Moon Bay. We're in the process of tracking him down. We've got APB's out."

"How long will that take?" Gene interrupted. "Or, are you just going to sit here on your ass and wait?"

Jarrett ignored the last. "That's what the rest of the force is doing right now, Dr. Corbett. We have men out now looking for your attorney, Lewis Arthur

Craswell."

Gene started. "Lewis Arthur? Arthur Craswell? Arthur?" It came out in a stammer. "I've known him most of my life. Arthur wouldn't hurt Sarra. You have to be wrong. He wouldn't hurt a fly."

Jarrett shook his head. "I'm not wrong. We believe he helped kill his mother. Regardless. Sarra's. . . George is one George Thomas Lowell, and his brother happens to be Lewis Arthur Craswell."

"Gene, Lad," Caruso interrupted, "you know this man?"

Corbett blinked stupidly at him. "Yes, as I said, for most of my life." He pointed to the top of the uppermost sheet on the notepad, laying on the table in front of him where Sarra had written the ledger numbers, putting their letters in a separate column. "That's his phone number right there."

"Phone numbers? Jarrett grated.

Gene nodded. "Yes. Why don't you call him? He still lives right next door."

"They're fucking PHONE numbers!" Jarrett swore as he began to move. "Next door? CJ!"

CHAPTER TWENTY-FIVE

June 13

If it was possible, Sarra's skin crawled when Arthur Craswell removed his hand from her mouth and nose. She gulped air and cringed as he leaned further over her to finger her hair and frown strangely. A moment later, he got to his feet and over to the window to peer out through the gap in the drape.

"Gone," he murmured, pleased. "I knew they would be. Can't hear a thing up here."

It hit her then, a wallop of cold reason. Yes, they could. If she had heard the banging on the door, the chime of the doorbell, they would most definitely be able to hear, if it was loud enough. Sarra filled her lungs to scream. Then, the same cold, rational clarity reminded her that he had said, "Gone." That someone had to be close enough to hear, and that he had turned and was looking at her again, but differently. Hideously, and with menace. She exhaled carefully.

"Arthur keeps warning George, you see, about the young ones, but he's just like our dad. George saw dad fuck his girl, Vicki. Tried to have a go at her too. Got her in the end, though." He shifted, moving closer to sit down again and look at his gloves and fuss with them. "Don't like these. Can't feel anything." He frowned at her. "I told you to leave us alone."

Sarra swallowed. Something very sick was happening. Why was he referring to himself as Arthur? Wasn't he Arthur? "But, you're Arthur," she dared and wait.

"No!" he yelled. "I'm Lewis. Arthur's weak. I'm the one who had to protect us all these years." She shivered violently as he leaned forward to pull at her hair and shake his head.

"Told you. . ." he repeated venomously this time, jerking to his feet to strip off his gloves and drop them on the floor. "You're a dirty fucking whore, Mom. You can't have George. You can't have Arthur. I won't let you. I'll stop you this time. I can do it too. You can't touch me, remember. Can't. You want to, though." He jerked opened a shallow drawer in the side of the table and pulled out a knife and some surgical gloves.

They slipped across the lawn with practiced stealth, Jarrett, and Caruso, with Gene Corbett following slightly less graceful at their heels. It was Gene who showed them the old, narrow gap in the hedge near the street end of the lawn. Once through it, they moved quickly toward the house with its darkened windows, lights from next door making yellow toned scraps of illumination between the shadows. They noted the open, empty garage and slipped up the front steps. Caruso pulled something out of a pocket and bent to jimmy the lock.

Moments later, they were inside. Closing the door most of the way, Jarrett set a palm against Gene's chest and pressed him back, as he flipped on his flashlight with the other hand, to shake his head, telling the other man to stay put. Alert and flanking each other,

Jarrett and Caruso prowled silently from room to room, seeing glimpses of a plain, tasteful décor, everything immaculate, magazines even precisely fanned on the coffee table in the living room. Dining room. Kitchen. Then upstairs where three bedrooms and their associated bathrooms showed a similar pristine emptiness, the beds made with military precision. At the end of the upstairs hallway, they found a window and next to it, at right angles a doorway that opened into a large storage closet. They headed back downstairs and pulled a wide-eyed Gene Corbett with them out through the door. With a hand signal and an exchange of nods, Caruso started around the side of the house. He paused for a moment to beckon to Jarrett then, looking up, froze.

He let out a low hiss, his pale hand pointing suddenly upwards. There, half hidden by foliage from the nearby tree was a black attic window with a pencil thin, vertical streak of yellow light showing down one side.

Caruso and Jarrett looked at each other for a fraction of a second, nodded, drew their weapons, and ran quickly and quietly for the front door again. Gene looked up at the window and followed.

He wasn't the same man at all as the sleek, cool lawyer Gene had introduced to her Sarra realized with a horror so deep it gagged her. She watched as he pulled on a pair of surgical gloves, found a rubberized apron from somewhere she couldn't see and wrapped it around himself. He had slithered into some other kind of entirely malignant persona.

"I remember you," His voice had shifted into an eerily flat monotone. "I took lots of pictures. Still got them somewhere. George fucked you. And the other guy. George said I couldn't fuck you." He picked up the knife. The light caught on the blade, and it flashed as he bent over her. "I didn't want to fuck you. I saw what you did. . . Bitch!" The knife pricked into Sarra's abdomen and she felt fabric give as it cut upwards while his other hand splayed around her throat. "Arthur likes you, Bitch. . . You can't have him. You can't hurt. . ."

And Sarra screamed.

Jarrett slipped into the closet, frantically searching. There had to be a way to the attic. Somewhere, there had to be a door. Being as quiet as possible he began shifting the line of suits and coats apart. Finally, hidden between two clothes racks on wheels, filled with hanging bags of clothes, he found a door. Behind him, Caruso had flipped on the closet light switch, when the high pitched woman's scream reverberated through the door above. Jarrett jerked it open and charged up the narrow staircase lunging into the room, gun raised and cocked, yelling, "Police!" at the same time.

Something smashed into his chest and shoulder, exploding, driving him backward to crumple helplessly. There was another succession of shots. He couldn't breathe. Then there was nothing at all.

Suddenly the monster twisted away. The hand left Sarra's neck, and she gulped in air as he dropped the knife. She saw him snatch up the gun, then whirled around. There was a sharp cracking, the gunshots shattered through the room. He paused for a moment, utterly still, and then dropped out of sight, becoming a loud, dull thud on the floor.

And then she saw the big cop, Caruso, and, just behind him, Gene, round-eyed and haggard.

Safe, she thought, just before she passed out.

CHAPTER TWENTY-SIX

Sarra came around abruptly to the realization that she was no longer tied down, and that she was being held and carried across a familiar threshold into bright light. That she could hear sirens. She flailed in reflexive panic, but she was securely held, and a familiar deep voice rumbled just above her head, "Steady, lass. It's over. You're safe now. I've got you."

Caruso. She went slack.

He carried her through the living room, across the dining room, and into the family room.

There was a high pitched shriek of "Mommy!" and then she was on her knees, breathing convulsively and shaking all over as she clung to Amanda.

The shaking hadn't yet subsided later when Amanda wedged against her. She attempted to drink the coffee Caruso brought her without spilling it all over everything.

Phone in one hand, he sat down in the armchair across from the sofa, having just told her that her abductor was dead and that the intruder had been killed as well.

Sarra swallowed coffee, ignoring sore abraded wrists, carefully trying to absorb that death was final. Dead couldn't come back. She set the cup down on the coffee table with still trembling hands.

"He was . . . mad," Sarra got out raggedly. "He changed into something else. I need to tell Jarrett. He was the photographer all those years ago."

"Jarrett was shot," Caruso said then.

"What?" Sarra croaked.

"He was shot. Twice. He's on his way to the hospital now. Your brother, err, Dr. Corbett, is with him."

"He. . . Jarrett . . ?" she couldn't get it out.

Caruso inhaled unhappily. "It's bad. He's still alive, though."

"Oh my God!" Sarra whispered. And then she couldn't see anything because she was crying.

Much later, when the crying subsided because there wasn't anything left, she looked up at Caruso, who was still sitting there, patient and concerned.

"I need to go to the hospital," she told him.

Gene signed off on the ICU orders for Jarrett Blackwell that he had just finished scribbling out. After more than four hours of grueling, meticulous surgery, of which extracting the bullets actually had been the least difficult job, he was cross-eyed with fatigue.

He passed the order to the ICU charge nurse and stared blankly at the watch he had yet to return to his wrist. It was somewhere around six in the morning, he realized, picking it up. Still in green scrubs, he got to his feet and meandered down the hall to see Sarra sitting on one of the waiting room settees, her daughter leaned against her side and curled under one arm, asleep.

She looked terrible, his sister. Pale. Drawn. Black circles under large anxious eyes. Rumpled. The big police officer, Caruso Jones, sitting near her, didn't look much better. There was another, an aging large black man sitting at right angles from them. Police too, from the badge he wore over his suit coat breast pocket. Numerous other police officers sat in chairs or leaned against the wall. All waiting, all anxious for news.

Gene came to a stop, thinking that it was curious how his sister and Blackwell had been drawn together like a pair of magnets. "He'll live, and he'll make a complete recovery," he told her. "There were two bullets. The damage was extensive. His left lung collapsed. Missed his heart, but there was some arterial compromise. He lost a great deal of blood. We're still transfusing. However," he tried a smile that was more of a grimace. "He's back in one piece, Sarra. He'll be fine. I promise."

Between the tubes, bed rails, bed covers, IV's, monitor and machines, there wasn't much to see, Sarra noted, her nose against the ICU window. Jarrett's head on a pillow hid a face that was far too pale, a tube in his nose under a mask. One hand and arm with all sorts of things attached lay across a chest that was rising and falling. Something beeped steadily. Seeing him breathe, though, filled her with momentary relief. Something inside relaxed a bit.

She barely noticed as Gene led her away. Didn't notice much as, later, carrying a mostly sleeping Amanda, Caruso steered her out of the hospital, then drove them all back to the Driftwood house. She had gone into a strange sort of limbo, where everything was suspended, especially feelings.

Still at the hospital, after checking on Pearl Ann

and on his way to check on Jarrett again, he was surprised to hear, "Dr. Corbett?"

Gene blinked and turned. The older, black policeman had risen and was looking at him. "Yes."

"Do you have an office? Somewhere private?"

What now? He wondered, nodded, and led the way.

Ten minutes later, Gene sat staring blankly at the door to his crowded little office after Captain Whitmore had left and closed it behind him. Helen was dead? Murdered? Dead. How atrocious that he had virtually forgotten all about her over the last, what? Two days or so. Whitmore had undertaken the courtesy of personally informing him.

They had located Arthur Craswell's black Mercedes Benz in a supermarket parking lot halfway between his office and Driftwood. Mrs. Corbett's body had been in the trunk. She had been garroted. Her handbag had been in the trunk as well. It had contained a set of car and house keys, a hotel key, and several thousand dollars in cash along with other sundries. Gene could collect it with all the other appropriate valuables at his discretion. A red BMW registered in his name was in the lot outside Craswell's office building.

He caught a ride back to the Driftwood house and picked up his car. The house was dark by then, and he didn't want to disturb his hopefully sleeping sister, so he backed out of the driveway.

He didn't know whether he was shocked or not, Gene thought later as he drove home through early morning traffic. Helen was dead. Gone. Murdered. Possibly by the same man, his attorney, he had seen lying dead on the floor of that horrible attic. There had been glimpses of Caruso freeing Sarra, and then, nothing else but trying to stop the bleeding from Blackwell's wound.

The house seemed far too quiet, even alien when he let himself in. And, as he looked around, he saw Helen everywhere. She had chosen the décor, the furnishings. All of it, and suddenly he knew he couldn't live there anymore.

Twenty minutes later, some clothing and toiletries stuffed into his car, he was driving away, on his way to the Driftwood house that had been home until Dad had died. And was home again now because his sister was there.

Parking his car, Gene hauled his untidily assembled luggage out of the back seat, got it and himself in through the front door. A minute later, he dropped his bags on the living room carpet, sat down on the sofa, then keeled over into the cushions, sound asleep.

He hurt, Jarrett knew, rousing slowly. He hurt in a way he had never experienced before as if every part of him was in a strange kind of concussed shock, and mainly his chest and left shoulder. It was a deep, pervasive kind of hurt that followed him with every breath he took.

He'd been shot, he remembered. A blur of impressions. A man in black clothing in a small room. Then scraps that involved a lot of pain and people fussing over him. He opened his eyes, blinking several times to feel tubes around his face, in his nostrils, the soft hiss of foggy air. He was in a hospital room, in a hospital bed.

And Sarra was there, right beside him, holding his right hand. The left seemed to be strapped down and had all sorts of things attached to it. Jarrett turned his head fractionally, startled to realize that even that small amount of movement took every ounce of strength he had.

He stared up at her, so very glad to see her.

"You're going to be all right, Jarrett," she said softly. There was a nimbus of light around her dark hair. She looked so beautiful. He couldn't even nod, so he tried a faint smile and squeezed her warm fingers a little and slipped away to where it didn't hurt anymore.

He was a brave, good man, Sarra thought, that faint smile still with her as she left Jarrett's room two days after he had been moved into it, no longer engulfed by such a battery of medical gear. Seeing him awake and knowing her.

"Ms. Gray?" Sarra swiveled to see an enormous, grizzled, very dark-skinned man stop close to her. "I wonder if we could talk for a few minutes. I'm Whitmore." He held up a police badge. "Homicide. I'm Jarrett Blackwell's boss."

Sarra nodded.

"I would like to get your account of what happened on the night when Blackwell was shot." he clarified.

Sarra swallowed, then nodded again. "All right."

"It will help us wrap this case up," he added with a remarkably kind smile. "The perpetrators are both deceased, but anything that will help us to make sure there are no loose ends."

"Yes."

In her own car, Sarra followed Captain Whitmore to the police station where, for two hours, in the privacy of his office, she carefully recounted every experience of that horrible night. She was startled somewhat to realize how she remembered almost verbatim, everything Lewis Arthur Craswell had said. And then, because it was still sinking in and she needed to plant the knowledge more firmly that George was dead, she had elaborated further, to tell the Homicide Captain about what she knew of the Blackwell Christmas nightmare eleven years before, including her own involvement in that.

A photograph of George's ashen face had been easy to identify. He had looked abominably peaceful, dead. Eyes closed, face smooth and revoltingly serene. Older than the man she remembered, but otherwise the same. She shuddered.

Caruso Jones, Jarrett's partner, Whitmore explained, would be concentrating on other cases. He asked if she thought Amanda might need to talk to a psychiatrist. He knew of a good one who could help a great deal.

Possibly, Sarra told him.

She drove to the now empty house that she and Pearl Ann had rented to collect more stuff, pack the rest for the movers that Gene had insisted on.

He was right, her brother. He really was her brother. She couldn't live here anymore. It wasn't home, not even as much as the lovely old house in Kentucky had been. It had been a hiding place and its association with all that somehow tainted it. It would make it difficult to realize that she didn't have to keep looking over her shoulder anymore.

She had been doing that for so long that it had become a reflex. One she didn't really know how to get rid of. It caught her at times, like the shivers. That was why she was so eagerly embracing the new.

"Jarrett, Lad," Caruso said, five days later, landing on a chair by the bed as Jarrett sipped at the ghastly, clear fluid diet on the tray sitting on the bedside table. "Tis glad I am to see you doing so well, Laddie. Your dog is fine. I brought your mail." He plunked down a huge pile of assorted envelopes and flyers.

"All of it?" Jarrett raised his eyebrows. It was still difficult to breathe. The wretched nurses had him taking inhalation therapy every several hours, and his left shoulder was a shambles.

"Including the junk mail," Caruso said agreeably, setting down Jarrett's cell phone on top of the lot.

Jarrett swallowed apple juice. "You're a teddy bear, you know it."

Unoffended, Caruso grinned, then sat back to inform Jarrett about everything that had been put together for the past eight days. Some of it, resulting from information Sarra had given Big John, had come as an unexpected and nasty surprise.

After Caruso had left, Jarrett lay back with his eyes closed, letting the painkillers do their work.

His thankfully dead uncles had been a pair of absolute monsters. It turned out that the house next door to Gene Corbett's Driftwood home had been deeded to one Lewis C. Thornton, an alias Arthur Craswell had used to keep the place off the police radar. Thornton, Jarrett now knew, was a name he absolutely hated. Craswell's driver's license had made use of his office as his listed address.

Thanks to Sarra's thorough recounting of Arthur Craswell's perverted monologue that night, Whitmore and Caruso had been able to resolve another unsolved collection of cases of missing children going back more than twenty years. Craswell, his brother, George, and Thelma Joan Poole had been running a child trafficking ring, abducting small children, mostly girls, and selling them elsewhere in the country. Thelma's daughter, Helen, a small child herself at the time, had been used as bait to entice and facilitate the abductions. That, Jarrett decided, was something Dr. Corbett didn't need to know about his dead wife.

It also explained the killings of both women.

Learning that both brothers had been involved in the nightmare that had caused the destruction of his own family was almost anticlimactic.

And, as Whitmore and Caruso had pored over the materials Sarra had provided and consented to be reviewed, they had also learned that Homer James had been the intermediary in a couple of George Lowell's blackmail schemes. One of which had to do with Ada Thornton, and had involved photographs of her long-dead husband doing things he shouldn't do to their young daughter, Vicki.

Mom, Jarrett thought, his mind braking abrasively

on that. Poor Mom.

But, in supplying Sarra or, Candace James, for that Christmas disaster, Homer James had gotten greedy and had turned on George. George had disposed of him. And had been chasing Sarra all these years because she had absconded with the evidence he wanted.

A further investigative dialogue between Big John and the NYPD had been able to establish that George had been likely responsible for several brutal killings of other, various young prostitutes years ago who had been pimped by the same Homer James.

And Lewis Arthur Craswell had been the perpetrator of the brutal rapes and murders of those very young girls that he and Caruso had been trying to put a stop to. Again, from Sarra's recounting about the personality change and the surgical gloves, Big John and Caruso had deduced that Craswell had been a fractured personality, one aspect functional, the other a pathological killer.

A thorough search of the Craswell house had provided evidence to support appropriately obsessive behaviors. There were boxes of surgical gloves and condoms, a collection of rubber and plasticized aprons, and a large quantities of disinfectant. A closet full of brand new clothes and towels. A stack of unopened bars of soap in one of the upstairs bathrooms. Whatever Craswell's alter ego had been, he had undoubtedly been fixated about contamination.

Sick! Thoroughly sick.

It was the next day after Sarra had gone that Jarrett reached for his mail to find among the junk and bills, a letter from his attorney. Opening it, Jarrett read the brief note requesting that he call as soon as possible, that Lawrence had been unable to reach him.

Picking up his cell phone, he discovered several old messages to the same effect and remembered that he had ignored a similar voicemail from his attorney the day before all Hell had broken loose. He dialed Lawrence's number.

Thirty minutes later, he lay back, slack against the pillows, the phone in his limp right hand, his eyes closed, trying to comprehend.

His grandmother, Ada Thornton, was dead. She had, apparently, fallen down the central staircase of her home in the middle of the night. Lawrence and her attorneys were untangling the will. He, Jarrett, was the primary beneficiary, but apparently, there were some issues over an old trust fund that had been set up many years ago for one George T. Lowell that had to be resolved.

George had killed her, Jarrett was sure of it. Those two, in every way, bastards, had killed off every last member of his family except him. Grandfather, barely remembered. Uncle Albert, surely. Maybe not Cousin Sharron, given how she had gone overboard while sailing. His parents. Now his grandmother. They'd been after him as well but had lost him until a few days ago.

Sarra had been the catalyst for that.

He swallowed hard, feelings welling up to overwhelm him.

CHAPTER TWENTY-SEVEN

Days passed. Pearl Ann had been discharged from the hospital with the minimal of information that her assailants and Sarra's pursuers had been taken care of and permanently put away. Interestingly, Sarra discovered, she had no wish to return to their rented home either.

"Too many ghosts of neuroses past," Pearl Ann had told Sarra pointedly and had settled happily into the Driftwood house, and once again returned to being Amanda's Gran. Amanda had picked the south corner bedroom, it had two windows, and Pearl Ann had taken the one next to it. Sarra had stayed where she was.

After crash landing on the living room sofa, Gene had moved in to stay. He had taken his old corner room with the balcony, insisting that Sarra have the master suite. Between stints at the hospital, he had moved his personal and favorite belongings out of his former home, and found a realtor to put it on the market, also disposing of everything that had been associated with Helen.

Helen's body, with her mother's, had been cremated. There had been a grim little service, and their urns had been placed side by side in a crypt at a cemetery, not too far from Thelma Joan Poole's condo.

After that, Gene took a month off. He hadn't had a holiday in years, he told Sarra. It was good to be home again. Pearl Ann kept calling him my boy, and he apparently loved it because he grinned whenever she did. Amanda too fell in love with her Uncle Gene, and Sarra was glad to see the two of them mesh so well. Gene even pried Amanda away from her video games to pull out medical books and teach her all sorts of gory details about anatomy and the workings of innards. And, he introduced Amanda to tree climbing.

Sarra and Gene had had an argument about that. Who won was hard to say, but Gene had agreed that climbing out onto the roof of the house would be off limits.

He took them all out in the boat, too. Lovely hot days sailing around the Bay spotting pelicans and dolphins. He also had been enchanted by Sarra's painting. Sarra was still a little amazed by that. Gene announced one evening, he had arranged for a studio to be added onto the back of the house for her, to one side of the stone terrace. No more working at the hospital for her. She should focus on her art.

Then, one day, and very solemnly, he asked her to help him decide where to hang their mother's portrait. It took hours. They finally agreed to place the painting, at the top of the stairs, on the back wall of the landing.

"That way, she can watch us," Sarra had said slowly.

"Yes," Gene had agreed, an arm around her shoulder adding a light squeeze. They had looked at each other, smiled, understanding and accord passing between them on the deepest, tangible level. Gene, Sarra had realized suddenly, looked like a much younger man.

But, like another ghost flitting across the landscape to remind them that the past had not been wholly exorcized, Gene learned that Arthur Craswell had embezzled the trust fund that had been willed to his sister. The money had been transferred to a Cayman Islands bank, which meant that the mess would take some time to sort out. Sarra didn't care.

Her job at the hospital abandoned, she went there only to visit Jarrett as he slowly recovered. They held hands. He asked about Amanda and Pearl Ann. She told him about the bits and pieces that composed her days. He listened, interested, but reticent. He had withdrawn somewhere inside that she couldn't reach and, quite honestly, Sarra wasn't sure she was ready to try. She was still in that strange limbo where she felt like an amputee trying to adjust to doing without a missing limb.

And so she painted ferociously. All sorts of subjects. On one canvas that she kept going back to and flitting away from, a portrait of Jarrett Blackwell was emerging, young, warm-eyed, open-hearted.

Then Jarrett was discharged from the hospital and moved back into his small house to continue his convalescence. Caruso moved out, and it was just the four of them, more tightly knit than she could have expected.

She stopped by his house to visit Jarrett. He looked thin and pale, his left arm in a sling. And Sarra found herself remembering it was here they had opened Pandora's Box of so much past atrocity. That this place had much in common with her last residence which she, happily, would never have to see again.

Jarrett was polite. And friendly. They sat in his kitchen and drank coffee. And talked about anything that was essentially unimportant.

Amanda was going back to school in two weeks, Sarra told him. She's very excited about that. She's itching to make friends her own age.

His arm was healing well, Jarrett told her. He was getting his strength back. Caruso got his groceries. Things like that.

Then Pearl Ann kept baking cookies, muffins, and insisting Sarra take them to him. So, she did.

She wasn't working at the hospital anymore, she told him. She was painting full time now. She hoped to get enough work together for a show next year.

He'd love to see her work, he said. He'd resigned from the police force. He'd had enough.

Sarra had nodded, understanding.

And that was that.

Until, December, when she finished his portrait.

It was a ghost too, she thought, studying the vibrant, handsome, whole-hearted man who looked back at her from the canvas where he had been captured so perfectly to reflect precisely the man in her mind.

He didn't look like that now, she thought.

Scars.

"Sarra, this has got to stop!" Pearl Ann said fiercely before she could respond. Gene, standing right behind her, gave a solemn nod. "I know very well the two of you belong together. Now, it's Christmas in a few days. Gene has packed all sorts of Christmas stuff in the trunk and back seat of your car. A tree, decorations. Some of my special cookies." She held out Sarra's' purse and car keys. "You get in that thing and don't come back until you've fixed up his house."

"And him," Gene inserted rather aggressively. "I

told his physical therapist that I was going to get a different one!"

Sarra stared and then gulped.

"Well, get on with it!" Pearl Ann scolded, shoving the car keys into her hand.

Jarrett stood, feeling both astonished and helpless as Sarra huffed through his open front door pushing two large cardboard boxes on top of a third long one with a picture of a Christmas tree on the side. She pushed past him, past Chance, who was used to her now, to plant the lot in the middle of his bare living room, where the TV was blaring out some sitcom. Even canned laughter was better than none.

"I've never seen such a green Christmas season before," she said, straightening to indicate the outdoors with one hand. "If it doesn't snow, it's all browns and grays in Kentucky."

Jarrett closed the door. "What's all that?"

"I've no idea. Christmas stuff," Sarra said awkwardly. "Pearl Ann and Gene sent me over with it."

Jarrett nodded and watched Sarra glance around. He wasn't ready to deal with . . . .

"They were right, I see," she interrupted his thoughts.

Jarrett shrugged and moved closer to her in the living room. He hadn't seen her for about two weeks. "Would you like some coffee?" Formula question.

"Sure." Formula response.

"You didn't have to do this," he said, indicating the boxes with one hand.

"Seemed like a good idea." Then she surprised him. "I can help you decorate if you like?" She eyed the television.

"Okay," Jarrett agreed, expecting to have refused instead.

A cup of coffee for each later, they both got down on the floor to open the boxes and pull out the six foot, artificial spruce tree. There was a diverse collection of ornaments, brightly colored balls, gold and crystalline angels, silver dancers, frosted reindeer, and a small, beaming Santa for the top of the tree.

"I love Christmas ornaments," Sarra said, pulling out and opening a large tin with Christmas sugar cookies. "Pearl Ann made these. Here." She held one out. He took it. "They come up with such lovely, cheerful things for decorations," she continued. "Part of it is Amanda's doing. They're magical to her."

Magic? Maybe to both of them, Jarrett thought, watching how Sarra handled the pieces. Suddenly he felt how thoroughly Christmas had been destroyed for him all those years ago and felt as well a surge of the same enchanted fascination he had known for such things as a boy. He swallowed and looked down at the cookie he was holding in his right hand.

"You don't have to do this, Sarra," he repeated, then took a bite of the cookie before closing the lid on the tin.

On her haunches, fluffing open wire and plastic branches, Sarra stopped what she was doing and looked at him. Saw where he knelt on the carpet a couple of feet away.

Saw her painting of him.

Saw the differences. And that the differences were all caused by pain. And loneliness. Like her.

"Yes. I do," Sarra said softly. "Pearl Ann was right."

His eyebrows flickered. "About what?"

"Us. What a mess we are."

He nodded fractionally. "Yes."

And then they shifted closer, leaned, and were hugging each other desperately.

He could feel her breathing against the neck of his sweatshirt. And how warm and alive she was.

She could feel the smooth firmness of him. And how warm and alive he was. And then, how unevenly he was breathing.

"They killed off every last member of my family, Sarra," he said raggedly into her hair, the one thing he hadn't been able to say aloud at all.

"Oh, Jarrett," was all she could manage. Hugging became clinging, and a quagmire morass of feelings coalesced into another direction. Every old hurt and fear had to be stripped away and replaced with comfort and loveliness, isolation destroyed with intimacy.

It was a shock to discover that when their mouths came together, the electric intensity was still there waiting for them.

"Sarra," he groaned, pulling her up with him.

"Jarrett," she whispered, following.

It was a strange and tenuous, yet desperate, lovemaking. Shy and fastidious, incredibly intense for that, and made prettier, perhaps, because of it. Sarra and Jarrett were discovering through touch what was real this time, and not imagined, just how thoroughly they could feel each other. It had little to do with pleasure, a fact they both somehow understood, and everything to do, through the most beautiful of sensations, with freeing each other from the isolating, rancid accumulation of their pasts.

How they managed to end up in Jarrett's bed, clothing scattered everywhere, still tangled together, neither of them had any idea.

"WOW . . !" Jarrett gasped when they lay sprawled on their backs, her head on his still tender shoulder, his arm locked around her, making sure she was pressed against him.

"I think everything's turned pink," Sarra said breathlessly.

"Pink?" Jarrett felt an unexpected urge to laugh.

"Definitely, pink." She sat up suddenly, and full of energy, to look down at him where he lay, still practically shivering and seriously demolished. "You look better," she said.

He studied her face in turn. "So do you."

He let his eyes drop down past full breasts to the stretch marks on her abdomen where Amanda had been. "Beautiful," he whispered, then realized she was exploring him even more intently. He almost flinched when she traced a fingertip across his scar, down his sensitive stomach, then shifted suddenly to grab one of his feet. "How interesting. You have hairs on the tops of your big toes!"

"I do?" Taken by surprise and unaware of it, and, suddenly very ticklish, he jerked his foot away.

"I don't," Sarra said.

"Let me see," he said, grinning. Happy. Delighted.

"Here." She shoved a much smaller foot in the direction of his face.

The bed was a shambles. The room had gone dark, light from the TV in the living room flickering into it. They lay curled together, unable to move at all to realize that somehow an entire afternoon had vanished.

"Sarra?" Jarrett said softly, his chin tucked against the top of her head.

"Jarrett?" Sarra sounded sleepy.

"I asked you once to marry me."

There was a short silence. "Twice, actually."

"Well, I'm going to ask you again. Will you marry me?"

"Yes."

"Good." Then. "I'm glad that's finally settled."

Sarra giggled a little. "Pearl Ann will be pleased. She's adopted Gene, you know."

"Sarra," Jarrett pursued, still serious, "there's something you should know."

"What?"

"I'm worth about twenty million dollars."

"WHAT?" She twisted around in his arms.

"My grandmother died and left me everything." He plunged in further before she could say anything. "It might well end up being quite a bit more." She was breathing funny, he noticed. "About double that," he amended. "Anyway, I want to set up a foundation with programs to help abused children and a service to help track down missing ones."

She was silent for a long time.

"Sarra?"

"Mild case of concussion," she mumbled. Then, she was hugging him. "Jarrett, you really are the most beautiful man!"

Just like his painting.

And, Sarra thought as they nestled as close together as they could, she suddenly knew exactly how to dispose of part of Homer James' million dollars she still had hidden away. She knew a particular redheaded girlfriend that was going to get quite a surprise for Christmas.

# # #